PIG IRON TRUCKER

A Jericho Book

T. F. Platt

authorHOUSE®

AuthorHouse™
1663 Liberty Drive
Bloomington, IN 47403
www.authorhouse.com
Phone: 1-800-839-8640

First published by AuthorHouse   06/09/2011

ISBN: 978-1-4634-0459-8 (sc)
ISBN: 978-1-46340-458-1 (e)

Library of Congress Control Number: 2011908056

Printed in the United States of America

Any people depicted in stock imagery provided by Thinkstock are models, and such images are being used for illustrative purposes only. Certain stock imagery © Thinkstock.

This book is printed on acid-free paper.

Because of the dynamic nature of the Internet, any web addresses or links contained in this book may have changed since publication and may no longer be valid. The views expressed in this work are solely those of the author and do not necessarily reflect the views of the publisher, and the publisher hereby disclaims any responsibility for them.

DEDICATION

This work is dedicated to my family.

Introduction

As in all books of the Jericho series, Pig Iron Trucker is fiction. The Jericho books were written in honor of the author's grandfather, Clarence Groner, and the author's mother, Edith Marie Groner Platt. The geography used in the books is similar to that of the communities in Michigan where Clarence Groner and Edith Marie Groner Platt and T.F. Platt, and others of the Groner and Platt families, resided or toiled through much of their lives. The books aren't biographical, although the real Clarence and Edith for a time lived on a road called Jericho Road and Clarence did work briefly in a paper mill nearby.

Pig Iron Trucker is a serious book lightened by humor, romance, suspense, and a wholesome revelry that is accomplished by means of interacting colorful characters. The story opens in 1956 with Del Platt and Louie Watkins, a.k.a. Danny Platt and Peanny Watkins laboring in a sweltering stand of aspens. Del is a nephew of an Athabascan Indian trucker from Alaska and soon joins his uncle as a fellow trucker. His transition from woodcutter to piloting an eighteen-wheeler is at first complicated by an elopement and further diced by inadequate funding, worn-out tires, pregnancy; all factors foreboding inevitable tragedy.

Jericho Books written to include events from 1944 through 1971 cover a time wherein characters in the book could be based upon the author or upon persons of the author's actual acquaintance. In Pig Iron Trucker some readers may see a bit of themselves in an otherwise fictional character. One such a.k.a. character is T. F. Platt and what that character does in the story is somewhat in line with actual events of the author.

Pig Iron Trucker is the ninth of the Jericho Books by T. F. Platt. The Jericho stories are intended for adults and young adults. The tales do not include explicit sex and they omit profanity.

Jericho Books, listed in chronological order, by T. F. Platt are:

If We Make it to Jericho

The Brown Mud of Jericho

I've Baked a Fresh Cobbler

I'll Always Take Care Of The Trees

It is Edith's Tree

She Wears It for Her Loved One, Oh So Far Away

The Three Door Dodge (1944–1948.)

You Did Okay (1948–1952.)

Pig Iron Trucker (1956–1957.)

ACKNOWLEDGEMENT

The author wishes to thank family members and friends; notably Rena Baker, Michael Baker, Buck Platt, Helen Platt, Violet Robinson, Peggy Schneider, Kathleen Heimendinger, and Bessie Moorehouse who have read one or more Jericho Books prior to publication. Their comments have been helpful and appreciated.

The author wishes to sincerely thank the Truck Museum at Auburn, IN, members of the American Truck Historical Society, the Wheels of Time magazine, and a host of truckers and mechanics for their patience as he drew upon them for information and insight. He especially thanks Dawn Ruth, lady trucker. The author also sincerely thanks and cherishes his nephew, Bob Platt, professional trucker; and the author's brother, Bob Platt, recognized expert on all things that have engines and move on wheels.

The cover with its big Green Mack was made possible by Ora Marie Pulley, a grand lady of our church.

CHAPTER ONE

Scattered wisps of pearly cumulus decorated an azure ski, the sky blue watering to pale blue, nearly stark white near the scorching yellow sun. The shady stand of woods wherein they labored offered respite from the searing sun but allowed no stirring breeze at all. That stand of trees near Yelrom, Michigan was an oven. The Watkins brothers, Sid and Louie, each had a crew in the oven. The stand was to be white pine under red oak but aspen and scrub stood in the way. A government forester had been through and he'd marked with yellow paint all scrub trees to be felled by the sawyers.

On one side of the woods Sid Watkins' crew assailed the trees the forester'd declared to be scrub; trees that were ill, too crooked or otherwise unwanted. All trees were to fall except the healthy red oak and young white pine. The oak would protect the pines from a weevil that'd otherwise ruin the pine. Removing the scrubs would foster quality oak and pine to build furniture or to be used in construction. Sid's crew assailed with chainsaws and they skidded out logs with an Oliver Cleat-Track crawler tractor. Across the woods Louie and crew heard the scream of chainsaws, the snarl of tractor, and they with envy imagined the cooling breeze pelting the face of that lucky guy driving the luxurious Cleat-track Oliver.

On Louie's side of the stand of trees there wasn't a whisper of breeze to elate a single soul of Louie's crew – and they could all hear the snarling tractor and all were imagining the stirring breeze to comfort that lucky driver. Louie mopped his face with his big red hanky. "Whooping juniper," he said, as if to no one, "it'd be hotter than a griddle all day on that darned Oliver." He glanced at Del Platt whose mouth was gaped in disbelief at Louie's comment. "Because of the heat from that miserable engine," Louie explained. "Best figure a way to tell the others." Louie's crew was to harvest

1

all aspen of sufficient bole to yield at least three bolts for excelsior. In Louie's hands a David Bradley chainsaw screamed brief seconds.

An aspen toppled.

Louie moved up to the next aspen.

Feeling somehow cooled by Louie's comment about a hot tractor, Del Platt tore at the felled tree by double-bit axe, neatly clipping away limbs until reaching a part of the tree too small in diameter to become excelsior. Behind Del, Dan Francis set tongs to the trunk then waited near his long eared mule. Del clacked the top from the tree simultaneous with Dan's "Get, you Nancy."

Louie called out, "Whoa!"

The mule stopped willingly and Dan peered back at Louie. "Darn lucky for us with a mule," Louie cocked his head to listen across the trees. "That old Oliver'd cook a body today what with that engine heat pouring back onto you along with old sol broiling down." Dubiously, Dan the muleskinner peered at his boss. "Let me take a turn with that Nancy, huh Dan? I could use cooling and I should check on them anyway."

Dan Francis stood in the oven with the David Bradley chainsaw and he followed Del's glance to the next aspen. Suddenly he envied the boss behind that cool Nancy mule.

That mule called Nancy could tow one to as many as six trees at once from the woods and out to the buckers and peelers. Those crewmen labored next to a tandem-dual forty-foot-long Lufkin stake-sided semi trailer. Near that trailer any remaining limbs were clacked off the tree trunks and marks were placed on the trunks so the buckers could saw out fifty-six inch logs. Next, using drawshaves, the peelers removed the bark to produce the pearly little logs, called excelsior bolts. The buckers then loaded those pearly white excelsior bolts onto the semi trailer. Louie pulled into view.

"Gee. Gee, Nancy."

He swung Nancy in with a hitch of four of Del's trimmed aspens. Mopping his face, Louie peered around as though listening, finally cocking an ear. "Whooping juniper." He mopped anew. "All that glitters is not gold," he breathed. "That hot bucking Oliver'd nigh kill a man today. What with the engine heat under this sun." He glanced skyward. Again he mopped with the big red hanky. "I've come up to give each of you a turn with this here mule; anybody who'd want it. Every dog has his day, you know."

Louie's crew labored the rest of that day in the oven, cooling off a little only by taking a turn behind Nancy. In late afternoon with the sun yet relentless the three peelers, two buckers, Dan the official skidder, and Del and Louie worked together to peel and toss the last of that day's bolts up onto the semi. Louie tossed the last of the last as it was a high toss. Del worked atop the load to catch and place the little logs. "That'll do her!" All were glad to hear Louie's call as sweat had soaked every item of clothing. Despite the heavy heated air Del still felt somewhat cooled by recalling Louie's ruse, chuckling silently at his use of Nancy to cause his crew to feel cooler. One seldom heard grumbling from Louie's crew. Del'd learned not to comment on his friend's methods, knowing Louie's caution, "The walls have ears, you know."

Finished for the day, the bulk of the crew was local and left straight away for home. Louie, Del, and a bucker named Wesley remained in camp. Wesley would've stayed on the crew even if he couldn't buck straight, this because he was a fine camp cook. Often he'd say something like, "Louie, if you ever get grand enough to have a good size crew, well then I'd just cook, but seeing's we're small then if you'll take some time off, please, and scout around for a bigger job, I'd be obliged."

Wesley'd been gabbing at Louie just as he, Louie, and Del were emerging from a dip into the Muskegon River. It was by then around nine-thirty and dark was coming down on their camp. The air'd cooled a mite, advantaging the cool they'd just acquired from dipping the Muskegon. "My, let me at that Mulligan." Del dashed on ahead and had used Wesley's long steel hook to swing the stew pot from over the fire and he'd thumped it to the planked top of the table as Louie and Wesley converged with coffee and biscuits. Already in place on the table was a box of Nabisco Crown Cracker, referred to as pilot bread. It sat handy to an expected dinner companion. That companion's empty plate was set beside Del and he served it along with his own generous helping of Mulligan.

They'd just dug in when a truck was heard from out at the roadway a quarter mile from their table. They could visualize the driver's muscular arms spinning the eighteen- inch diameter steering wheel as he maneuvered around the curves. The over-sized steering wheel, the special gear ratios for the transmission and differential along with a host of other modification and lights and chrome doodads made the truck truly a wonder for off-road trucking. The driver had heard that in a time anon cars and trucks could all have power steering but for the present arm muscles rippled in steering trucks, especially in off-road conditions. His thinking about his marvelous red Reo raised a grin as sweat pushed salty droplets from his gnarly arms. In another few minutes the red 1948 tandem-dual Reo tractor pulled dimly into view. Within another minute or two he'd unhitched an empty semi trailer. Expertly the Reo was attached to the load of bolts. The truck driver was their expected companion, an Athabascan Indian from Alaska. His name was Helio C. Outhe, pronounced out-he. Del Platt called him Uncle Helio or, as often like the others, simply called him Helio.

"Full load, I see." Helio slipped in behind his plate and reached the pilot bread. "These bolts here'll go to Muskegon." He sat with a grip of pilot bread in one hand and a tablespoon in the other. He mouthed a heaped spoonful of Mulligan topped by a chunk of pilot bread. "Next load's for Otsego," he spoke around a mouth load. Another heap passed his eager lips and was crowned by more pilot bread. "They'll want three loads," his Adam's apple leaped, "and then I've arranged two deliveries at Grand Rapids." His effort to converse went seemingly unnoticed as none of his companions had paused their Mulligan pursuit to be conversant. "By then they can take more at Muskegon."

"Which part is the semi, or is it the whole rig?" Del Platt had polished off his second full plate, now slurped coffee while awaiting a reply from Helio.

Having finished his plate, Helio set aside the box of pilot bread and reached a buttery flakey biscuit, another pride and joy of Wesley's. He slurped warm coffee then squared around to see his nephew. "Semi refers to part trailer." Helio loved an opportunity to explain. He was especially responsive to queries by Del as the young man wasn't typically a joker; at least not with Helio. Helio was of a different culture and he hated those times he'd inadvertently butt a joke. "A full trailer, that is, not semi, would have four wheels that carried the full weight of the load whereas a semi uses the tractor to bear part of the load. The truck attached to the semi trailer is often called a tractor. Either tractor or truck is okay for that, and to provide confusion a semi trailer is often called a trailer 'cause folks don't know better."

"We'll finish here tomorrow with only part of a load," Louie interrupted. "Then we've contracted to work a stand east of Bruin City. When'll you be back?"

"Noon or early afternoon. I'll sleep in my cab as usual then haul out of here by two in the morning. Get there before daybreak. Cooler to unload in the morning."

Louie spoke around a mouthful of biscuit and stew. "Del and me'll be here breaking camp. Wesley can start the crew on the new trees. Dan will take Nancy in the pickup and trailer."

"Louie and I and all this camp plunder'll ride with you to the new stand then, Uncle Helio."

Helio nodded his understanding and agreement then said, "Sid out is he?"

"No, two days and he'll have half a dozen full loads of logs for pallets and crates. That's the Coopersville mill."

"Been in there. Better use the Mack for it."

* * *

With the first sounds from the truck that morning, Del'd hopped up from his bedroll to help Helio thoroughly check over the rig and its load. President Eisenhower had just announced his ten-year plan for rebuilding the Country's roads, ending with efficient Interstates, but his plan didn't alleviate the presently atrocious road conditions. The roads were so bad a trucker had no trouble at all going slow enough to read the Burma Shave signs like: "Don't lose your head to gain a minute you need your head your brains are in it." Their brains were fully to the task as their flashlights probed into every nick and cranny including conditions under the hood of the willing Reo.

The inspection over, Helio heaved into the cab. Del stood outside his mentor's window, ready to wave him on his way. "After this next excelsior load, Del," he grinned down at his nephew, "The two of us, we could get busy on Sid's logs. Haul bolts like mad and fill in with loads of logs. I hope I'm thinking what you're thinking."

"Sure." By the sound of Del's voice, Helio wished he could more clearly see his nephew's face. Even without a clear view, the face seemed to glow in the dark. "Sid and Louie's crew will combine on bolts," Del said, "and load them high while the bark still peels freely. There'll be a lot to haul." He stood quietly a moment, wanting to be sure of himself and Helio before saying, "I haven't driven the Mack much, but I want to."

"Plan to drive the Reo on this next excelsior run to Otsego. Then make a run with me with the Mack and logs. After that, say on Monday, you can choose the truck." Helio pulled away with his load long before the sky began paling in the East. Del plunged back into his bedroll, planning for a precious late snooze before pancakes awakened him.

By early afternoon that day the stand was harvested and most had left for the new location. Louie, Del, and Helio tossed the remaining bolts onto the rig. In the background of their noisy tossing they heard Nancy fussing as Dan tore out with the wobbly rattling horse trailer. With the waning rattle and bray Helio mused: "I wonder how valuable this field is we're standing on."

"By mule? Not for me; and for what, a crop; wheat, maybe?" Louie peered at his friend. He knew Helio wasn't a joker.

"No, for nothing. I sure wish I had some land so's to get paid not to farm it."

"Helio, making a joke? Why, I'd not thought it."

"No, by gosh, no joke. Just like these woods. The forester was paid by the government to mark the trees to be cleared from the woods, which you just did. Next the government will buy the fence for the farmer to fence in the woods so that cows cannot go in there. This field, the farmer is paid so much an acre not to farm it. It's the Land Bank program of 1956."

Louie rubbed his head. "I wonder how one gets to be a farmer."

"I wouldn't hurry into that," Del said. "You know my brother Albert delivers milk from the Toberton Dairy; that's a big farm actually. Well, he heard farmers are paid so low for their crops that Uncle Sam has loaned three hundred million dollars to India. That's so that India can buy our excess farm commodities. Trying to get higher income for the farmer, you see. Eisenhower needs to get selling prices up for the farmers if he expects them to vote him back in this November."

"He works like a beaver for his 'I like Ike' slogan, but I just wonder when that Ike will think to help a poor woodsman like me."

"Or a poor struggling Athabascan trucker that I know about."

Helio pitched in with Del and Louie to toss the camp on top of the excelsior bolts for the trip to the new stand of trees. Their conversation was vigorous and continued as the Reo ground across the field and onto the graveled dusty roadway. Their voices jarred and jiggled due to the rutted washboard-like condition of the road. Talk was loud because the cab windows were wide open daring a breeze to cool them. The day had grown predictably hot and was whipped to a breeze only by the truck moving along at thirty, or less, miles per hour.

Louie and Del were old friends having been neighbors as kids and as buddies all their lives. As kids the boys were called Peanny Watkins and Danny Platt. They reared in rural venue near Ellington, Michigan. In high school Danny's name briefed to Dan and at work on the excelsior bolts he elected to be Del, his middle name - after Delibar Platt, his grandfather. Simultaneous with Del joining the crew was Dan Francis who joined as the muleskinner. Dan didn't want to be called Fran and the other Dan felt proud to be known as Del so the arrangement of their names had gone without hassle.

Back when as a high school sophomore Del joined the crew, Peanny had already elected to be Louie, his front name being Lewis. On contracts, paychecks, and other transactions he signed with a formal Lewis Watkins. Del Platt was on the crew only during summers, and was presently doing his third stint. From the beginning it was assumed by the others that Del was second in command whenever he was aboard, but lately Louie had begun to alter that assumption. That change commenced to occur on the day Helio C. Outhe began hauling for the Watkins brothers.

Helio was born in the Alaskan interior and reared along the Tanana River. He was on hand when his father and grandfather helped the U. S. Army engineers construct the Alcan Highway. Shortly after World War Two the Alcan became public highway Rte. 2, the Alaska Highway, and Helio grew up to become a trucker doing maintenance on that big road. In Alaska researching for a book, Del's Aunt Anna Mae Groner met Helio at a fish camp on the Tanana, a short way from his home at Northway Village. They married and settled into a home in Michigan; located across the street from Del's grandparents, Delibar and Ella Platt. It was crewman Del who'd mentioned to Louie that he knew of a trucker with a red Reo semi needing work.

It wasn't any time at all before Louie noticed that Del was fond of Uncle Helio and that he seemed as fond of the red Reo truck; and he saw Del dote even greater fondness on the big green Mack when it'd become a part of Helio's stable. Del and/or Helio went over the inside of the Mack and the Reo cabs everyday with a polishing cloth and Helio washed the trucks weekly, if not daily depending on the unsightliness of dirt and mud which could cling to the beautiful beasts. When he had a minute or two Louie enjoyed cleaning and polishing beside his friends, signaling that he also liked the spunky red Reo and the big green Mack. The big Mack carried a huge squared-off highly chromed radiator grill. The grill gleamed in compliment to the large air cleaner on the left side of the cab, the sparkling chromed oil cooler on the right side of the cab, and its highly chromed Grover air horns that decorated the roof. Adding to the gleam its towering pair of chromed exhaust stacks were positioned up each rear corner of the cab. The cab looked new inside with every chromed knob radiant and the dark green paint unscratched and polished and blending with the medium light green seat cushions.

Louie knew he'd soon lose Del altogether to the trucks. That's why

Dan went with the pickup and horse trailer where before Louie or Del would've moved that mule. And Wesley'd gone on ahead to start the crew at the new stand where before Louie or Del would've done so.

"Hear about um blasting off that darn bomb?" Helio's query broke into Louie's thoughts.

"Huh?"

"H-bomb. They touched one off out someplace in the Pacific; just to see her go, I guess."

"Big blast?"

"Pacific, that term, that 'pacific' used to mean 'peaceful' but not anymore."

"I'd heard that the bomb's to prevent war," Louie advanced.

"You know," Del said, "Nathan's due back this summer from serving in Germany. He's an army medic."

"So could the H-bomb help him?" With the road so rough, the men were fairly shouting back and forth to each other.

"No, I doubt it," Del called. "It seems to me you'd best try to scare some one specific with it, not just countries in general, that is. Nathan's written saying it was the UN that saved his neck. To do with the Suez Canal, that was."

"Isn't he in Germany?"

"Isn't that canal in Israel? I wonder if it isn't the way they got their country; by some treaty or some such, I mean; not like won in a war, I mean." Helio rubbed his chin.

"Nathan didn't say so," Del said.

"Israel became a country in 1948 as prophesized in the book of Isaiah," Louie said.

"So what were you saying about Nathan?" Helio called over the still louder noisy way the truck was now called upon to tackle. "Not in Germany, did you say; where it's safe?"

"Yes, in Germany. Safe's what he thought until one day he said trucks bigger than he'd seen before came onto his base hauling huge earth moving machines. Before nightfall they'd built an airport with a steel mat runway. He said at daybreak he hurried outside at the sound of airplanes. C-119's, Flying Boxcars, they were and they landed; then he said all that's holy broke loose. Full alert and deployment it was. His whole outfit was combat ready at all times but didn't expect action out in the middle of occupied Germany. Well, everybody lined up and began marching toward those aircraft. They all wanted to know, 'Where're we going?' Then he heard somebody say, 'The Suez Canal.'"

Helio looked worried. "When did you say that happened?" He slowed the truck in an effort to quiet the willing Reo.

"Just a year ago now. They didn't get all loaded into the aircraft before they were ordered to turn around and go back. They heard then that a UN Emergency Force had moved in to settle things. By things, I mean that disharmony between England, France, Israel, Egypt, and a big lot of Arab nations, I heard; so Nathan's outfit wasn't needed."

"So, what do we conclude?"

"That a UN Force applied in a specific locale stopped the bloodshed. They didn't need any old H-bomb. Also, it's essential to keep the UN forever healthy."

"Well, I'm glad it's us, not some one else who has that bomb. I'd hoped they took pictures. Why just think if that UN Force could've shown off pictures. It'd be as scary as Noah's big adventure."

"It wouldn't look pacific, I'd agree," Del said.

The truck maneuvered around a tricky-tight turn to follow where Louie pointed. "Well, back to the farmers," Helio said as their way again straightened. "For the first time in history a group of farmers own an international business. Guess what business, what company?"

Louie touched a hand to his chin. He looked at the ceiling. "Well, I'll guess it's pulpwood producers. Most of U. S. pulpwood comes from Canada; used in paper. Some farmers, Canadian and American, could've gotten together, I'd think."

Helio grinned. "Good guess, but, you listen now, you listening? It's grapes."

"Grapes?" Louie rubbed his weary head.

"Welch's grape juice company is apparently largely or completely farmer owned. 'Welch's Grape Juice goes international,' I heard on this truck's radio this morning."

"My business could use such help. You know there's an end in sight for excelsior, the plants tell us, so we pray another market develops for our aspen. They say other packing materials are being tested. Del's brother Nathan saw some testing on that at Michigan State – cheaper ways to make packing stuff; plastics, maybe.

"Helio, you haven't met Delt Watkins, our dad. Well, there may be hope. That's because he's gotten into a group that's trying to make log cabin type buildings from aspen wood. They can make a good looking building

9

already but it won't last long without preserving the wood first. They're working on the best way to do preservation. They want to build the walls then truck the assembled parts, roof, too, to the build sites. Could be some work for you truckers yet."

"It's a relief to hear it. Line me up with their address, if you would."

"Sure." Louie touched Helio's arm. "Now look ahead, pard." He pointed. "Right by that tree with the shirt flapping. We're back in there half a mile, or so."

* * *

Helio left his semi trailer on a nearly level stretch close to the aspen stand and a hundred yards up from a babbling creek. Wesley belly flopped the cool creek on his way to set up camp near the parked semi. On the third day of aspen tree harvest the crew size would double; half working with Sid from the north end of the aspen stand while Louie's crew harvested aspen from the south.

Wesley whistled away at "Heartbreak Hotel" as he worked. Camp cook! The whole day, every day, he was to be camp cook. His whistle rivaled the sweetest passerine love song and his mind assembled provender unparalleled in the annuals of camp. "Too bad old Del'll miss opening night of this," Wesley mused.

On the afternoon prefacing Wesley's opening night, Helio was out on the road with his eyes boring the endless centerline of Michigan Rte 57. He was a bit antsy, wanting to travel near enough to Ellington, Michigan for a local call. Out on the open road as he was, he was the only one of the group anywhere near a telephone.

His mind began a muse in focus of his wife. Anna Mae, the author, had urged him to do as she said instead of drumming the steering wheel. "And now don't get mesmerized by boring some foolish road sign or some shiny knob in your truck," she'd cautioned. "Think up trivia like it was right here in Michigan, near Trenton, Michigan, that is, when they painted that very first centerline in the United States of America."

Helio grinned as he turned the rig south along a county road. "They created that very first centerline in 1911, thank you, dear." The big red Reo held to its side of centerline on the now narrow tarmac and his eyes cleaved ahead to a lonely country store he knew about. His call from the store wouldn't be long distance.

"Who?" Naddy Platt jammed the receiver to her ear; listened with a hand pressed to the other ear. "Huh? Well, I . . . wait." She switched ears. "Now, speak up. Say again."

He called into the phone, "Naddy, it's Helio! I married Anna Mae, you recall?"

"Oh, hi."

"I want to say Del won't be home Friday."

"Friday? Del is home. Why he . . ."

"No. Your son, Del, not grandpa. He's going with me into Otsego with a load of excelsior bolts. I'm teaching him to drive heavy truck."

"Del is?" Naddy called into the phone, "Del can't drive. He's too old!"

"Del is? Huh, who is? Oh no, not your father-in-law, but your son is driving."

"Well, I'll have Del call."

"No need. I'll catch him here." Helio rubbed his ear to still its ringing as the red Reo drove on for the camp.

With the loaded semi hitched and with Del at the wheel, Wesley handed in a bag of sandwiches. He was determined that no crewman miss out on his opening full day's spit-roasted beef round. The sandwiches were thick with sliced beef, dripping browned juices, and that sack of provender was nestled between them as he handed in two thermoses of black, black coffee. "You've spoiled us already, brother."

Sid and Louie were handy to wave them out with the load. Del had the Reo in low range low to avoid any wheel spinning in the sandy soil. Even a slight spin could drop the four pair of 10 x 20 Cooper-clad tandem duals into the sand and stick her there to be jacked up and planked for another go; and such mayhem would put them late into Otsego. Helio looked proudly across at Del as he brought the rpm of that beautiful beast to the next shifting, settling smoothly into high range low. They rammed ahead to the gate and on into the narrow dirt roadway, beginning the first leg of a one hundred mile roll for Otsego.

* * *

Del's mom, Naddy Platt, was yet confused that evening about the telephone call received from Helio C. Outhe – was it about her father-in-law or about Dan, the son who insisted upon confusing her life by changing his name? Her father-in-law, Delibar Platt, was often in a dream about one scheme or another, but at age seventy plus she'd not thought he'd take up truck driving. Her son Dan, though, that a.k.a. Del son of hers, likely wouldn't be truck driving either as he was working a good job harvesting excelsior bolts. They'd finished supper and sat stirring their coffee when she made forth with an idea: "Denibar we should drop in on your folks."

Den had just finished a hard week at a planer sizing steel to a forty-thousandth of tolerance at Oliver's Machinery in Grand Rapids. "Sure, maybe tomorrow."

"Let's ask your folks to a movie." He repositioned the ear of his cup then peered at her.

"Movie?" He raised the cup an inch from the tabletop. "Maybe tomorrow."

"Tonight's the last day for van Gogh. They wanted to see it. You know they don't drive." His cup clacked down.

"Where's Del, uh, er, Dan?"

"Del, well, I'll ask your dad or Anna Mae next door. Where's got me stumped."

Her comment raised a mystery in his mind. "Some girl, I'd bet, has taken our boy."

She ignored the comment about the girl, although the thought had sharply crossed her mind. She'd seen her Del looking longingly at his cousin Dosia; his cousin! By jiminy, what could be after his mind, anyway? Her mind snapped back to the present: "The movie's 'Lust for Life;' about Vincent van Gogh, and starring Kirk Douglas. Let's hurry along as I may want to confab with Anna Mae, as well."

Pulling in at the Delibar Platts, she saw that visiting Anna Mae would be easy – she was seated on their porch swing beside Ella, Den's mom. The ladies were sipping lemonade. Propped in a rocker was Delibar and he obviously wasn't in shape to be a trucker. Arthritis had him scrunched to a question mark configuration, so compressed he'd not see above the dashboard of even a midget-size truck.

"Anna Mae, where's your Helio?"

"Why, do tell, sis, I thought you'd know. Why he's with your very son, Del, on a roll for Otsego with excelsior bolts."

"I'd feared it." She slumped into a folding chair facing the others. "What's a body to figure on? Sent to cut wood and he goes trucking it."

Anna Mae's smile was radiant. Any mention of Helio brought that happy grin. "Helio says he's a natural truck driver. They've enough work, Helio says, to put both trucks on the road, so he's glad Del's proving out."

Den moved along the porch to clack open a folding chair near his father. "How's things, Dad?"

Delibar raised his copper bracelet vested wrists in a wave of hello. "Bees help." His arms slowly lowered, placing his hands once again on the padded arms of the rocker. Weekly he drove an old John Deere B across Jericho Road and to the apiary located far out behind the home of neighbors Clarence and Clydis Groner. There he'd tease the bees into stinging him. "Bees help."

Father and son visited but moments before Johnny Cash burst into the consciousness of those seated on the porch. All heads turned to view a Cadillac approaching from Jericho Road. Front seat occupants, Clarence and Clydis Groner sat with their heads cocked toward their Motorola as the large black car ghosted to a stop. The porch sitters watched those heads bob in concert clear to the last deep note of "I Walk the Line" before one of them switched off the Motorola.

"Howdy neighbors. Come on up," Delibar creaked, looking over the top of his glasses. "Den, clack open a couple more chairs."

"No need, we can't stay. Heading for that movie, Vincent van Gogh, so we stopped to see if you folks want to go with us."

"Anna Mae, where is that pretty daughter of yours? She's welcome to come."

"Already there with friends. I've not seen it. I was hoping Helio'd have time to go with me."

"Lets all pile into two cars," Naddy said.

South of Grand Rapids on U. S. 131, Helio suddenly thumped his knee with his fist. "Darn it, Del, I'm in trouble." With his forehead instantly crinkled, Del looked over at his tutor. "You know that movie at the Dawn? Well I'd hoped to take Anna Mae to it, but we've missed it."

"That movie about that artist? Well, better luck next time, Uncle Helio. We could check at the Paradise in Ryanton, though. They're often right after Leadford with the movies."

Helio leaned comfortably back into his seat.

Del kept the throttle in.

Fifty to go for Otsego.

* * *

From the Motorola, Doris Day's clear sweet voice filled the car with "Que Sera, Sera (What Will Be Will Be)" on the drive back to the familiar farm house on Jericho Road. They slipped in past an arborvitae that all referred to as Edith's tree. "That tree became as much your tree, dear, on our long wait while you glorified Alaska," Papa said as they'd turned into the drive. Anna Mae smiled, knowing his statement to be true; and feeling a slight pang of regret in knowing she'd stayed away so long. Suddenly she smiled a tiny private smile. She'd been in pursuit of Helio as much as for information needed to round out her Alcan narrative.

She coaxed Helio out of Alaska and they now owned a nice brick home with a fireplace, located in the development across Jericho from the Groners. During their four years of wedded bliss Anna Mae and Helio'd lovingly shared their home with adopted daughter, Dosia.

Anna Mae and Helio were already feeling the duress of loneliness in knowing that Dosia, beautiful, vivacious, and eighteen would soon be on her way. Many a beau was already lurking. Dosia and crowd were sitting far behind Anna Mae at the movie. Anna Mae'd looked carefully, however, and purposefully, and was able to single out Dorsia's exact location because of the unique silhouette of her daughter's close-combed hair-do. She'd said she'd be with friends, Anna Mae'd thought, and she'd turned again to peer back at that young crowd bent close about the pretty daughter. Boys, really; all boys?

Upon the fear that Dosia's surround was indeed all boys, powerful loneliness had swept through Anna Mae and that feeling yet haunted her as her Papa pulled up beside the rear steps of the Groner house on Jericho Road.

Immediately upon entering, Clarence turned on the RCA radio and worked the dial. Their hearts rejoiced at hearing Elvis Presley singing "Love Me Tender." By then, ice cubes were afloat in glasses of root beer Fizzies. The soft-drink tablets scurried around until they disappeared where upon Papa Clarence and Momma Clydis held the beverage high in salute of the young superstar singer. The station rushed on to hawk Comet cleanser, the latest competitor for Ajax. All through Elvis' song and then all during the commercial, Anna Mae'd sat slowly spinning her icy glass, seemingly amused at seeing the glass turn faster than did the floating ice cubes. "Did you notice any girls with our girl?" Her voice had a sigh to it, instantly alerting Momma and Papa who still pined for a return of either or both of their two daughters.

"She had me worried, too," Momma said, "until just as the lights were coming up, I saw a girl on her right. You likely missed seeing her. I was a step or so behind you as the lights were coming up."

"Short hair? I thought she sat with a boy to either side."

"Yes, I'm sure I saw a girl, perhaps the Benson girl. Constance, I believe."

"Oh good." She still hadn't tasted her icy glass of Fizzy. "I just wondered."

"It's good to wonder and even to worry a little, even sigh a little," Papa said. "We did."

"About me?"

"About Edith and about you, although away in the Yukon and in Alaska, we worried mainly about your being harmed in some way. That's because we'd no inkling of Helio." His comment brought a sly demure smile from his beautiful youngest daughter. "I looked back," Papa said, "after holding the car doors for you sweeties. She came out with Constance and the two of them got into a car; boys got into a car across the street. They'll all be sitting in the Buena Vista by now."

Her chair scraped as she stood up. "I'll get on home. I feel that I should go there to the Buena Vista, their favorite restaurant, but I won't. I'll be brave like you were, but I do fear that Mr. Right will appear." Her Fizzy untouched, she hurried out the kitchen door, beginning a brisk block-long walk, returning to her lonely house.

Chapter Two

It seemed that every bolt-bearing semi in the region had decided on an evening run to Otsego. "Well, I would've thought they'd gone to a Friday night dance, or something." Helio rubbed his head as Del pulled into the rear of a line of rigs. They counted ahead twelve rigs to the one just unloading.

"Be all night, you figure?"

"Likely till daybreak. I'm usually first in line when I arrive at daybreak. Now we sit here while my Anna Mae sits through that artist movie with lonesome beside her."

He made a rare joke for his uncle. "She's to get all the popcorn, that's sure, Uncle Helio."

"Del, I'm prideful sorry about this." His sad face confirmed the truth of his statement. "There're blankets behind this seat," he sighed, "but only one pillow."

Del opened the driver's side door. "Take a rest, Uncle Helio. I can use a folded blanket for a pillow if I decide to snooze. I'll go to see what's up."

Once settled across the seat of the cab, Helio fell asleep, missing that Del hadn't promptly returned. Hardly noticing even when from time to time his feet were raised to Del's lap and the Reo eased ahead toward the unload zone. Finally, that is to say, about four in the morning, Del shook him awake. "Huh?"

"We're next. Uncle Helio."

"What?" He pawed for his pocket watch, peered at it by flashlight. "Four? Gosh, they're unloading faster that I'd figured."

"They've good help." Head rubbing ensued as Helio watched his nephew disappear into the night. Moments later he thought he glimpsed

16

Del trotting into view under the floodlights of the unloading area. But Del at five foot seven and one hundred fifty-five pounds, and with his thick brown hair to move with the breeze, looked much like all the other workmen. He again blinked, thinking that he did indeed see his nephew blending in with the gang of workman milling under the floodlights.

As the truck ahead pulled away, Helio was sure he saw Del grab a bolt and swing it onto the bolt stack. The stack was about eight feet tall and would measure the length of a city block. Had he stood upon his load to look over the stack, he'd see that the pile was perhaps wider than long, but the size of the stack didn't interest Helio. He wished his nephew would get out of the way of the workmen before being clobbered accidentally by a flying bolt. Answering a hand wave of another workman who resembled Del, he eased the Reo into a position indicated by yet another Del-like workman.

Deciding he wasn't seeing Del at all and thinking Del'd be right back, Helio scrunched into his corner of the cab and settled back with his warm blankets tucked about him. He stirred next to a throaty roar. The factory was coming awake. By that time he was again stretched fully across the cab seat, and had been oblivious to all but his dreams. Coming now up through his sleep fog he paused at the edge of slumber where his mind's eye saw bolts moving from the far side of the stack. The bolts were in concert with the mill's awakening. Bolts from that far side of the stack would've aged about five years and were ready to be sawn into chunks and the chunks shredded to become excelsior. While still in sleep fog his Indian brain was sorting the din of mill venue into a distinct cadre of sounds even to his hearing the cheer of robins busy with morning chores. That before his slumber again deepened.

"All set," Del slipped in behind the steering wheel where he sat with Uncle Helio's feet in his lap. Helio popped fully awake. He scrambled into a sitting position. He squinted into the early rays of morning. His head came around to rest his eyes upon Del just in time to see him pushing dollars into a shirt pocket.

"What, they paid already; paid in cash? Very unusual. A check is sent usually. Did you sign the slip?"

"Yes, Louie will get a check in the mail." Del grinned over at Uncle Helio. "They paid cash just to us roustabouts. $2.50 an hour." He patted upon the stuffed shirt pocket. "It was a good night, old sleepy uncle. You snoozed right on through it." Helio grinned.

Del crossed the Kalamazoo River on a brief joy ride past one of two mountains near Otsego. "That's around 1400 feet, I'm told, but I don't know how much above sea level. Sure some sight, huh?"

"We Alaskans just think of Michigan's mountains as hills."

"Pretty, no less; I'll enjoy what we got." After a few minutes Del gunned the big Reo out onto U. S. 131 where he began working his way up through ten gear shifts, settling into top gear by three miles, or so. "Keep watch for a diner. I'm starved. My treat." By then the sky was radiant blue and cloudless.

The cab began to heat. They wound down the windows and each rested an arm on a window frame to let breeze pelt the arm and to cool the face. They were just into the south side of Bradley, Michigan when: "Diner, my side. See it? It's a good one I've been in before." Helio licked his lips. "Trucker's delight is this one." Del coasted the big red to a stop out in front of Maxie's Cuppa.

A sign boasting, "Breakfast all day," acerbated a growl in Del's vacant belly as he was exiting the truck. His paced quickened, darting him on past his uncle.

They took a window table in view of the truck. "That Reo, out there," a stranger greeted. "Seldom see one. She okay?"

"Grew up driving Reo," Helio said. "Up Alaska way. My granddaddy and daddy drove U. S. Army Reo building the Alcan and on to maintain it as the Alaska Highway. I cut my eyeteeth on a big army Reo. I came south here to marry and near went back home for want of a job to do before a neighbor showed me an ad in the Press for this big old Reo. She's a 1948. Her service began in California and she now has just two hundred thousand miles on her. Sure a good truck, I'll tell you."

"Better than Mack or Kenworth, you think?"

"Oh, now I'd say not," Helio admitted. "I'd guess that pound for pound they'd all three equal out; other makes, too, I'd say. We have a '53 Mack for hauling logs. Hard to beat a Mack, I'll say. There were some big bruiser army trucks by Mack up on the Alcan, too. I've not had the pleasure with a Kenworth, as I see that might be yours out there, but I'd driven Mack some up there in Alaska before coming down here."

"I'd like to try a Mack some time. Cut my eyeteeth on a Kenworth Bullnose like you've seen right out there," he nodded proudly. "Hard to change brands as you know, but I do like that cute bulldog hood ornament on the Mack."

"She earned that bulldog name back in World War One," Del put in. "Bulldog tenacity. That hood ornament, though, I heard's since 1932."

18

The man nodded but said nothing as his heap of pancake, egg, and bacon had arrived.

* * *

Dosia Outhe, adopted daughter of Anna Mae and Helio C. Outhe lay without covers, and with the sunshine blinking her eyes awake. Birds chirruped outside her window and a pleasant gurgle reached her ears from the Black Sucker River that flowed nearby. Her pink silky pajamas flashed in sunbeams as she sneaked a peek out at the birds prancing in the apple tree near the empty feeder. She whispered, "I'll be but a few minutes," her lips forming a graceful smile as though the birds understood and were grateful, as was she.

Her eyes scanned pink-painted shelves along a side of her room. A hard cover edition by A. A. Milne stood behind her stuffed Winnie-the-Pooh bear. Her half-filled scrapbook rested under a plastic Hasbro Potato Head family of Mr. and Mrs. and children Spud and Yam. The Potato family group was a permanent setting as now-hardened Silly Putty'd subbed for potatoes. She'd recently pulled her scrapbook from under the potato family to scotch tape in an article about Mr. Milne. Christopher Robin, a main character in the Winnie book was based upon Mr. Milne's son. Mr. Milne had died on January 31, 1956 and she'd felt moved to retain a record of him, and she'd dusted off her Winnie in commemoration of the bear's creator. Other toys rested amid a tangle of Slinky, bobby socks, saddle shoes, bird books and a scattered Erector Set from which she'd been fabricating the frames for bird houses. The Jackie Gleason show'd been the first to advertise a toy, Mr. Potato Head, on TV, and momma Anna Mae'd been quick to order one for her daughter. The Erector Set she'd received from Papa Helio. The bird house idea'd been the only project she'd dreamed up to make use of it. She reached for the Hip Bumper.

Years ago on a birthday, Momma had presented her with a wooden hoop measuring some thirty plus inches in diameter. Momma had seen the contraption at a craft shop in Montréal, Canada. The device had been an English improvement over a vine-fashioned hoop made in Australia, and, fashioned of plastic, it would soon be widespread as the Hula Hoop. Dosia's version was known in the Oute household as the Hip Bumper.

Close at the east window of her room her slender hips whirled her rose wood Hip Bumper. She whirled while beaming at Red Red Robin's tug on a worm from the dewy grass near a shading hazelnut bush. She paused her hip bumping and the hoop clattered to the floor. Her eyes lifted from the energetic robin to the blinding sun.

Dosia saw the stark bright sun as van Gogh would have seen it, and knew why he'd painted it boldly. She touched her ear, grinning that she found it all right, not missing as had been poor van Gogh's.

Wanting bright color to compliment the red robin and to honor poor Van Gogh, she stepped to the closet, selecting a bright red blouse and her newest, brightest blue Levis.

She stood five foot four and weighed a hundred and a few pounds. Her eyes were brown and she wore her slightly wavy dark brown hair cut short and combed close as a bid to stave off hairdo maintenance.

In the kitchen, toast clunked into the four-slot Toastmaster and from a refrigerated Tupperware she flipped a slice of Lisbon lemon onto the saucer beside her Blue Willow cup. Milk, sugar, and a Tetley tea bag joined hot water in the cup and she tossed in the slice of lemon.

She pulled a pair of substantial size three brogans over her white sweat socks and then sat stirring the laden drink. Her huge belt buckle of pearl with a sterling inlay of an Indian chief scraped against the edge of the table as she rose to attend the buzzing toaster, it having popped her seared bread handy to her slender fingers. Approaching the chromed toaster her belt buckle flashed its reflection, and her mind reflected on wonderful Indians she'd met from Alaska and in the northern tier of the forty-eight where she'd ridden on truck trips with Papa Helio. On one trip to Minnesota she recalled Papa saying they'd reached the highest point of the lower forty-eight, just a stone's throw from Alaska. He'd grinned but she knew he missed his home lands. "Someday I'll get to go there with you and Mama," she'd said.

Her muse of Alaska waned, and her attention focused a slice of the delicious peanut buttered toast to be consumed with the tea. The remaining three slices were clutched in her hand as she pushed out the door and onto the rear porch where stood a tin storage box of birdseed. She filled a small paper sack.

The birds were fed quickly and she turned away, hurrying toward the riverward edge of the lawn. A bench sat handy and she planked upon it, turning in time to see that black cap chickadees were, as always, the first to brave an approach to the feeder. Other birds watched from the apple tree until hunger, and their apparent confidence in chickadee bravado, brought them cautiously from their snug tree limbs.

With the wonderful birds busy, the substantial brogans on her feet proved their worth as she began to tramp around in a woods nearby. Beyond the woods cows idly watched her hike across their pasture. Past the lowing cows she climbed a fence stile to arrive at a willow fringe rooted along the Black Sucker River. Peeking through the springy willows, Mrs. Mallard and her trail of precious ducklings held the girl spellbound until a gleam of red focused her eye upon Lead Bridge, far to her left. The Reo was just off of Highway 131 and her heart raced. Helio, her dad, her favorite Indian, would be home in time for lunch. Suddenly, her heart bounced; perhaps Del would be aboard too.

Del was her favorite cousin. She loved him and knew she wasn't supposed to. This time she'd be good, she thought.

Helio swung down from the cab just as Anna Mae skidded up with her ancient Ford sedan and just as Dosia darted into view from the direction of the river. Helio's arms amply held both slender beauties as he explained about his and Del's fortune, that of being near home just at lunchtime.

Dosia stepped up to Cousin Del and pecked his cheek. He returned the peck although this time, and it seemed every time lately, he wanted more than a mere peck. His face blushed slightly beneath his coppery tan and wasn't noticed by the others; but he felt the heat and he felt the twinge in his loins and the quickened pace of his heart. She's your cousin, stupid! His mind raced to tell his heart to be still. Your cousin. Your cousin. Stupid, don't forget it!

Not really; the sides of his mind began to tug his thoughts to and fro, 'your cousin, stupid,' being pitted against her origin: French, from France, she isn't blood related, but adopted: Did that make a difference?

Born Theodosia Amarante Robespierre, she was adopted by Del's Aunt Anna Mae and Uncle Helio. Anna Mae and others, Grandma Clydis and Aunt Edith among them, and with their friend Maggie, had assisted Dosia in her transition from Paris street waif to American teenager. She'd joined Anna Mae and Helio soon after their wedding. They formed into a wonderful family. At the time of her adoption, Del saw Dosia merely as a fencepost-shaped girl cousin. Del's friendly peck at that time had been more of obligation than of pleasure.

But now!

Wow! What four nurturing years had done for her!

But she's your cousin, stupid! Sure, sure, she is, but she's no longer the shape of a fence post. Her shape now graced the whole pasture, the whole landscape, the whole of his heart. He sat across from her at lunch.

'Dose' like a dose of medicine, then 'sea' then 'uh,' dose-sea-uh ('uh' like the 'a' in media), his mind reviewed the lesson his aunt had taken him through, wanting him, and everyone, to get her daughter's name pronounced correctly. 'Dose-sea-uh,' she was then a fence post, now a – What? Did she? Tap my toe with her toe? Del sat with his size ten Wolverines as stationary as Gibraltar. Tap-tap-tap, YES!

His return tap was hasty, clumsy; and he hoped it'd not bruised her petite tiny toes. Feeling no return tap, he tried again but his move missed her brogan and thumped a chair leg. He held still, hoping she could find him when her warm finger grazed his in her reach for the gravy bowl. "I saw Mrs. Mallard and several ducklings just as you were crossing Lead Bridge so I didn't get an accurate count, but I think nine." She caught his eye – jolting him!

He stammered, "Er, uh, n . . . nine, huh?" His shirt was growing damp, clinging to his shivering back.

"Yes, the egg shells are in the willows just off our east lawn; real close to the house. It's so surprising. So close, I mean, and I never noticed them before today."

"Nine, huh?"

"We could try to count them."

He nearly leaped from his skin: "Well, er, sure."

Momma Anna Mae'd heard the location, ". . . real close to the house," and she silently hoped the location wasn't too close; a selfish thought for a mother, she knew. But she loved Helio, and she, they, needed time. "Dear, you may show me sometime; maybe tomorrow." The youngsters were at the door by then. "Don't be long. Be back by one." Her hand was over Helio's.

"Yeah, one. Let's shove off around one, Del."

Outside, the kids ran across the east lawn toward the willow fringe along the Black Sucker. In the house, Helio and Anna Mae had already forgotten the ducks, the springy willows, the world.

One o'clock was an hour away.

*   *   *

That night around their campfire located some one hundred yards above Bellyflop Creek, Louie again cautioned Del, "The walls have ears." They were discussing the fact of Del's going over to trucking and that the boss should select a new second in command. "I'd like to decide what to do tonight while Wesley's in town on a date."

"You shouldn't choose one," Sid opined. "Like on my crew, Hedden

Burpmeister just slipped right into place; like Del, here, did. Old Burp simple assumed leadership, natural like."

"The proof of the pudding is in the eating, we might say, huh?" Louie tossed a stick into the fire, signaling finality about his decision to let the second in command pick himself.

"Guys, I think you're right, that it'll work" Del said. "I've never considered myself as any sort of boss or sub-boss, but the boys took to me so I tried to side Louie. I've never sensed any resentment over that, have you, Louie?

"No. Paid him in his own coin, you were. Kindness and cooperation were reciprocated."

"Where in the world do you get those sayings? They don't quite fit in yet they always fit in enough so's one sees your meaning. Clear things up, they do."

"I use them too much, I'm sorry."

"No, no, I like them. Wish I knew some. From your reading, huh?"

Louie always had a book with him. Idle moments with him were seldom idle. "For our thirst of books, I thank your Aunt Edith."

"Well, my brother Nathan, same as you, took to it better than me. I'll let her know. You read about those sayings, do you mean?"

"Yes, 'Don Quijotes de la Mancha' is considered to be the first true novel, your Aunt Edith told me. Miguel de Saavedra Cervante of Spain wrote it. Well the first part of it was written in 1605; the last was in 1615. That song she plays on the record player, 'The Impossible Dream,' is by Mitch Leigh and Joe Dariam, from the 1928 opera. She told me all about that opera and gave me the book. In the book Don Quixote is a Spanish nobleman, a knight, and he traveled with a squire to combat the world's injustices. To Don Quixote, windmills were giants he had to battle, and country inns were castles; and stuff like that. But even more interesting to me, I copied down about twenty of those sayings. The story is just jammed with those sayings that you've heard me use from time to time, er, uh, really, too much, I guess."

"No, just right," Del said, bumping his friend's knee.

"Same here, brother." Sid lightly popped his brother's shoulder.

Del stood up from his log seat. "Well, guys, I worked all night last night. That bedroll looks a country inn to me."

* * *

Del slept like a log a few hours then roused to a restless night. That little gal, that Dosia, she had his sleep dreams all mashed in with his day dreams. Out in the willows that day he whispered into her ear: "Nathan said your name, Theodosia, in French means 'gift from God.'"

"Really?" She kissed his nose. "I didn't know."

"Nathan's all the time looking up stuff." Her warm breath on his neck pulsated something high in his chest, putting a quiver to his voice, jarring his words. "Your middle name, Amarante, has to do with flowers." She placed a hand over his trembling lips.

"Don't say my last name. I won't keep it anyway. I want us to set Robespierre aside, along with Outhe."

"Will you marry me?"

"Yes, silly. Didn't you study biology?"

"That's college prep."

"Well, farming then. You know what I mean. They'll be madder than hops at us but they won't let us marry." She kissed his forehead. "Let's elope. When will you come?"

He grinned, thinking; of course, to elope seems the best solution. He kissed her, glad she'd thought of a solution when he'd thought only of endless tryst. "I could stop for you on my first solo trip into the Coopersville mill." He giggled, she giggled, and they snuggled. His breath fluffed her hair when he spoke, "Your dad'll have the Reo on hauls to Muskegon and Grand Rapids. I'll have the Mack and loads of logs for Coopersville."

She sat up straight and with hers palms on his chest; caught his eye. "Make it a Monday if you can, so that day we get the license and try to get our blood test. Megan Stokley, the head librarian, I know will witness our application and will keep our secret. I'll go see her tonight. She'll know all of what to do. You pick me up on each trip around ten. On Friday we'll say we'd planned to go see 'The Ten Commandments' at the Savoy in the city after the truck's unloaded. They won't even have to know we're married."

Their kiss was long; breathtaking.

"We'll have to make it work."

"It'll work." She was puffing. She spoke into his ear, shivering his back. "I've ridden with Papa all over the north tier of states, even to the most northern point in the lower forty eight, so they'll not be surprised I'd want to ride with you." Going over and over the plan, Del tossed and turned, finally coming to his feet near dawn when Wesley arrived driving the rattletrap pick-up.

Wesley bought supplies weekly as the best way of avoiding weevils and other buggers in the flour. "I don't never need no bay leaf, that dried laurel stuff, to preserve my flour," he boasted.

"Good film?" Del reached into the cab for a sack of groceries.

"Yeah, but I didn't pay much mind what with Jo beside me. No 'Giant' film, James Dean or not, could be as entrancing as she is." Wesley led the way to the larder, a box made of two-inch thick oak lumber to guard against varmints, raccoons in particular. He released a clasp and swung the lid upward. "I didn't dare to ask tonight, but I'm going to. To marry her, Del, you bet."

The campfire soon crackled and Wesley placed two rashers of bacon and hung a pot for coffee. "I'd like us to run a little restaurant." He spoke dreamily, and to no one in particular even though Del'd settled onto a bench of the nearby table. "I told her all about what was going on when we ate at the Brazier in Ryanton. She knows I know that work." Del had by then drifted deep into his own thoughts, not stirring as Wesley continued toward breakfast. "We did see a preview of that Charlton Heston one, that 'Ten Commandments.' Looks to be a good show."

"Me and Rose are going to see that sure," Louie said as he was coming out of a yawn and stretch. He planked down across the picnic table from Del. "You know, we went over to his town. St. Helen. Folks there brag about that Charlton Heston came from there. Little town about fifty miles east of Cadillac. It lies near lakes Haughton and Higgins, too. In there with Dad's crew while Sid was in Korea. Dad got us a good winter of work harvesting pine for telephone and power poles. Folks sure talked on about that Heston, claiming that his going to college at Northwestern some place near Chicago wasn't as important as where he was born." He reached across and tapped Del's shoulder. "Been moping here all night? You act like she's left you. Who you moping over?"

Del perked up. "Leaving this crew. You've a good crew, Louie."

"You won't be far, you know, and you stop in whenever you can to eat Wesley's cooking." Despite Del's smile, Louie guessed that more was troubling his friend. Gotta be a woman, he thought, and the thought brought a grin to his face; and a far off look to his eyes.

The Reo, grinding its way in from the shirt-marked gateway a half mile out, came to everyone's attention. Del looked to be sure the box of pilot bread was next to Helio's plate. They heard Wesley's command: "Pour!" Sid just then arrived from his morning ablutions near Bellyflop Creek. He grabbed a cook's mitt and commenced with pouring coffee. Wesley ladled batter for six pancakes onto his griddle. The Reo's twin solid brass highly chromed Grover air horns located atop the cab popped into view from behind a low hill. Del watched the cab rise into view, saw the morning air wavering above the stack. His grin widened yet more as the red wonder came on. Wesley, wiping smoke from his eyes, flipped the pancakes.

In a jiff Wesley'd pitched the first six onto a platter and ladled the next six onto his griddle. "Go ahead on," Wesley advised, as he set the platter of cakes amid his clientele. "I'll be right along." After five repeats of his pancake delivery he sat down and grabbed into a stack of three. "More if you need them," he said as he mouthed the first forkful.

Helio stopped at two pancakes and a triplet clasp of bacon, the whole consumed with several chunks of pilot bread. Del'd kept his eye on his uncle's progress. Noting when a slurp of coffee was to take place, he said, "Uncle Helio, which came first, diesel or gasoline?"

Helio's quick grin caused a portion of his slurp of coffee to dribble down his chin. He set his cup simultaneous with mopping his face and neck with his denim shirt tail. "Uh, well, you mean engines like in trucks and cars and such. We were up in Alaska, mind, and watching them harvest salmon from the fishwheel; Tanana fishcamp, you see. Well, Anna Mae up and told me about Wilhelm and Wilhelm of Germany, counting them in heavy on inventing the first internal combustion engine. It ran on gasoline, she said. A junked Mercedes car was found and she wanted to see if it had a place in her Alcan story is why she studied up on it. Those Wilhelmses, that's Daimler and Maybeck worked with Nickolaus Otto to build that first internal combustion engine. It burned gasoline, mind. It did 130 rpm, but the Wilhelmses went on to form a company and produced an engine of 900 rpm by 1882. Those guys made the first car, too. It'd do eleven miles per hour.

"They added a four-speed gearbox and launched the Daimler Motor Company in 1890. That was the first car company. Carl Benz, an acquaintance of theirs lived nearby. He built a car in 1893 and his car was the first production car. Then in 1895 Benz built the first truck. Soon Steinway, that piano company in America, Long Island, New York was producing Daimler motors, Benz cars, and Daimler trucks. Wilhelm Daimler died soon after, but Wilhelm Maybeck, still in Germany went on to produce a special car that was called Mercedes after a guy's daughter. Mercedes may've been made in the company on Long Island as well as in Germany, but Anna Mae never did learn that for sure nor how an old Mercedes come to be junked along beside some Alcan stuff way up in Alaska."

Louie slurped his coffee then set his cup. He looked at Helio. "Isn't diesel simpler?" Ignoring the automotive details Helio'd extolled, Louie said, "You'd think diesel'd come first."

"No, diesel was later, in 1894. Rudolf Diesel of Bavaria patented an internal combustion engine where fuel was ignited without spark. By pressure-ignition, he called it. Then in 1919, Clessie Cummins purchased manufacturing rights so diesel was birthed in America, Cummins diesel, you see."

"That Mack of yours is a Cummins diesel, is it?"

"No, a Mack. Mack builds its own diesel engines; transmissions, too. Our Mack engine's called a Thermaldyne; other Mack trucks have a Thermodyne engine; spelled slightly different."

"I noticed those twin exhaust stacks. V-8 engine, is it?"

No, the exhaust comes into two pipes. I like the looks of twins sticking up there and it does keep most of the exhaust smoke and sulfur and such away from your load. Seems like a good idea to me. I first saw twin exhaust stacks like that during the war. About in 1942, a fellow had one in Alaska. Civilian, he was, not military. Boy, I sure liked those twin stacks. When the Reo needs exhaust work on it, I may install twin stacks; snazzy her up a little like I have the Mack."

"I can smell that Reo is gas, right?"

"Yes, and I like the smell of both gasoline and diesel fuel and their exhausts." Helio stood up from the table. "Almost as much as I like your cooking." He let his belt out a notch, his grin to Wesley.

"I guess I favor the gasoline exhaust odor over diesel," Wesley said, "but no smell for me beats a spit roasting beef round or a griddle of breakfast. Is there other kinds of diesels, maybe better smelling?"

"All smell just wonderful," Helio grinned. "Besides Mack, there are three other makes of diesel I've come across; that's Cummins, Detroit, and Caterpillar; all good, and I'd think there're others. That front end loader Del and I are going now to use is a Caterpillar." He nodded to his nephew. "You ready to roll, Del?" His glance encompassed the other three. "Boys, I'll be back later to pull away with the bolts. Today Del's making a roll to Coopersville with logs."

Once settled in the truck cab beside Helio, Del observed, "Going to be a busy day around here." The Reo was approaching the gateway and its flapping shirt. The double-sized crew was by then pouring into the rutted way; headed for the aspen forest. Speaking of kinds of stuff, Uncle Helio, I'd say about each of those workmen's vehicles is a different kind; sure a lot of kinds." The Reo pulled onto the dusty washboard and Del began climbing the gears.

"That's nothing," Helio spoke loudly and with his voice chattered by the road. "A lot less kinds now, I've found out, than thirty or forty years back. Cars and pickups and trucks, I don't have numbers, but your Aunt Edith recalled about a truck problem that helped old Poncho Villa. He's the guy who attacked the USA back in 1916, you know." Del slowed the truck, the better to hear Helio.

"In that Punitive Expedition to get Villa, in 1916, General Pershing used 550 trucks of 128 different kinds and it was about impossible to get parts to fit any of them. Pershing's head ached even worse in France for World War One. He used 100,000 trucks made by 200 different companies. Outstanding among all those kinds, though, was White and Mack. That bulldog Mack, you know."

"Should've just ordered more of those two, I'd think." The truck was creeping along by that time, the road being especially atrocious. Del hung tight to the vibrating steering wheel, the truck ground along in high range third gear.

"Well, that's sort of what was done. I never did see a Liberty Truck, but that was the solution. Just one kind of truck that was assembled with parts from many different companies, but all of the parts for finished trucks were the same; parts were interchangeable truck to truck."

"If roads there were like this one, they'd sure need parts. I wonder that the tires held up during a war; worried too about the tires under us."

"We have it made," Helio called, "but you need to watch those tires on the Lufkin semi trailer. She carries my oldest tires. No problem with flats during that War One though, I'm sure. Those trucks were all on solid hard rubber. It must've jarred the socks right off those drivers. After the war, Goodyear decided to try pneumatic tires on trucks. This ride here would've seemed like heaven during that so called 'War to End All Wars.'"

Del turned into a gate marked by a tin can on a stick. Ahead lay the scatter of logs, but by then she, not the logs, not the Mack, again caused his heart to be thumping high in his chest.

CHAPTER THREE

Dosia fed the birds then hiked no farther than to a position affording a clear view of Lead Bridge. It was a cloudy Monday morning and she wished not to get soaking wet, but rain or not, she wasn't about to relinquish her view of that distant bridge. Ten o'clock ticked away into memory while another memory set her to pacing the grass off the sod beneath her feet. A raindrop smacked her forehead, and that drop called to others yet her feet refused retreat. Her eyes squinted, suddenly asking – is it? Yes, the Mack and the logs.

And my man!

She clamored into the cab, leaned over and kissed his cheek. She spoke into his ear, "I left a note for Momma saying I'm riding with you."

Del eased the big green Mack from her narrow street and into the back route to Conklin where he'd drop down to Coopersville. The whole way she kept one side of him deliciously clammy with rained on clothes and perspiration while his arm on his window frame and his face in the breeze were kept cool. Through it all she seemed as cool as a cucumber. She didn't cease a merry chatter the whole way. Nearing the mill she told him about "a sleeper cab she'd seen on a 1948 Diamond-T that Papa'd looked at before he saw the Mack. That Diamond-T was from out west."

"Likely a western truck would have Budd wheels like the Mack; that's ten lugs a wheel."

"You truckers, you're just like Papa." She squeezed his bicep. "I want to talk romance, not wheels."

"Why didn't he want it?"

"Gee, you're sure romantic. He said that it had split rims. Is that so bad?"

"You got me; I'll ask him about the rims." He placed his arm along her shoulders. She plunged to him, not needing her man to draw her in real close. "If we miss the mill by about three miles, sweety, we'll reach the Grand River; find some shade maybe. We're plenty early for the mill."

"Why, three miles is like nothing. Cross country trucking is like driving on and on forever. Lots of shady river banks along the way, I'll bet." An hour later they pulled to a stop in the mill yard. "Just my man and me, we'd just go on and on forever."

"Sounds good." He gently squeezed her knee. "Dear, with those river banks abundant we wouldn't need a sleeper cab."

She squirmed beside him. "We can be together until we get children." She wriggled closer, "then you could work more local, like now. That's why Papa came to stay local; because of me; and of course, Momma."

He wished he could think up plans easily, like she did. His hat lifted and his fingers mauled through his thick dark brown hair. His eyes beheld the silvery shiny Mack Bulldog hood ornament but he didn't see it. "Sounds good," he said. He'd been hearing her plans but couldn't think of any except to keep on hauling wood; and trysting, of course. She seemed to be filled with plans while he could drum up nothing about the future, about the coming fall, about the winter or of their course ahead. His ambition was limited to immediate desire rather than to perennial security. "Sounds good," he said. His mind struggled but couldn't get beyond immediate tryst, and of hauling more wood.

Wearing leather gloves he began unchaining his load. A yard workman joined in the task while close by a diesel front end loader sat waiting. The chains were removed and pitched up toward the truck cab. With pitching the last of the chains, the yardman left. The guy was a big bruiser and strong as an ox. When all was clear of the load, Del's hand signal would invite the loader to bite into the logs. Del signaled although he didn't see the big guy.

A strong rack on the rear wall of the cab was used to store the chains and he began hoisting them onto the truck, placing them such that a man standing in the limited space in front of the fifth wheel could grab them. A gloved hand grabbed a chain the instant he placed it within reach.

She was there!

Her tiny arms looked like broomsticks sticking from the man-sized leather gloves. He stood in shock seeing her raise a loop of chain to its hook. In fear the tiny arms would break, in awe that arms so tiny could do such work, his hat left his head and his strong fingers mauled the dark brown hair. "Here, let me."

"Huh?" He saw the big yardman take his place beside his woman. She hit him hard with a tiny sharp elbow.

"Sweetie, let me do that." Del could hardly see his mate lost in the bulk of that man being so nice.

Again, the sharp elbow. "No, I have help. I have my man."

The man winched and glanced down to size up Del, seeing him a twerp compared to Yardman Brutus. "Him?"

His snicker was cut short when a chain end rapped across his cheek. "He's my man," she said. Blood dripped from where the chain end had connected.

With a final glance at Del the man disappeared. Del took a step toward the truck but not seeing his quarry, he dashed around the truck, arriving just in time to see the gent leap back aboard his front end loader. "Let's get on with these chains," she called.

She hung all of the chain before hopping down from the truck. They walked together to the mill office to see that the load was recorded, assuring that Sid Watkins be sent a check. By then the truck was unloaded.

That yardman was not in sight.

"Looks like our booger has bugged."

"Dear, you handled him well but we can figure someway to arm you, if you like."

She walked beside him, silent for a time. "Chain end'll work for me, I guess."

"I'm keeping a club handy. A man his size may need clubbing. I'm getting a club shaped like a double-bit axe handle. No man better than me with a double bit axe."

"First, let's try diplomacy."

"Oh?" He peered at her.

"Well, but with the chain end handy, axe handle too." She squeezed his hand.

He boosted her up into the cab.

* * *

That evening Louie, Sid and Del sat around the campfire. Nearby, Wesley snored, catching up on sleep, his windup alarm clock near an ear. Wesley was usually first to bed, and he was always first to rise. Just at the fringe of firelight, Nancy's mule eyes shined. Dan had picketed her in close for the night. She waited now impatiently, expecting a sugar cube, some oats, and a brisk curry. Dan had driven off with the rattletrap pickup hoping to see Wynona at the feed store where he'd gone to buy oats for that precious Nancy mule. Louie looked over at Del. "Del, what you got there? Axe break, did it?"

Del had been sighting down the length of a handle that'd fit a double-bit axe. "I came here special tonight in hopes I could talk on something," Del said. He leaned the axe handle against his log seat. "I got me a girl," he said, "but can't tell nobody that'd get word of it back to Uncle Helio."

Surprise was in Louie's voice, "Why, you not getting along? Can't be."

"I'm eloping with his daughter."

"Gee, your cousin?"

"She's adopted; really she's from France. We've been together."

"Oh?"

"She wants to get married. We have the license. The librarian met us at the courthouse as a witness. She's Megan, the one Dosia works for sometimes. We can wed on Thursday or Friday."

With their study on the axe handle, his friends ignored details of the wedding. "That axe handle isn't for Helio, I'd think." Sid reached and nudged it with his toe.

"No, some big ape at Coopersville mill yard who fancies himself a Don Juan. He went after Dosia. She busted him with a chain end and he backed off, but we don't trust him. I'll leave here tomorrow after Wesley's breakfast. Go hitch on my logs and be at her place near Leadford around ten. Today we bought the marriage license and had blood drawn for some test. Doing a little everyday so on Thursday or Friday we can wed."

"Not without me," Louie was emphatic. "I'm to be best man."

"Okay, I'll let you know where and when."

"Bride's maid?" Sid hopped to his feet. "Maxine, I could ask her."

"Swell of you. We figure that once we're married, their learning about it shouldn't be too bad."

"How about, illegal or not, first cousins, I mean. Maybe there's a special paper, or something."

"Detail to clear up if necessary after the wedding."

"Gotcha, pard. And best of luck to you both. The whole affair is mum's the word by me and Sid."

"I sure wish it was happening to me," Sid's voice sounded sad. "She wants to wait till winter so's I'd have time to be home." He plowed his fingers through his hair. "She's right, I guess."

"No, she isn't, brother. I've kept mum, about like old Del here, but I asked Rose and she's accepted. Let's put some pressure on Maxine. Being a bride's maid might put her in the right mood. Go for a double wedding when we finish this year's bolts."

"Wow, well, darn it. When Dan gets back with that pickup, I'm going in to see her."

"Gee, aren't we all three like Don Juan here?"

"No, none of us," Louie said. "More Romeo, I'd say. That Don Juan was a Spanish nobleman, obsessed with the seduction of women and he felt no moral restraint in his seducing; bad apple, I'd say. Shoot, us three are just plain old ordinary lovesick loons, now aren't we? Can we ever have too much of a good thing?" Heads nodded in agreement.

"But Del, I'm somewhat dithered by your ape man, that big ape you mentioned. You could kill him with that axe handle; spoil everything."

"He's right. Just leave her home, er, away from the mill yard, for corn sakes. Get her a room, maybe."

"We thought we'd settle with him once and for all." Del lifted the axe handle onto his lap.

"Now, you be careful," Sid and Louie chorused. "And about apes," Louie continued. "Your brother Nathan visited us after he'd been to that college a while. So now I disagreed about apes being relatives; and about clobbering them too."

"Like you, he's always looking up stuff."

"There's a quote from Queen Victoria of what she said in 1842 after she saw an orangutan in a London zoo. She described it as 'frightful and a painful' and she went on to call it 'disagreeably human.' You heard that, 'human'? And her comment agrees with a book I read during last winter, 'The Hunchback of Notre Dame.' I'm waiting for old Nathan to come to visit again so I can explain to him my collaboration. Victor Hugo wrote that Hunchback book back in 1831. The hunchback's name was Quasimodo. It means deformed and Hugo described him as a 'hideous Ape.'"

"So? So is that crumb down at the Coopersville mill yard; ape, I mean."

"I'm agreeing with Nathan; that no human is an ape even if you don't like um."

"Huh?" Del and Sid were mussing their hair.

"Remember we were all warned by the Baptists all through our Sunday school years not to read anything by that awful Charles Darwin. Well, that was one of the first books Nathan read when he got to college."

"That'd be my brother, all right."

"Not in a class, mind, but on his own he read it in the library. Well, people think Darwin thought humans developed from apes. Nope, clearly stated in Darwin's book, he said that humans didn't develop from apes or from monkeys either."

"So where from then."

"Don't know accept in the Bible, and Darwin didn't know either. But the idea of apes ancestry to humans was persistent long before Darwin came on the scene. Forty years before Darwin, mind you, forty years, Darwin hadn't even written about it yet. Well, old Hugo described Quasimodo as a hideous 'ape' and, also, about thirty years before Darwin Queen Victoria had likened humans to an orangutan, a type of ape."

"Well, I really don't care, Louie."

Louie half stood, striving to make his point: "'Spartacus,' did you read that?"

"No." Del stifled a yawn.

"He was a slave and the Romans believed that slaves were not humans."

"So?"

"Well, they said not human because they didn't have a soul; only humans have a soul, you see? So in their opinion, slaves weren't human."

"So? Louie, it's getting past my bedtime."

"Wait, you'd agree that all humans have a soul, huh?"

"Sure."

"Well Darwin said that two characteristics distinguish the human from all other living things. The human believes in God and the human has a soul; and Darwin found no evidence at all that those traits were handed down through any natural selection process, by no ascending organic scale, he said; no evolution, that'd be."

"Gee, that isn't nothing like the pastors told us, is it?"

"Nope, and I'll believe old Nathan any day because I'll tell you why. He's read the book. I've read it too, now, and I agree. Besides, Nathan said, when I wrote and said I'd read the book, that as far as he can tell, only two people have actually read the book; that is him and me, yet thousands of yahoos bellow their stupid guts out about it and Darwin just about daily. Makes me sick."

"Well, it's made me groggy," Dell said with a grin as he gained his feet. He left the axe handle leaning on his vacated log. "Good night, you guys."

* * *

Del opened his ears and eyes to the growl of a heavy truck, the truck grinding in from the shirt-marked gate. He drew the blanket up over his eyes, hiding like the proverbial ostrich. Helio was expected that day, but later in the afternoon. By then Del would've been well under way, even he would've by then had her beside him, but why was Helio here now?

He knows!

Del griped the blanket tightly. How could he? Surely he'd not learned about it from her. She's cool as a cucumber. He lowered the blanket an inch and peeked out at the morning haze, his gaze coming to regard Wesley at the fireside positioning his rashers of bacon. He saw Dan sitting a bench of the table with his head in his hands; could be he'd had a fair evening with Wynona; and the mule was quiet so he hadn't forsaken old Nancy in the bargain; good guy was Dan. Ooooh My! The Reo was loud now and pulling right up toward the forty-foot Lufkin crammed with bolts.

Del counted to ten, daring himself to walk right up to Uncle Helio, to walk right up to him the same as usual – but he stayed put, his bed roll his fortress.

Coward. Get up.

You loon.

Act natural.

The warm covers went flying. He jumped into his boots, not even tying them, and was tucking his shirt as he trotted out past Nancy to greet Uncle Helio. During the whole trot he pondered what to say. What was it that was natural to say?

"Del, glad I caught you," the words came as tonic to his troubled soul. He'd let Helio talk.

Though he couldn't think on just what to say in return, he did manage: "Good morning. What's up? Why the extra semi trailer?"

Helio, with his familiar un-tucked shirt tail hanging over his belt, stood half out the door of his truck. "Powwow. I wasn't going to go this year but World War Two code talkers are coming and they know about other code talkers, some from World War One. All code talkers were Indian, you know. Also Clarence Groner asked me to help find somebody to take over for him. You know about Indians? You know about that annual Roughwater Powwow?"

"Yeah, I guess."

"Anna Mae and I've been going to it. These last two, Dosia went, too. The idea of it is to practice being traditional Indian yet getting along with non-Indians. Del, that's still not all that easy to do. Also, Grandpa Clarence needs help. Your brother Nathan was picked by Clarence to be the interface between Indian and non-Indian, but he went on to college and the army so we talked and decided you'd be a worthy replacement for Clarence. Clarence needs someone to break in a few years before he gets too old. How about it?"

"Gosh, I've no idea." His grin when he was saying that, however, caused Helio to believe his nephew was delighted to do it. Well, indeed, Del was delighted, delighted to be talking about anything other than his relationship with Dosia. Almost giddy with delight, he was. "Well, well sure, I guess." His mind was in a panic: Darn, now I'm sunk! It'll likely ruin our plans!

"I've been up all night trying to plan ahead on hauling bolts but I'm behind or I will be if I sit around in the woods thinking instead of hauling. Fellow's tractor went belly up over at the Muskegon excelsior plant. I've rented his Fruehauf for this summer as an extra to be loaded with bolts. It'll be less a hassle hauling them sandwiched in with our hauling logs. I'd bet you're loaded with logs right now, right?"

"Ready to roll after breakfast."

"Well then tomorrow can you make a haul with bolts to Otsego? I mean with the Mack and this thirty-four foot rented Fruehauf; bolts instead of logs, I mean. There's stake racks for this Fruehauf stashed in our garage. Stop on the way back today for the racks to get her reconfigured for bolts. Meantime the guy'll put bolts on this Fruehauf instead of on the ground; be easier to square um up once you get the stake racks installed."

Del knew that scheme'd louse up he and Dosia's plans, but what could he say? "Well, sure, I guess."

Right after breakfast and with Del still clutching a savory biscuit, Helio led out with the load of excelsior bolts. Del in the Mack fought Helio's dust until the turnoff at U. S. 131. Here Del turned north toward Yelrom to hitch his load of logs while Helio poured for Muskegon. Del pushed the Mack, wanting to be on time for Dosia.

A short time later at Leadford nothing seemed amiss as she watched the big green Mack cross Lead Bridge. Running, she timed the truck's approach and leaped aboard before the truck even stopped. At once Dosia grabbed onto Del, smashing her lips to his neck. A minute later, coming up for air, she noticed he'd chosen a different route to Coopersville. "We need to change plans a little, dear, to help Papa Helio. He'd say not to if he knew about us, but I didn't want to tell him just yet."

She leaned away so's to see him better. "What?"

"Helio's to meet some Navajo code talkers so he has to go to powwow. I'm to work in extra bolt hauls along with logs. This route to Coopersville takes us near that doctor's."

"Let's go in together. I'll give him calf eyes. You give him wild eyes to push him along with the testing. If we get the results today we can wed maybe tomorrow. Will that help?"

"Tomorrow it's to be bolts to Otsego. I'll pick you up around ten. Louie wants to be there as best man. Maxine is Sid's gal and they're pushing her into being bride's maid but I can't see them until tonight."

"I want to wed tomorrow, if possible. Bring Louie. Maxine if you can. I'm wearing new Levis, shined brogans, and a bright pink shirt. I bought new jeans for you and a red shirt. Can you polish those boots?"

"I've a new pair. I've holed the soles on these. New are behind your seat. I'm to stop at your house later today to get racks so's I can configure a rented Fruehauf for bolts. Then I'm to rush back to the aspen stand so's to install the racks so they can finish loading. I'll go on to pile a load of logs onto this Lufkin. Likely, then, I'll have a load of excelsior bolts hooked on tomorrow morning."

"Great. I'll push your new stuff behind the seat. I wish I could ride with you to Bruin City and Yelrom."

"After tomorrow, huh?"

"Sure." She squirmed nearly into his lap.

They grew silent, she with her hand on his thigh. His arms were busy threading the loaded Mack through Grand Rapids traffic. The rig pretty well blocked the street in front of the doctor's office. They left the Thermaldyne at idle. Diesel exhaust sweetened the air as they rushed on into the doctor's.

The blood test results were ready. Her calf eyes and his panic ones were saved, replaced by merry eyes and broad smiles. "I had a hunch you seemed rushed," the doctor said. "Congratulations."

She pecked his cheek and they rushed back to the Mack.

At the Coopersville yard she telephoned the preacher from the mill office, setting the wedding for eleven the next day. She began a trot back toward Del and the truck.

Nearly finished with unchaining his load, he failed to hear her yell over the chain rattle and clang.

Mill yard ape had grabbed her!

The chains removed, he looked toward the office, glimpsing her foot disappearing behind the front end loader. He didn't think to grab the axe handle. He dove right over the loader and from mid air latched onto Ronnie Perkins' neck like a python.

His big Perkins face scrubbed into gravel then raised just enough to catch her brogan in the eye. Del kicked him hard in the cheek bone. The two held to each other, kicking and stomping that crazy brute, but he came up a bleeding maddened bull, roaring mad with his aim for Del's puny face.

Del went down and dull just as she found a heavy five-foot-long pike pole.

The giant went sprawling.

Del boarded the front end loader, commencing to off load the logs while she took care of the chains. Perkins lay out in the yard, his head bleeding.

Later that same day, Louie said, "Don't worry I'll be with you tomorrow. Go tell Sid so he can go now to tell Maxine. She'll be glad it's to be a Levis wedding. Now she'll just need to fret her hair." He cuffed Del on the back. Del whose jaw felt swollen into the shape of an ape fist, trotted on toward the sound of Sid's crew.

All went well the next day. Louie, Rose, Sid, and Maxine arrived at the Methodist church in Leadford just when Del and Dosia pulled up in front with the huge Mack and with a Fruehauf loaded sky high with bolts. After the ceremony Sid handed Del the keys to a room in the Wayfarer Motel, easy to find on South Division, and he pointed the couple toward a gray Buick that was parked next to Louie's Chevy.

Just about suppertime that evening the gray Buick pulled in at the Outhe home near Leadford. From inside the neat brick house first Helio craned his neck to see who but hadn't said who before Anna Mae said, "Hon, who is here?"

"Er, well, er, come and see, uh, well, it's Dosia and Del, uh, I don't see . . ." He muttered off into speechlessness.

She joined him at the window.

"They're, why, they're holding hands. My dear, what is this?" They stood side-by-side and speechless, mouths agape, as the door opened.

"News, Momma, Papa.

"We're married."

CHAPTER FOUR

In mid summer, driving the big red Reo, Helio pulled into the unloading line at the excelsior plant in Grand Rapids. Del eased the Mack in tight to his father-in-law's bolt-packed forty-foot Lufkin, but thought to park slightly out of line to see past Helio's rig. In a moment Papa was climbing into the Mack. "Good, you can see when I'm to move along." With the Mack's idling Thermaldyne setting background tempo, Helio picked up a conversation where he'd left it a time previous.

"Like I was saying Del, on the old ground of the Choctaw, McCurtain County, Oklahoma, you'd most likely run onto Corporal Solomon Lewis. If any of the other World War One code talkers are yet available, he'd maybe know; according to Carl Gorman. Gorman's one of the Navajo code talkers I met at this summer's powwow. I wish you could've met him. Well, he said Solomon Lewis may be the last of the World War One code talkers so we'd sure like a visit with him and any other possible Choctaw talkers at the next Roughwater Powwow."

"It'd be maybe great if we could find Philip Johnston, as well. Lucky he recalled the Choctaw contribution to World War I."

"We're lucky, all us Americans, we're all lucky he knew the Navajo language. It was while his folks were Navajo missionaries, he said, that he learned the language then was to hear the tale of the Choctaw War One code talkers. Remarkably, just in the Meuse-Argonne battle is all they were used, but it led to Mr. Johnston alerting those marine officers at Fort Elliot during World War Two. The marines then trained the Navajo talkers for use in the battle on Iwo Jima."

"Saved a lot of lives, that's sure, and it makes my job with the Indians seem ever more important."

"Your Grandpa Clarence said he's never regretted a day of his involvement with the Indians and Roughwater Powwow. He says the same for Robert, his father. Robert Groner, you may know, knew Jody Roughwater all of his life, until Jody died. Robert and Clarence Groner are like a saint or shaman to the Roughwater Indians. It's wonderful, too, that now as husband to Dosia you really are of the Groner family."

"Say, you're right. We kids have always thought of Clarence as Grandpa; now, by golly, he is. Three grandpas and three grandmas; we really are lucky."

"Speaking of luck, are you going to need some help to get the rest of the logs hauled before snow?"

"Don't worry, with this the last of the bolts, Sid and Louie will soon be honeymooning. I'll easily finish with the logs before snow. How does snow figure in your plans?"

"My plans infringe on your plans, I'm afraid. I'll want the thirty-four foot Fruehauf to go west. It's the right size for the Pittsburgh haul my dispatcher arranged. I take a load of Continental aircraft engines from Muskegon to Lock Haven, Pennsylvania; then pull in to Pittsburgh to load the saw mill parts."

"I can get by with the Lufkin. You sure favor Fruehauf, don't you?"

"Habit, I'd think, or, more likely, history; and history right here in Detroit, did you know? Anna Mae's chucked full of history stuff, you've noticed. Well she said Fruehauf of Detroit invented and named the fifth wheel back in 1919 and they coined the term of 'semi' because the tractor bears part of the load. You know before the fifth wheel they say it took several men just to hitch or unhitch. I guess I just feel good about that company's history."

"I'll be happy with the Lufkin."

"Sure, okay. I can't see any company building bad semi trailers. Ours have both held up well this summer. You know, I've never hauled as many excelsior bolts before as I have this summer. They say 1957 will be a lean year, though. New products, plastics, you've heard, will be coming into use. Del, you work wholesomely with your dispatcher. Logs, freight, anything you can get, and always be kind. You know, I was just kidding one day when I asked our dispatcher to find a load for Anna Mae and me to haul clear to Alaska."

"Gee, what; maybe a load of pilot bread, huh?"

"No, but we carried plenty of that along. That first fall with the Reo; I'd just installed the roof horns, you see and was shopping around for some work. Anna Mae located Dolly Reams, never dreaming she'd send us home to Alaska; but she did. Dog sleds, you'd never of guessed it. Michigan ranks first in dog sled production, one factory is in Jackson. Many others are around Michigan's upper and lower peninsulas." Del rubbed his head; looked over at his father-in-law.

"My dispatcher, that's Dolly Reams," Helio continued. "Yours, too, now. Well, she teamed with one in Oregon to set Anna Mae and me up for the winter. We'll take the Reo out there with the Fruehauf loaded with the mill parts from Pittsburgh.

"Once out there I'll use the Reo and a company semi-trailer to haul wholesale groceries up and down the west coast. I'll stay on the job too with the Fruehauf hauling anything the Oregon dispatcher can arrange. Meanwhile my dispatcher has landed a log hauling job for me; filling in for vacations. Out there they run a lot of Peerless equipment designed for logging the big stuff and often use Hayes tractors built for tough off-the-road application. I've driven Hayes."

"Tough going is it?"

"Sure. You sit up straight and drive all the way and with your butt clinching the seat, no moment of relaxation. In off road conditions, like this'll be, I wouldn't bet a set of those new belted radials to last more than 30-45,000 miles. Grades up to 20% you'll handle but steeper and a crawler tractor will pull you up then put a drag on your tail to ease you back down. You go in weighing around 29,000 and come out loaded to a gross of 80,000 to 100,000 lbs. That's what logging the Pacific Northwest is about."

"Wow."

"You can believe it. A Hayes truck has 550 horsepower, burning No. 2 diesel at sixteen gallon an hour. Top speed is around 45. You don't need speed as much as staying power. Loaded, you're in low range low gear most of the time because you can't get momentum enough to shift up.

"Brakes! Brakes!" Helio slapped his knee. "If they fail you'll maybe not stop short of disaster. Like most logging trucks, the Hayes carries a reservoir of water on the back of the cab. The water's held at a pressure of seven pounds per square inch. Press a button on the dashboard and all eighteen or more wheels get a squirt of water onto the brake drum. That cools the brakes. Hot brakes and you're like sliding on rotten plums right to the gate of Hell.

"Still; I'd rather drive the forest non-roads than to drive anywhere else, except when it's rainy, that is. Then it's worse than to be on sand. Rain is the biggest problem for all off road truckers. You can't tell what its doing or has done to the road; worse than to be on sand.

"You're good on sand, by the way. Low range low gear and don't jerk it. Start to spin, STOP! or you'll just go deeper. By jingo, I'll take a forest to drive in any day!"

"I'd think a dispatcher'd have a hard day finding logging drivers, huh?"

"You gotta be proven. That Oregon dispatcher is a woman; I prefer a lady dispatcher. She's been in the business some fifteen years. Began dispatching for her hubby but she found more over-the-road loads than he could take, let alone trucking off- road like in logging. I'm lucky, having off-road experience in Alaska, the Yukon, and some in British Columbia. She'll find an easy go, however, to get me started again. Meanwhile I'll be trucking those groceries and anything else coming our way.

"Dosia's a good dispatcher, by the way. She worked in with Dolly Reams during last summer. Dolly says she's a natural. I know she'll want to be on the road with you, but get her into dispatching as soon as you can. Courtesy, honesty, mutual trust, and respect are required of both dispatcher and trucker. Dosia understands that. You remember that and the dispatcher'll have your next load waiting."

"Dolly got your load to the Pacific Northwest then, huh?"

"Yes, and she found us the lady dispatcher, too, that we'll have in Oregon. We'll be leaving for the mill parts a week next, so you kids move in. I suggest you set Dosia to work finding a south-going haul for right after the logs. Don't worry about the house when you go. Your three granddads, Cliff, Del and Clarence will be looking after it."

"Whoops, Papa, they're calling you ahead."

Helio hopped from the Mack. In a moment Del eased the Mack along behind Helio's load. He could see now, four trucks ahead to the end of the 1956 bolt hauling season.

* * *

While the men waited in the unload line, Momma Anna Mae was on the edge of her seat, immersed in an episode of 'As The World Turns.' Dosia sat on the sofa quietly occupied with Readers Digest, waiting for the next commercial message to take the air, releasing her Momma. The Procter and Gamble ad for Crest toothpaste was interrupted by Dosia faster than the announcer could mention stannous fluoride. "Momma, you'll see, the timing will be perfect." Momma Anna Mae peered at Mrs. Del Platt, her daughter.

"Dear, you should move here today. Aren't you afraid of bears? And I worry about you in a tent as the nights will grow cooler. And isn't this the last day of hauling bolts?"

"Yes, it's the last of the bolts, but Wesley's moving the camp to Yelrom to finish logging. I like helping Wesley. Louie and Sid's double wedding is next week. Then we'll move here because Sid and Maxine will be tent honeymooning in the Upper Peninsula. Momma, it'll just be another week."

Anna Mae's frown of concern vanished with the resumption of the program. By the clock that would be the final segment, the part of the program which introduced crises enough to draw Anna Mae another day. Despite herself, Mrs. Platt also yielded to that final segment, sitting with a finger hold marking her place in Reader's Digest while her head cock homed an ear for 'As The World Turns.' Momma turned down the next, and last, commercial. Dosia continued:

"Louie and Rose want to go tenting in Alaska on their honeymoon trip, but not until early spring. They'll take a short trip now and do Alaska later. They mentioned hoping to see reindeer and other native Alaskan animals like mountain sheep and bears."

Momma clicked off the radio. "Reindeer were introduced in 1890 so they aren't native. I didn't see one all the time I was there. Maybe Papa would know where to look."

"Anyway, Louie and Sid's wedding will both be next weekend then we'll move in here. When are you leaving?"

"During that first week you'd be here. By then our load will be ready in Pittsburgh by way of Lock Haven. We'll be in the Pacific Northwest, as you know, but in a cabin not any awful tent. Aren't you or the boys afraid a bear may enter the tent?"

Dosia had opened Reader's digest to the page she'd held with a finger. "This magazine's harder to read now with the ads cluttering it," she said. "No, we didn't see any sign of bears during our camping, but Sid and Maxine hope to see some in the Upper Peninsula."

"And they still plan on tenting? Dosia, that's not bravery, it's naivety."

She thumbed the Reader's Digest pages. "I'm glad Del and I don't smoke. At least Reader's didn't include cig ads. I thought Del and I'd go to Alaska when you and Papa can go. Is it really a backward place, undeveloped, I mean?"

"Progressive, we've thought. It'd surprise you. Alaska, for example, had women voting by 1913, way ahead of the forty-eight. I wish you'd help me with a perm this afternoon."

"You look as cute as any starlet right now. I'd bet you were a knockout in Alaska."

"Mr. Wilt of Detroit invented the cold permanent in 1886. Back then getting a perm was an all day job, not simple like today. A perm's likely how the stars' hair always looks so nice in western TV shows and in movies. The venue for those movies was set primarily in the late eighteen hundreds. That's after the trail herds were no more. Gone too were the heroic robbers, two-gun law officers; and the stage was set for the decked out cowboys in fancy western garb with tights and stripes and such, which never were, and for the beautifully curled women that one sees in the movies or on TV. Alaskan women also perm, by the way, so I had no trouble getting waved while in that wonderful setting."

Momma began removing bobby pins and a barrette from her hair. "How about around two o'clock?"

"Oh, sure." She flipped shut the magazine and placed it on the end table. "Right now, if you'd rather. I've time."

"No, I want to Clairol first."

"Miss Clairol, really?"

Momma chuckled, "'Does she or doesn't she?' Yes, love; there's been a touch of gray lately."

"Del and Me?"

"No, just age. You shocked us but now we're glad; and we want to help more, if we may."

"You've done a lot lately and a lot while I was a Robespierre and then an Outhe, let alone loaning the house and the truck. We're blessed, Momma."

"Your mother-and father-in-law say the same opinion; so glad they are to have you in the family. This updating of my hair is because of Del's grandpa Delibar's birthday. He thinks Marilyn Monroe is a goddess. Momma and Papa Groner want to take Delibar and Ella to see 'Bus Stop' at the Savoy. If our men aren't totally bushed when they pull in here from unloading those bolts we could go too tonight or tomorrow night. What do you say?"

"Fine for either. Then we'll stay that night here and now Momma that isn't because of bears or cool air. It's because we, too, want to eat with Del's grand folks on his Grandpa Delibar's birthday with a special cake and all."

"While I get personal with Miss Clairol you bake a cake. I'm assured he likes chocolate with chocolate icing."

The ladies, each humming a favorite tune, set to work, one to seek a transformation back toward youth, the other to brighten a day for a dear old man. Fifty miles to their south, a Reo hauling empty began climbing the gearbox, its aim for Leadford and Anna Mae. Behind the Reo, Del clicked into higher gears, each gear spaced at a habitual 150 rpm, edging the big green Mack to a cruise homed for his Dosia.

* * *

Grandpa Delibar Platt pranced around the house as briskly as arthritis would allow and with an ear cupped for any vehicular sound from the driveway but it was Ella who said, "Aren't you ready yet? They're here."

Delibar stood with his white shirt buttoned to the neck and with the knot of his crimson tie snuggled to that button. Below his shirt tail Ella viewed his gray and white striped boxers, his green and black striped garters, and his thick gray socks. "Del honey, I laid your pants out on the bed, I told you."

"Well, loud, huh?" He tried to sound disgusted but a grin foiled his sarcasm. Marilyn Monroe! Her day, day of the goddess! It couldn't be a sad day if he tried. Holding to the bedroom door frame, he struggled into the freshly pressed dark brown pants.

"Delibar! Happy birthday!" Clarence and Clydis Groner had just entered. She planted a wet one to Delibar's forehead while Clarence pulled gray suspenders up onto his friend's shoulders.

Wriggling his shoulders, Delibar said, jokingly, "You reckon Bus Stop's still on today?"

"You mean that Marilyn Monroe picture, that goddess? Why, I don't know. We'll have to go see."

Delibar looked worried. "At the Savoy, Ella said."

Clarence continued his tease. "Well, we'll go see."

Delibar looked at Ella, looked at Clydis. Ella placed an arm around her husband. "Miss Monroe wouldn't leave without seeing you, you old fossil."

Across the road, Anna Mae looked from her window. "They're going now."

"Let's hurry on over."

Wanting also to be arriving after the old folks had left, Naddy and Denibar pulled in just as Anna Mae and Dosia were nearing the Platt house. "I pray we're not late."

"They've just left for the Savoy. Plenty of time," Anna Mae said.

"I sure hope he doesn't sleep through the picture," Den said. "He'd be pretty low if he'd missed his goddess. Old age, I'd think, causes one to dream of Marilyn." His glance came to rest on Naddy and he stepped toward her. "But she doesn't stir me all that much." His arm came around his wife who stood beaming.

Gosh, Dosia thought, even in old age the pulse can quicken. Dosia walked up to her in-laws. "Papa Den, your dad was dressed to the nines; your mom, too."

"They don't get to the city often nowadays."

"Papa Den," she said, "I'll do the ladder work while you hand the paper ribbon up to me. We thought a line in from each corner with the paper mache bus hanging in the middle."

"Like a piñata, huh?"

"It is a piñata shaped like a bus. He drove school bus for a while before his arthritis grounded him, but also at the Savoy right now they're seeing Bus Stop with Marilyn Monroe. My folks decorated like a school bus 'cause they didn't know what Marilyn's bus would look like. They used a lot of Elmer's glue to get the hook at the top on strong enough to withstand his bashing the piñata bus with a cane."

"You know that Elmer's glue was named as a spouse for Elsie, the Borden cow. Kind of romantic, huh? And it's good glue-all glue. It'll hold all right."

"I sure hope so. It's heavy; filled with beef jerky, smoked fish, and like that; Papa Helio's idea. He and Momma made the grand thing of mache several days ago; nearly worked all night." She grinned, thinking, wondering, what else they may've reveled into while waiting for various stages of the work to get dry. Her gaze swept past father-in-law Den, hoping to glimpse the big green Mack approaching. A sigh escaped her as she stepped to the ladder.

"He'll come," Den said.

Del and Helio arrived without being noticed so engaged were the party preparers in their pursuit. Replacing his father, Del handed a length of orange paper ribbon up to his wife. She took the ribbon then dived onto him, smashing him to the floor.

"Hey, I'm not that Ronnie Perk . . . ."

Her lips crushed against his, preventing him saying, 'Perkins.' Del had confirmed the amorous bully's name as Ronnie Perkins, son of All Perkins, a Leadford resident. She held a delicious hand over his mouth. "No Ronnie talk."

He wrestled out from under her, wondering anew as to where in her slim construction she hid muscles as strong as his own. "Let me up, you meany."

They pulled each other upright. "That guy's name's Ronnie Perkins, for sure. They say we sent him to the hospital that day. Now he's okay woundwise, but grudgewise, I don't know."

"I know that family," Papa Den said. "His dad was of that swinery family; but that's gone now, of course, but that family's noted for being good workers, but quite stupid. I'd keep away from him. They're also noted for being stronger than any ox."

"He looks to be that all right, Papa Den. He tried to get me but Del and I laid him out with neck twisting, kicks and then a bean with a pike pole."

"I hope he doesn't keep on with work there," Del said. He handed more ribbon up to Dosia.

"Likely he's a good worker and they'll keep him." Worry lines pestered Den's forehead. "Son, can't you haul to a different yard?"

"Could be. We'll soon be done hauling into there for this year. Next season could be different. He does well at the saw mill, I'd guess, because I saw a new dark blue and cream Ford Crown Victoria there. The office man said it belonged to that big guy Ronnie Perkins. That's how I learned his name."

"Well, stay as clear of him as you can. Dosia, well, I'm very worried."

"I can out run him, Papa. Run right to Del, you bet."

The room was completely decorated and the table set with a chocolate iced chocolate cake as the center piece and gifts were crowded around his plate and onto the side board behind his chair. The group began to watch professional wrestling on television. The bad Russian had just beaten the skinny blond Adonis to a cringing blood-smeared pulp as the door opened to admit the movie goers. Jumping to their feet, they missed a sudden thrust of energy from Adonis to pin his opponent. 'Happy birthday' was yelled in chorus, but the 'Delibar' was mottled by on overlay of Dear, Papa, Del, and Grandpa. He caught who they meant, of course, and stood beaming yet shaking with a mix of embarrassment and pleasure.

Actually, a tear trickled. He felt so wonderful. "This," he said, "is my very first birthday party." Del wondered at hearing the comment, he wondered whether his Grandma Ella had ever had a birthday party. He silently vowed to be sure that many whom he knew would have one. He could see that his grandpa was really tickled pink. He even walked more upright, as though he'd finally been dealt a cure for his arthritis.

As usual Anna Mae interjected some history, this to do with the Happy Birthday song. "Mrs. Hills and Mrs. Hill wrote it in 1893. It's the most sung song in America." Folks looked at her wondering: What? What of it? Until Dosia came to her rescue by calling,

"Hey, let's sing it again!"

They sang it while Del and Helio were lighting the candles, the candles representing his age if one figured some meant two years, some three, and the rest likely one year each. There was a heap of them, no less, and Grandpa's biggest breath hardly bent the flames. On a three count several blew at once. The conflagration was brought to bay. "Piñata next, Grandpa Del!" Anna Mae was anxious to see her handiwork tried. "While we get set up for the refreshments."

It took only moments to realize that blindfolding a wobbly arthritic man armed with a cane with which to strike a red, white, and blue bus piñata located somewhere amidst the guests was a dangerous game. He missed the fool thing even when they stood him advantageously but he missed the guests only because they were spry. With his blindfold removed he opened the thing after a few determined bashes. He jumped straight to the beef jerky and Ella had a time convincing him that at a birthday party one ate cake first.

Then, in assembly line fashion; Ella and Clydis on cake, Del and Dosia on ice cream, Grandpa Clarence on lemonade, and Anna Mae and Helio on nuts and coffee, the treats were handed with expedition. "Gifts next," Ella cooed, her arm around her hubby. She'd noticed the signs and knew poor old Delibar was by then about pleasured into a deep sleep.

They lugged Grandpa's gifts into the living room where he opened them.

During the oohs and aahs that subtended, the grand old fellow fell asleep.

Clydis went to the phonograph and started his gift record, 'Love is a Many-Splendored Thing.' Del and Helio carried Grandpa over to the couch and laid him straight and with his head pillowed. Ella flung an afghan over him. "I'll rest in the rocker here beside him," she said.

The party had lasted less than an hour yet each guest was satisfied. Grandpa Delibar had had his first birthday party and it'd made each of them feel as grand as he.

CHAPTER FIVE

"You know while we were watching that fake wrestling match before they'd returned from the movie my tummy growled for Swanson's instead of cake." Anna Mae rubbed her tummy.

Helio mocked his offence at her opinion. "Fake? No, I don't believe it. It looked like blood to me even showing up as black on TV; must've really hurt. That Swanson's more likely a fake."

"Oh, do tell?"

"Campbell's Soup Company bought them out. It sure troubles me that Swanson's is gone."

"No more Swanson's, are you sure?"

"Papa Helio, it's because of the Motorola in your truck. It doesn't cover every thing. The Grand Rapids Press says they'll keep the Swanson's label and expand the product line. Campbell's is big. Why they invented canned soup, I've heard. The first such soup was tomato and they've sure been big ever since. You'll have a steady diet of TV diners along with your pilot bread; maybe you won't ever be without them."

"See there, Papa, you listen to that grown up daughter of ours."

"Good to hear. What a relief. I'm for TV dinners and pilot bread all the way across to Oregon. Plan on staying in housekeeping cabins. Triple-A has supplied a list of them all the way so we could telephone ahead every eight hundred miles or so; make sure each cabin has an oven, too; and a TV, of course."

"I'm packing in a jar of Smucker's strawberry and a double loaf of white bread, just in case we run shy of Swanson's."

"Huh?" He looked worried.

Ignoring his dubious expression, she continued. "And Vernor's ginger ale. That's your favorite pop."

"Yours, I'd say. We always pack Vernor's. I like it, too, however."

"It's history. They both are; seeing's our family has eaten Smucker's right along with homemade since 1906, and in 1866, James Vernor of Detroit invented Vernor's ginger ale right there in his pharmacy. Vernor's was the first carbonated soft drink in America. Vernor's was also this country's first diet, sugar free, soft drink, invented about when Del was a freshman in high school."

"They're just side dishes, be sure we pack plenty of Swanson's."

"I don't think Del and I like the TV dinners all that much. There's usually a restaurant associated with truck stops. Papa, that's the way you and I always went before. Why the change?"

"TV dinners. I simply love um."

While chatting, Del and Dosia were packing up, making ready for an early morning departure. Del still had many loads of logs to haul. Suddenly Del remembered an item that he'd wanted to relate to his father-in-law. "Papa Helio, did you hear about the uranium ore in Saskatchewan? I wonder if that'd be like that Pacific Northwest forest trucking you told about."

"Yes, it's around Lake Athabasca. They've found the biggest uranium ore deposit in the world. I caught that word 'Athabasca' which is about like Athabascan; Indians, like me. Trucking there is all off road but it's just haul ore, haul ore; you don't get to go anyplace. Not for me, but I'd bet the pay's good. You might ask dispatcher Dolly Reams about it."

"Yes, just to know the details just in case, but no, that kind of haul doesn't sound right for me either, but the word 'Athabasca' grabbed me so I wanted to be sure you knew about it."

"You could ask Dolly Reams more about it."

"I'll ask or Dosia will; then write you the info after you're settled in Oregon. Right now, I'm hitting the sack."

They could hear Del's shower running and Helio put the TV volume up a notch. "Hey, Sweety, toss in a beef Swanson's won't you!" Helio stretched out in his easy chair; watching a Colgate commercial, waiting for Ed Sullivan's variety show.

She pushed a dinner into the General Electric oven and set the temp and timer, turning then back to Dosia.

"Dear over the last four years I've been saving Good Housekeeping and The Reader's Digest for you. You may leave them here, if you like, or take some along on the road." She looked hopeful, desiring that her daughter be happy.

"Well, gee." A finger came to her chin. "Well, gosh, well that may be just the thing; especially if we get to drive a sleeper. I thought we could sort of set up housekeeping in a sleeper, one like that Diamond-T you and Papa looked at. They look really roomy."

"I kept that ad about the T so you can take it along."

"Thanks, we could call there just to see if there's a chance."

"Good Housekeeping is the first magazine published that was intended just for women. I don't know as to women on the road, but the mag's mostly for dreaming anyway; like catalog shopping."

"You know, Momma, I never knew Sears had so much in it for homemaking. I've started to look at such as that."

"Catalog dreaming is good to do; it gives one goals to strive to, dream about. The Leadford library has most of the Good Housekeeping issues, from May 2, 1885, that first issue, if you want to dream historically, but I like to be getting catalogs and a really current mag or two at home. Your Aunt Edith passes Reader's Digest on to Del's mom and then it gets passed on to the grand folks. It's fun to pass them along so I wouldn't care if you did."

"We'll see how crowded the truck gets."

Del and Dosia returned to hauling logs.

Helio readied the Reo and soon purred for Muskegon to pick up the aircraft engines.

* * *

During late summer and into fall the family had kept an eye out for Nathan Platt to return from Germany. He did return but his folks and a few were all who saw him. Nathan'd rushed right on to Michigan State at East Lansing where he had a job waiting. "I'll be shoveling for a time before I begin milking cows." In the Yelrom woods, Nathan was frequently mentioned in confabs between Louie, Sid and Del. Hearing of Nathan's return, they clearly wished Nathan'd had time to visit. Del especially wanted Nathan to see Dosia as Mrs. Del Platt. Fall was relentlessly descending. Soon snow would clog the off roads and bury any newly cut logs and then he and Dosia would begin hauling loads to the southlands; thus missing Nathan should he manage a visit. Del glanced out a front window one day just as a dark green 1947 Oldsmobile coupe pulled into the driveway. "Why, it's Nathan."

Just into the house, Nathan said, "Dan, uh, er, Del, I'm sorry. I was surprised when you became Del. I thought of you all while I was away as Dan. I'd best shape up."

"No problem. Great to see you."

Dosia gave her brother-in-law a moist peck on the cheek, finishing with a pull of his sleeve. "This way to coffee and eats in the kitchen. You guys get started while I put unmentionables to soak in the Whirlpool."

A waft of Clorox reached them from the laundry. "Man, I do like that smell, huh Del? Momma'd wash every Monday morning during our entire childhood."

"Clorox bleach since 1913," Dosia joined them at the table. "Instead of a wash day, we wash whenever we can happen onto a washer that doesn't demand coins."

Nathan took a grateful sip of Maxwell House. "Well, enough of washing. That sounds like a hassle. I stopped in to ask you, Del, if you want to go to college." He dipped a doughnut into his coffee. His eyebrow was raised to Del.

"No, no, no, I liked high school not at all. It's trucking for me." With a wink at his older brother, Del plunged his own doughnut.

"You've registered for the draft?"

"Yep, but they'll have to come and get me. Why?" Del popped in a bite of his soaked drippy doughnut. He wiped a finger across his chin, in a copy of his brother.

"I'm to begin milking cows now in a few days," Nathan said, "replacing a friend who is migrating to Canada." Nathan finished his doughnut and his eyes sought another. "The guy says there's a dirty war brewing in a place called Vietnam. A place, he believes, that the United States has no business budding into. He put his draft card into a manure heap there at Michigan State. Granted his situation is different than mine was back when I entered college, yet I can't agree with his logic. Back when I started at the college, I set aside any thought of military obligation. I hardly noticed that war raged in Korea. I hadn't thought about the army until it came to me that I needed the GI Bill to make it on through college. So I volunteered induction. I went to college in the first place because I didn't want to be a farmer. Now I'm working at farm work at the university to supplement the GI Bill. Del, I'm patriotic, as patriotic as most, and I see you as perhaps even more patriotic than me. But, Del, I don't want you to fight in any war at all."

"No problem here. I'll keep on here unless they draft me. How about you? I heard about the C-119's. How was that, anyway? We're glad you're home safe; are you?"

"I'm in the reserve and could be called back in. When they said to get on the C-119's, I wasn't scared and I wasn't feeling patriotic. I just felt that we had a dirty job to do. 'Getting it over with' was my main thought. I've talked to guys since. One was a survivor of the Bataan Death March. He said he was so mad and filled with hatred that he survived. He didn't think about patriotism, only hatred. Sid Watkins, as you know, was hit hard in Korea, out there in that stone frozen wasteland under hordes of Chinese. He said he was there with a job to do. The idea of patriotism came later when he saw others being called in."

"You'd go?"

"Yes, as I'm sure you would, but I'll wait until they find me. Once in, it's just a job. Sometimes that job's bossed by Lucifer. But the guys and gals do that dirty job and most come back home." Dosia startled them by fumbling her cup, splattering coffee as she clacked her cup onto the table and came to her feet. With eyes to Dosia, Nathan continued: "They didn't come for me for Korea, apparently because I was in college." She walked around the table and came to behind her husband, placing her hands on his shoulders. "That's why I mentioned college to you."

"Well, no college for me." Her hands moved to his chin. "And no trucking in Canada." She pulled his head way back toward her and she leaned over him and planted a noisy wet one upon his forehead.

"You're my man."

Nathan and Del grinned at each other. "Now, let's get off this gruesome topic," she said. "Nathan, how is Amy?"

"Married. She married one of her professors. Both are math nuts and will spend their lives happily wandering around in one massive equation after another. A lot of guys in the service received Dear John letters. I didn't. Amy and I exchanged letters right up to her wedding. It just worked out that we decided not to marry."

"Nathan," she said, "I hope some one finds you soon."

Having drained the last drop from his cup, Nathan stood up from his chair. Obviously he was ready to depart.

"Darn, it, stay a while."

"Can't. Studies and work. Stop in when you can. The barn that I work in is the farthest to the east, the Experimental Dairy Barn. The cows are milked at four in the morning and at four each afternoon. That's so that visitors can watch the milking. Starting in a day or so and then on and on, you'll be able to find me in that barn. I won't get a break from it until the powers decide that the farm crew needs to be expanded. The farm manager said that budget considerations power all such decisions."

* * *

Soon after Nathan returned to Michigan State, Dosia and Dell delivered the last of the logs. They rested the log chains in November right at the time when President Ike was re-elected, returning to an empty house as the folks were by then settled in Oregon.

They'd caught glimpses of Ronnie Perkins each time they were at the Coopersville saw mill. His job had changed. Instead of unloading trucks, he was set to moving logs from the yard to the debarking machine. Even when they didn't see him, they knew he was around because his highly polished Ford Crown Victoria was always parked near the office.

"Whoee, I'm glad we're done here," Dosia'd said. "And the monster didn't try anything, thank Goodness." She'd patted her husband's shoulder.

"Well, I'd think we're done with that old Ronnie Perkins," Del said, returning her pat with a hug for measure. "Next stop is East Jordan to load cast iron components. Then we journey on to Ardmore Oklahoma with the cast iron, but stop to see a Choctaw code talker on the way."

"Papa Helio said that he thinks cast iron is also called pig iron. Del, why is that?"

He pinched his bottom lip. "Gosh, I don't know. Dolly just said cast iron to Ardmore. We can ask at East Jordan while they load us."

"Okay, good, and at Ardmore, Dolly has arranged the swap. It'll be the very 1948 Diamond-T sleeper that Papa inquired about. With a load of home furnishings, we'll roll on across to California." Hand in hand their feet skipped and their eyes swept hungrily along the distant horizon.

* * *

East Jordan, Michigan was located on an arm off Lake Charlevoix with the lake really a long deep bay of Lake Michigan. They cruised through marvelous scenery to arrive at the town and were but moments within before espying the East Jordan Iron Works, Inc. at 301 Spring Street. The Lufkin was snuggled to the loading dock shortly after the clear dawn had awakened a brisk morning. Del trotted to the office, returning after several minutes to swing open her door of the cab. "Pig iron is what they get from the smelter. Here they melt the pig iron and cast that iron into molds, cast iron products, you see. Cast iron's also called gray iron because of its color." She smiled at him, and then shivered at seeing his arms huddled close about him. "You'll need your warm coat," he said. "Hand out mine, will you?"

They scrunched deep in their mackinaws, turning shivered backs to the breeze, having spotted the cafe a long block ahead. It seemed to take forever beating their way to that cafe. Settling at a table, she said, "Gosh, I know it's warmer in Oklahoma." They were still huddled into their mackinaws when a large pyramid-shaped waitress arrived at their table.

"Good morning. Chilly, huh? Coffee? We have regular or decaffeinated." She stood alertly in her light yellow uniform and with her order pad poised. They read 'Jacqueline' from her name tag. The tag was of black plastic and with the letters cut through its surface to a white under layer, spelling out JACQUELINE in bold, block white letters. The tag suggested permanence in her employment. A concurring independent thought of Del and Dosia was that she'd worked there a long time, and expected to work there perpetually.

"Yes, both, and cream and sugar," Del replied. "Regular, for me."

"All my life I've heard of decaf, but never drank any. Decaf for me."

"The breakfast special looks fine."

"Same for both of us."

She jotted the order, stabbing the period with her green No. 2 Ticonderoga brand pencil.

Her suspected long experience as a waitress was confirmed when she said, "Coming right up, but that special will sure stuff your tummy, ma'am. We can halve the flapjack portion, if you'd like."

"No; I'll give Del any extra."

Del looked up from where he'd begun reading his place matt. "Sure, I'll take care of it. I see you've an ad here for lake fishing excursions, something I'd want to do someday."

"Sure, fun all summer. This town booms all summer. You'd like the excursions, but I prefer the winters." She rushed away with the order, returning swiftly with the coffee. "Did I hear Oklahoma? I'll bet it'll be warm there; but no snow and ice, I think, so I'd stay here."

"It'll average around forty in mid winter. We're truckers, delivering road building stuff from your foundry to down around Ardmore, not far from Texas," he explained. "We're dreaming of a warm winter."

"Then we'll shoot on across to California," Dosia added. "I hope we get even too warm. Gosh, the wind's cold off this lake." She stayed cuddled in the mackinaw while reaching a small slender hand to caress the warm mug of coffee. Yet shivering, she clutched her mackinaw close around; "and you like it?"

"Less people," she said. "Less guys." Their eyes followed her movement toward a doorway to the kitchen, both accessing her broad beam and seafarer's stride.

His eyes flicked to his pretty wife and back to the waitress. Sure wide, all right, and instantly he was ashamed for thinking that non-Christian way; until Dosia voiced the same notion; "Broad beam, huh?"

"Er, uh, yeah. Too bad." He reached across and touched her hand. "I'm sure lucky."

"I went after you."

"So? Well, I'm glad."

"If she went after a man he wouldn't think about width."

"Er, well, I think not. I think you're right, just right. You aren't thinking I'd - ?"

"No, you're my man. She knows that. So would any other."

They grew silent, pensive, each with private thoughts about Jacqueline until gradually their lovebird's chatter returned, bending their thoughts anew of the Oklahoma sunshine. Presently, with the sound of her footsteps and the swish of her crisp yellow uniform, their thoughts shifted wholly to breakfast.

They stuffed in pancake, eggs, and bacon before leaving by way of the cafe rear door. "Warmer back there," Jacqueline'd said. "Cut right across to the foundry."

At the foundry they walked around their load, checking every inch. She continued the scrutiny as he sought the busy office. "News, good or bad depending on the weather, or our tires," he said, settling into his seat. Over the accelerating diesel engine, he explained, "They'll have three or more loads of stuff during the winter. I signed us on for them. The first in January right after we're due home from Lufkin, Texas."

"Well, its work, dear, and we'll see spring on each return south."

"I wonder where, that is warm south or cold north, that tires wear the best. We've weak rubber on this semi trailer, but I'd hoped we could wait until nearer spring."

She looked at him. "Oh?"

"They could put on fresh rubber during servicing at the Lufkin Company but we'd have to borrow the money. We may need to. These heavy loads of cast iron road parts may wear the tires faster than Papa and I'd thought."

"Good thing we can live in the Diamond-T cab. It'll help us save all we can toward those tires."

"That's what I thought, too. The tires are the bad part I mentioned. Wanted this to be more like a true vacation. Sorry."

"Our honeymoon on wheels. No mind, love." She reached to grip his bicep. "We'll be close together, and that's a treat. And we'll sure see some country this winter, and that's a treat." His arm moved from the wheel and across her shoulders. She cuddled close. They began a long roll to Oklahoma.

Nearing the Oklahoma border Dosia checked a road map. They'd planned for a brief stop in McCurtain County. There they'd make contact, hopefully, with Corporal Solomon Lewis, a Choctaw code talker of World War One.

Of the dozen or so Choctaw Indian code talkers used in the Battle of Meuse-Argonne in 1918, six were from McCurtain County, Oklahoma and, as they'd hoped, at their lunch stop just into the county, mentioning a few of the names rendered quick recognition. They were just to dig into slices of peach pie ala mode sided by Pream laden instant coffee when a slight young man, much younger than they'd expected, approached their table. "Solomon Lewis," he greeted, "at your service."

Their heads reared back. "Well, er, well, we'd thought your father, I'd guess, Corporal Lewis of World War One."

He grinned. "The same," he said. "I was the youngest; joined the army at sixteen. My hair has stayed black but just look at these crow feet wrinkles. Young indeed, my good gosh!"

"Well have a seat, pard. I'm Del Platt of Michigan, from near the site of the annual Roughwater Powwow at Leadford. I'm training under the wing of Clarence Groner, blood brother of the late Hawcho Lakes."

They shook hands as Del pulled a chair for him. "Sit a spell, will you?" Del waved to catch the attention of the waitress: "Belle, more pie here," and he placed a hand on Dosia's shoulder: "My wife, Dosia," he introduced, "my full time partner."

"How do?" They exchanged a nod and smile. Solomon reached into the air to snap his fingers: "Belle, make that Hills Brothers. Use that Pyrex Silex drip pot we gotcha and Pream, that new non-dairy creamer. And mincemeat pie if you have it."

"Gotcha, Cousin Sol."

"She's my second generation cousin; runs this place which we're trying to modernize since her folks've died. They sure resisted investing. Why, Hills was the first vacuum packed coffee; before I was even born. Since 1900, yet cousin Burl's family never adopted naught but instant. We of my own family always had drip coffee; bought a Silex when that coffeemaker first came out in around 1908, so I always thought cousin Burl was behind." He looked toward their cups. "Instant, I'll bet." Again he snapped his fingers into the air. "Belle, and bring these two a refill of that good drip Hills, too, okay?"

"Gotcha, Sol."

Sol turned back to the truckers. "Since 1906 and the first instant coffee his family most always drank instant and my cousin still preferred it till he died, but now I decided his daughter should go modern seeing's how I've invested in the place. I've introduced decaffeinated now, too, as I see you've discovered and we're prideful that we sell a few groceries, mainly baked goods, and we give out S & H Green Stamps. Those stamps've been around since before 1900 yet they didn't get offered here until just lately."

Now he spoke so she could hear: "She's a good kid, learning fast." His attention swung back to the truckers.

"Now there's four of us code talkers left that I know about, all here in the county. I'm amazed that anyone had heard about us." He dug into a generous slice of mincemeat pie.

"Carl Gorman, a World War Two Navaho code talker came to the Roughwater Powwow," Del said. "Dosia here, well her dad is an Athabascan Indian from Alaska. He met Mr. Gorman and they talked about the Navajo contribution. The Navajo, as you may know, code talked for the U. S. marines on Iwo Jima. The Nips sure couldn't break their code. Well, Gorman mentioned that during War Two, the U. S. Army, not just the Marines, used talkers, and from several other Indian tribes. 'Even lucky enough to get Choctaw,' he said, 'as in World War One.' We were surprised he'd mentioned code talkers 'as in World War One.' That's the first we'd heard about Indian code talkers being involved during that earlier war, WWI."

"Yes, we were there in France. You know we'd not bragged about it so we'd not thought any one had remembered. Sure, we Choctaw were in War One and in World War Two. In War Two, besides us Choctaw and the Navajo, there was Hopi, Comanche, Kiowa, Winnebago, Seminole, and Cherokee, and we're all justly proud of what we did."

"You bet, and the native Indian languages made a code to be talked openly over the radios and walky-talkies, a code that not a one of German or Japanese could even come near to deciphering. We'd like to honor as many of you guys as possible at the next Leadford powwow. That'd be in June next summer, 1957, up there in Michigan. A friend of ours, by the way, Jade Pickerel, a Mohican from Wisconsin is the present chief of Roughwater Nation. He and I'll become blood brothers at that next powwow. We'd sure be honored to see you there."

"Our pleasure and, you folks couldn't know this because we just received word yesterday in the mail. Chief Jade found out the address of Tobias Frazer, fellow Choctaw talker, and wrote him. Chief Jade, and that wife of his with a helicopter, and with Tobias and me helping, and others, too, helping, will get as many found as possible and we'll surely be at the powwow; you bet. Dog gone, you bet. Why, we're tickled pink."

"Chief Jade may have mentioned then that we also seek Philip Johnston. His folks were missionaries at a Navajo reservation in California. He speaks Navajo and recalled hearing talk about you Choctaw code talkers of War One so he contacted the marines near San Diego. That led to the training of the Indian code talkers for World War Two."

"By gosh, I'd shake his hand, that Philip Johnston; hope you locate him."

"We hope he's still near San Diego."

"We're truckers, by the way, Dosia said, "in case you're wondering how we get around. We'll be taking a load of household belongings to California pretty soon, so while there we may be able to meet Mr. Johnston."

Talk among the three whipped on until suddenly Del espied the restaurant wall clock just ticking at two in the afternoon. "Oh, golly, Solomon, we've got to get on with the trucking." They pumped hands all around and Dosia hugged him. "Thanks," she said.

They rolled on for Ardmore, Dosia with the sleeper cab, their rolling home, sweetly on her mind.

* * *

They found the road crew foreman at the office of 'City Police' just as they should have and were about to ask the why of such an odd meeting place when the foreman said, "Me and Allen, the Chief here, own the movie theater. That's the building you're parked in front of. We get you unloaded then youins are invited to see 'In Old Santa Fe' with us, starring Gene Autry. Free, of course. Folks right and left hereabouts are Autry fans, you'd guess, being so close to his town and ranch, but us of down town

Ardmore want to grab a little spin off. So we began the theater and curio shop; all to honor Gene and Tessie."

"Gene Autry? Gee, around here?"

"Sure, he and Tessie ranched near here and Gene was a telegrapher before he became the Yodeling Cowboy. We see more of Tessie, though, as she doesn't go out all the time to Hollywood and such."

"Tessie, his wife?"

"Sure. She's nice as he is; always nice, the both of um, but we wanted to get some of the income from his fame here in our town instead of all out at the town of Gene Autry. The road improvement will boost that. The load you have is for Love County which borders the Red River and is close to Fort Worth and Dallas, Texas. Then to our north there's the Arbuckle Mountains that you can see from the town of Gene Autry. The Autry's, those mountains, and the seven pretty lakes around here; all that with good roads and we'll all benefit all right."

"May I use that telephone?" Dosia moved toward it. She held a slip of paper. "We need to contact a man about a Diamond-T."

"Sure." The chief pushed the instrument her way.

She had just reached Mr. Diamond-T as the foreman was leading Del from the office. She stole glances their way and saw them begin a walk around with the bill of lading checking to see the items listed.

"Manhole covers, manholes, sewer grates, fire hydrants, iron pipe, catch basins, you loaded right. Are you bringing the rest? We ordered more."

"We've signed on with the East Jordan foundry for an additional three, or more, loads."

"Good. We're to begin construction in January. Stop at the chief's office each time. He or me'll know where the gray stuff goes."

He climbed into the cab with Del. "Follow that there yellow bus. That crew's to unload." They'd traveled but a minute when: "Say, your name is Platt. Do you know of Platt National Park?"

"No, around here?" Del eyed his companion.

"North a bit. This area's loaded with things to see, things to do; pretty country. Platt National Park was designated in 1906 by Teddy Roosevelt. The park is located right within the Chickasaw National Recreation Area. We sure need improved roads. Folks are missing a lot in this area."

"Well, it's sure our pleasure to haul the stuff in for you. We'll see to fit in a visit to the park and to visit the Chickasaw Indians on one of our trips. And, by the way, do you have the check for this load of gray iron?"

"Check? Er, or, oh No! We sent the money to the foundry up at East Jordan. Sorry. I can show you the check stub so's you'll know for sure but I'm sure we sent it." His mouth gaped as his eyes fell upon Del. He gripped Del's shoulder. "Sorry, son. Really sorry."

Del looked about to implode. His hands and arms quivered at the steering wheel. They needed fuel, food, and they were approaching doom as the semi trailer treads transformed to cords, cords that'd show up stark white, as white as his face when he said, "I just don't see how we'll make it." Instantly, he was shocked that he'd blurted his feelings to a near stranger.

"Son," he jerked at Del's shoulder. "You're not abandoned here, no you're not. Loosen up a tad. I'll get right with Chief; see what's to be done. We're regular folks here, you hear? We won't leave you stranded with no money, not one of our own such as we see you are. Youins are with us now. By the time you get out of "In Old Santa Fe' we'll have this problem fixed for ya."

The foreman seemed to have taken a personal interest in Del and as the foreman talked, Del was obviously responding, his tension slackening. After a short pause the foreman felt he could brave a return to a discussion of local attractions. "As I was saying, son, you'll see that the Chickasaw area's big and with Platt Park nestled within it. Why Platt National Park alone is 800 acres and it's located good; less than an hour from Ardmore and Ada; about the same from that big whopper Texoma Lake. That lakes right on the border with Texas, as you know, right with the Red River and its population's grown some since 1944. But with good roads, well, I'll tell ya, son. That area and this area all around'll surely draw big when there's smooth macadam."

Del was indeed back to near his normal constitution, calmed by the foreman's jovial nature and convincing narrative. "Concrete surface?"

"Huh?" He peered at his new friend: What's with him now?

"Er, why no, tarred surface, don't you know?"

"Really? I'd heard that macadam referred to the base under the surface; built up solid yet with good drainage; dating back to roads the Romans built that are still good."

"Oh, I get ya. You're OK now. Yes, well I've heard of that, I guess, but I've heard to associate macadam with John McAdam, of Scotland. He built such roads as early as 1822 in Boonsboro, Maryland; had tarred surface. But that base you've spoke of, we'll go with that for sure. It's the way to build alright." They drove on for a time. "Turn ahead, see um? We've a yard set up there. What's your wife saying about Diamonds?"

Del was glad Dosia hadn't suffered the money shock along with him. "A truck called a Diamond-T, she's looking into."

"I wish I knew trucks."

"We're borrowing, or actually trading our Mack for it; just temporary. My in-laws sent payments to Lufkin, Texas, completing a deal that came with our Lufkin semi trailer. The trailer's used but with a paid-up contract for reconditioning, that to occur while we're out west in the Diamond-T. The Diamond-T has a sleeper cab so we can rest in it on across to California; saves time and money. Getting back from there, we'll be right soon at making our next run with road stuff for you."

"Honeymoon's what I heard; uh, er, Chief guessed."

"Yup, you bet."

At the yard were several farm tractors with front end loaders and a Caterpillar fitted with a derrick. The foreman and Del worked up on the load attaching hooks and unchaining various components. The work was dangerous and noisy, noisy right to the final snort as the Caterpillar lowered the last catch basin onto the bed of a lowboy trailer hauled by a diesel Ford farm tractor. "Hey!" At her yell, his head popped around, catching at once that she leaned from the passenger door of a bright red Diamond-T.

Massive chromed bars of the grill glistened no less brightly than the over-size twin Grover air horns on the cab roof; obviously the man was proud of his truck and took good care of it. All was polished to an eye-shocking gleam and that gleam spread as well over the black fenders and black front bumper. Del readily saw the new deeply treaded tires all around, six tires in all, not ten tires as on the Mack. He felt a twinge of shame in knowing that the rubber was weak on his Lufkin. He wanted to tell the man that "When you pull in at the Lufkin trailer works have them toss on a new set of Coopers" but he knew his wallet was too thin. He couldn't have guessed that Mr. Diamond-T also was aware of the Platt couple's hand-to-mouth trucking venture and of their honeymoon idea.

Mr. Diamond-T, ignoring Del for the moment, walked right over and began to examine the Lufkin's tires even to crawling underneath to get a real close-up look.

"I'm glad you know your business." His voice rolled out from under the Lufkin and shivered Del, so pleased he was that the man would notice.

Del confirmed the man's statement: "Easiest way to keep an eye on them."

"You bet," he grunted, swinging out and coming to stand facing Del. "Always keep your worst tires in plain sight." He extended his hand to Del. "Glad to meet you. Honeymoon trip, I take this."

"Del Platt; you've met Dosia. Honeymoon, you bet. About wore out our dispatcher finding you."

"I, er, and my wife, was glad to help. More power to youins. We remember a time long past, but a good one, a honeymoon for us. We trucked a load of southern pine lumber north to Chicago. I'm sure we would've enjoyed a sleeper, but we tented; gets kind of chilly on up there near Chicago. Oh, what sweet memories. Your wife's a good gal. She said right off that I'd plainly like her man. I'm hauling hay, I'm not sure you'd heard. Six or eight loads of East Texas hay to go west. Bad hay year, as often happens, down around and south of San Antonio. My loads will be a sight lighter than all that cast iron I see here. Your tires will make it, but I'll carry two spares just in case. I might have the spares to sell before you go north for more of the iron."

"Sure, we'll surely talk about it when we come back to Texas" he grinned, so pleased with himself at being showered with southwestern generosity. "You'll be at Lufkin, when we return the Diamond-T, huh?"

"No, but close. I've relatives west of Lufkin. Dosia has the address and telephone number. My wife's already out there. Her brother is a ranger in the Davy Crockett National Forest located a bit to the west of Lufkin. I'll finish the hay hauls then set your semi trailer in at the plant then I'll cool down on a shaded porch in the park where you'll find me. "

"Good, and I'll want to start you with full tanks on the Mack. Those are thirty-three gallons to each side, adding to a full barrel of fuel. And, now darn it hang on to those spares until we can arrive with a pay check."

Mr. Diamond-T bumped Del's shoulder. "Sure enough. I've bolted twin forty-gallon tanks onto the Diamond-T because I hope to get in some long hauls. The minute your dispatcher called me I decided not to sell the T and I installed the tanks. Youins'll be the first to go long distance with her. Sure good that old Ike's making new roads. I just topped off the T at my favored pumps, a Gulf station's just north of here."

"Good. My ma-in-law tells me that the very first drive-in fueling station in the US was a Gulf; 1913."

"That early?"

"Not too early, about time, she says, because Standard's had gas stations since 1907; but not drive-in though."

Beep! Beep! The foreman had swung aboard the yellow crew bus and was waving from the driver's side window. "See you at the show! We'll start the show when you get there!"

Del returned the wave. Both drivers swung aboard their stallions. Del gunned up the Mack and followed after Dosia in her Diamond-T.

CHAPTER SIX

While the Gulf attendant was topping off the tanks of the Mack, Del received a crash course in the intimacies of Diamond-T operation, that while answering similar questions about the Mack. Dosia took in modicums of the male conversation while she scurried about in the sleeper compartment of the T. As Del took the wheel she hopped into the T cab to wave goodbye to Mr. Diamond-T. During the drive into town she continued in the sleeper compartment, popping her head out but briefly to view the passing scenery.

Throughout 'In Old Santa Fe' with Gene Autry and later, during their bout with hamburger, malted, and chips, her man listened to her wide-eyed glow of the spacious sleeper while staying from any mention of their money and tire troubles. He was as excited as she about trying out the sleeper but knew that not telling her right out was keeping his revelry short of her fervor. His aim was to not spoil her, their, adventure.

She was bounding around in the truck like ricocheting black hat bullets in a Gene Autry thriller. Later they pulled off the road at a sign announcing entry into the Chickasaw National Recreation Area. Eventually they stopped beside a neatly stacked pile of cordwood. They were near a creek in what they thought must be within Platt National Park.

With their aim to snuggle into the sleeper, her big and fancy western decorated belt buckle raked Del's shoulder. "Ouch!"

"Oh darn; sorry." She pulled the belt free and stuffed it behind the mattress.

They snuggled into the sleeper.

He awoke when she stepped on his arm and then raised his head in time to be raked across the face by a set of her ruby-painted toenails as she

67

scurried from the sleeper and into the cab. He stood in front of the driver's door mirror in faded Levis and unlaced boots. He was without a shirt and noticed the scrub from her belt buckle, and wondered whether she'd look okay without wearing the precious thing. Memory of cozy willows wherein he enjoyed his first close-up of the buckle brought a grin as he applied his Bam roll-on and then rubbed a dab of Brylcreem into his luxurious hair. His comb motion matched the tempo of the song she warbled from behind the stack of cordwood. Peering her way he was suddenly jolted by her orange blouse flopping atop the wood. The blouse was joined momentarily by a pair of wrinkled jeans. Sunlight caught the flash of a pink garment and a white being tossed up after the other clothing.

He held onto the mirror but his feet pranced and his pants began to drift down his thighs. To steady himself he shoved a Colgate vested toothbrush into his mouth. He'd brushed and was wishing for some water to rinse when she popped from behind the stacked wood carrying a pail half filled with creek water. She was dressed in bright blue denims and a bright pink blouse, her wedding outfit. Her brogans were untied. Inside the brogans was a pair of white sweat socks, the socks over her nylons. In her hand with the pail bail she carried a hairbrush, that lot balanced off by her other hand's grasp of her soiled clothing and the accouterment of her bathing. "Isn't this fun!" She was prancing as though on a fine picnic.

He grinned at her, thinking Skip to My Lou as he rinsed the Colgate from his gape. Reaching for a printed green plaid cotton shirt, he answered, "Sure," himself as happy as she, "like a picnic." Accept for the dual woe of scant money and balding tires, he thought, but his broad grin and sparkling eyes beamed over to her.

At the right-hand mirror she rubbed a dab of Jergens lotion into her delicate supple hands. Helena Rubinstein mascara went on along with eye shadow and a Rubinstein colored face powder to set a faint blush to her cheeks. She opened her lipstick tube. As usual he loved seeing her move her lips deliciously in applying his favorite red lipstick. She pushed her short hair into acceptable array and placed a tiara-like red barrette studded by sequins crosswise in front of her delicate ears. She was attaching the second of two red teardrop earrings as he hugged her to him and kissed an ear lobe. "Always on a picnic with you, sweety. This should go on forever."

"Let's eat in Norman. We meet the movers at the White Castle burger stand. That's the oldest franchised burger-type establishment in America."

"The very first kind of burger stand, you say. Ought to be good."

"While they're loading us we could eat. Will that be alright?"

"Yes," his lips grazed her ear. "We're a couple of hours below Norman. We'll be in there around nine, to the minute, if we stay lucky. We could drop the semi-trailer at that house. Could all work out just great if I can grab a shave at the nearest gasoline station on the way north."

Further along the road, upon exiting the rest room with his toiletries bag he caught her inquisitive expression. His heart jolted. His shaving had given her a moment to reflect on their circumstances; even, he guessed, she'd been able to discern the slightly dulled edge of her hubby's good nature. At times she displayed a powerful version of extra sensory perception, ESP as penetrating as Superman's. Before she could say "Out with it," he said, "Dear, I wish I didn't have to say about it; the money, er, well, we only got half."

"Oh?" She moved to touch his face. "You old smoothie, you," her fluttered heart caught in her voice, betraying her labored charm, but she kept a brave face. "You smell great. The lavender? I like the smell of my man."

"Yeah, well, I couldn't find the right moment, honey. They sent our pay for the load down clear on up to the East Jordan foundry, wanting to pay in advance, for some unclear reason. Well they gathered up half of it somehow and slipped it to me at the movie. They said to stop back on the way north and they'd have the rest, but I said to send the remainder to the Lufkin factory with a note for us. Sorry, dear. This money will hardly more than feed the truck all the way to San Diego."

"It's good of them to send the balance to the Lufkin factory to hold for us." She placed her palms against his chest. Her lips were very close to his. "Good thing I'm acquainted with Indians," she whispered. Abruptly she bounced to the fore as though a jumping jack. "We'll trap bunnies and such and fish the creeks and lake shores all across. In Norman let's look for a used goods store. We'll need a Dutch oven and a kettle. Buy ten pounds of whole grain flour, some lard, baking powder, and salt and pepper. Dear, this honeymoon's to be the best ever. Why, it sounds to be better than my wildest dreams about it!"

"You're a caution!"

They hugged.

"You're my man," she said.

Feeling much better about their situation, he set the gleaming red chariot north, chewing the miles to Norman, Oklahoma.

* * *

From Norman they telephoned Dolly Reams, their Michigan dispatcher. She'd found a light load of World War One era Curtiss Jenny aircraft parts in San Diego, California to be delivered to the Stinson airport in San Antonio, Texas. They were to contact dispatch every other day after that, seeking to add on to the aircraft load to San Antonio and to find a haul from San Antonio to east Texas. Awaiting happy dispatching results, their bellies grew thin. Hope held a dull edge.

Cash from hauling the household goods flashed from their hands as they topped the tanks of the T. They splurged in eating a much needed husky meal in a restaurant, stretching the meal while they poured over telephone books. Remaining illusive was the whereabouts of Philip Johnston whose memory of World War One code talkers had led to the use of Indians as code talkers in World War Two. Dosia sat in the truck cab to write the mayor in each of several towns where a librarian had suggested he might be reached, but their hope of finding Mr. Johnston wore thin by the time they were leaving San Diego with the aircraft parts and with the addition of two antique automobiles for their load.

Meanwhile in Michigan, Louie Watkins had paid a visit to Delibar and Ella Platt. "Call their dispatcher," Grandpa Delibar advised. "I got the number; er, uh, Ella, where is it?"

"Tacked at the telephone." She dialed. "Dolly Reams?"

"Dispatch. Yeah, me, Dolly."

"Louie Watkins is here with a load for Del and Dosia."

"Logs or bolts?"

"Logs."

Just into Yuma, Arizona, they stopped at the Colorado River crossing for a chunk of ice to cool a jug of water. It'd been a blister all of the nearly two hundred miles across California. Coming steadily across, they stayed too thirsty and miserable to detect their own hunger accept for a desperate hunger for good news. Dosia slapped icy water onto her face. Sweltering inside a public telephone booth, Del waved a towel to cool her as the swung the blister-hot Bell dial. The Bell ate her coins at Dolly's pick up.

Hanging the receiver, she grabbed the water jug and guzzled, letting water splash to cool her front. "Loads of logs," her voice echoed from inside the jug. "Louie and Sid," she lowered the emptied jug. Her grin was stretched to where he could hardly understand her. He looked into the empty water jug, studying as though her voice may yet reside there and hoping it'd translate her jubilee. He caught enough finally to know they were to load a family's goods in San Antonio and drop the stuff in Nacogdoches, Texas, a thriving town located in the vicinity of Lufkin.

In the morning they munched hamburgers while plying dust clothes to fetch a glistening gleam to the bright red and glimmer from the black of the T and to polish the windows. From Nacogdoches they dropped into Lufkin and soon had collected the paycheck owed by the Ardmore foreman and his buddy the chief. Under blistering sun they swung into the Davy Crockett National Forest, giving sighs of relief at seeing pine tree shade ahead. Beneath that shade stood a modest log home with the biggest front porch they'd yet seen. The shiny gleaming green Mack stood beside the porch with its chrome whetted to startle the eye. "Howdy, neighbors," Mr. Diamond-T grinned at them over his glass of icy lemonade. "Come on up, sit a spell. Meet the family."

"Be right up," Del said, but he walked on over to the sprightly looking refurbished Lufkin forty footer where he stopped and knelt beside a set of tandem duals. He was passing his palm along the deep crisp tread as Mr. Diamond-T knelt beside him. Ignoring the tread, Mr. Diamond-T's fingers ran along the nearest twenty-inch rim.

"Split rims, do you see?"

Del scratched his head. "Papa Helio cautioned against such as those."

Their toes served as pivots until the men faced each other. "Never try to change one." He eyed Del straight on. "The tires came to me already mounted onto the Diamond-T, mounted on ancient Budds. I put new Budd wheels and Goodyear rubber on the T and stored these split rim jewels as spares. Sure, good tires sure, on the T, but one cannot longer rely on these prewar ones I've mounted on your Lufkin. The tires look good, as you can see, but don't expect any pre-war tire to last very long. Just by age alone they seem to weaken."

"So I've heard; about changing one, I mean. We hope to make it through until spring and with paydays adding to all new 10 x 20, twelve ply Coopers."

"There're a good make of tire. I didn't have any flats on my hay hauls. Your best two are mounted on the racks underneath as spares. Both are nearly treadless. Of your others, four are corded or nearly corded, all twelve ply being now just road dust along the trucker's roadways I'm afraid, but still have air. You could carry all of those as spares to await the new Coopers."

"Sure, you're right."

"And when you get new Coopers, don't attempt to mount 'um onto the split rims; just throw the old tires away, wheels, rims, and all." He spoke as though he were an older, more experienced man advising a son or other tyro just entering the trucking profession.

Dell took it that way. "Thanks. And you've answered another of our concerns; that's the difference in tire wear on hot roads or cool. Cool wins, judging by how quickly the tires finished up on the hay runs. We'll be mainly north for the rest of the winter, but down here with three or more loads of gray iron products. I'll keep my fingers crossed, you bet."

Dosia contacted dispatch, seeking a load from Texas to Michigan. Found none. They rolled from Texas with a glistening Mack and shiny like-new forty foot Lufkin and with a lard pail of commercially reared earthworms. The worms were nestled with a hamburger supply and an ice block inside their larder, the worms potentially the more valuable. Halted at a hundred south of St. Louis, she'd just hooked into a good puller when he yelled across the cadre of semis parked like giant sardines across the parking lot of the Dixie Truckers truck stop. "We got a load!" and "I'm into a big 'un!" crashed together over the trucks snapping heads around to either direction and with truckers heading opposite directions seeking to share in the fortune. Many followed Del, that shouter running, but it was a Missourian who saved the day, or say, 'saved the fish.'

"Don't haul on him! Don't haul on him!" He reached across her shoulder to test the strain on the line and the pole, his hands coming to rest over hers. "Just taut, gal. Just taut. Your line's not near strong enough."

Taking turns, the three hopefuls fought thirty pounds of Mississippi catfish for an hour and a bit more. Finally the fish dangled below the twenty-foot bluff from where she'd been fishing. "Easy, easy," his hands once again tested the strain. "Easy. Easy."

He had the pole, gently turning in line, praying the fish wouldn't again struggle for its Mississippi venue until suddenly, daringly he walked back from the precipice and the beauty lay upon the gravel of the lot. "Whew! Beautiful job, ma'am. Beautiful fish."

The fish lay like a Nativity scene with Del and Dosia, she backed up to him, he with his arms around her, standing with the Missourian and with a crescent of goggle-eyed truckers in a semi-circle, gawking, and all with reverent admiration of the fish. "Gosh, Dell," she wriggled against him. "Thank God. Where do we cook it?"

"Please allow me, ma'am, to say. The Trail of Tears State Park is near here. You could be my guest. I'm called Cherokee and I ranger there."

"You Indian?"

"Yes. The park is pleasant, a real contrast to the story of my people. I was born this side of the Mississippi River, an Oklahoma Cherokee, and it is with honor that I tend the Trail of Tears Park here in Missouri."

Del and Cherokee using jackknives and pliers soon had the big catfish skinned and filleted. Throughout that process the men were discussing the 1838 removal of the Cherokee from Georgia to Oklahoma. Many died along the way. "I believe this Trail of Tears Park was one of the stopping places," Cherokee said. "And cutting this fish apart is like they were cut from their home country. I've made tears myself more than a few times thinking about them. Least I can do is to take good and honorable care of their park."

Cherokee began frying slabs of fish in a bath of melted oleomargarine. She saw Del begin to open a can of pork and beans and to break up leaves from a head of lettuce. The men seemed so content in their efforts that she chose not to bud in, but what to do? The magazines! She reached behind the truck seat, musing that she'd not opened a single one on the whole trip, and she'd brought along a half dozen each of Reader's Digest and Good Housekeeping. She'd not finished the first article before Del announced; "Come and get it!"

She hopped from the cab: "Smells delicious, gentlemen."

The men grinned and nodded while Cherokee kept to their conversation. "Yes, indeed I've heard of the Nation of Roughwater but I've not been able to go to a Michigan powwow."

"It's held near to our home." She turned from her plate and reached into her purse. "Our name, telephone, and address are on this card." She passed it across the picnic table. "May we exchange for your name and address?"

"Sure." He jotted the information on a slip of paper torn from a grocery sack.

"We can arrange for you to ride to Michigan with someone coming by your home or this park."

"We'd look forward to seeing you again," Del said. "I'm training under my Grandpa Clarence Groner to take over as the interface between Indians and non-Indians. Clarence Groner is the son of Robert Groner. Robert was a personal friend of the honorable chief and shaman, Jodie Roughwater."

"Wow; and to think I've actually went fishing with a relative of that great man. The Manitou is smiling upon me."

"Talk about great. Pard, this fish is excellent."

Cherokee nodded his head and his grin leaked fish juice onto his chin. Patting with a napkin she'd quickly passed to him, he said. "Will you folks be long here in Missouri? I can arrange a campsite."

"Sure wish it, but we've around 275 miles or so to go yet today. We'll load Caterpillar tractors and implements at Peoria first thing in the morning. They're for Tillageville, Michigan, located some hour and more from our home."

"The new chief of Roughwater Nation lives in our neighborhood." She wrote on the back of another card. "Jade Pickerel, a Mohican, is chief, and his wife is a helicopter pilot for the Roughwater people."

"I couldn't have imagined this fortune."

"Nor us," they chorused.

The fine lunch completed, they departed with their larder stuffed with ice, cooked catfish, earthworms, and a chunk of lettuce, beginning a 270 mile roll for Peoria.

* * *

Pulling to a stop at Louie's house on Perch Lake, their air brakes had hardly ceased hissing before Louie was pulling at the cab door. His strong arm and Del's met in a firm grip of hello as Del swung down. Louie's Rose stood at the other door as it opened and her arms reached for Dosia. Dosia fell into arms made short by the bulge of a baby. Dosia thrilled that it kicked against her own tummy, and wondered how joyous it must be for Rosie. "Yes, I've joined the La Leche League," Rose said. "Come in. I've a pamphlet on it."

"New to me, that La Leche."

"The latest, or the oldest idea, I'd say," Rosie talked while leading the way toward the house. "It's a league to encourage breast feeding. I'd thought such a group as not necessary. You may know that the first baby formula to feed the baby instead of breast feeding was invented by Nestles in 1867. Since then I guess the use of formula has become sort of vogue so that's why the league. My doc says that a lot of moms don't breast feed, but for me, I'm looking forward to it."

A tingling passed through Dosia's breasts. "Gosh, I'd sure think so," she said. Crossing her arms, she passed a forearm across each breast and felt the firmed nipples. She glanced over at Del but he was strolling along with Louie, their eye upon a new truck.

"Four wheel drive diesel with a winch that we'd thought up uses for. Might replace that old Nancy mule or the Oliver Cleat-Track on occasion.

Sid picked it out. Said he seen 'um like it in the army. Big Dodge, as you see. Sid said they're undaunted by mud, snow, or terrain, but I think he liked the bright yellow color."

"Sure looks handy. You have a lot of logs down?"

"A finger in every pie, I'll say. We can't venture all eggs in one basket, what with the excelsior business iffy for next summer. So we cut logs, there's a couple of dozen and more loads stacked at Yelrom, recall where that tin can on a stick marked the gate? We skidded all the logs out to that good loading area. No brush there to scratch your Mack. The Caterpillar loader's there for you. The aspen logs we've grouped separate, to haul into Dad's mill and plant near Bruin City. One of us will show you where his plant is located.

"Sid, me, and some of our crew have been helping to assemble log buildings. Recall Dad and his buddies were making prefabricated buildings. Woops! I boo-booed. They're called 'pre-constructed' buildings. To dad, that name seemed to sound like a time saver while the former term sounded artificial; so it's pre-constructed. Well they cut and stack the aspen lumber until it dries then soak the stuff in preservative; dry that, then build the things in sections. He'll have a load of buildings for the Upper Peninsula when you can work it in. Hunting cabins."

"We've likely three runs down to Oklahoma to mix in with your loads. We're hauling cast iron components from East Jordan, road building stuff. Old Ike started something with his road building idea. Best roads in the world, we can figure on."

Louie snickered. "Pard, we loggers won't ever see such roads as that! I'd like to get old 'I like Ike' into this yellow beast here and bound him around some. Give the devil his due, I say. The proof of the pudding is in the eating. It's time somebody came to notice that most people in the nation live and work along thunder-busted darn roads. We're forced to drive upon them to make a living." They'd by then arrived at the war surplus gleaming yellow Dodge. Louie slapped the hood. "I'd sure like to give him a ride in this 'un."

"Helio said old Ike was sort of a road building officer. He went on that famous three thousand mile cross country truck trip across the North American continent in 1919 and he also built roads in the Panama Canal Zone."

"Sure, I know. Nathan sent descriptions about Eisenhower while he was in Germany. An acquaintance of his was a sergeant in a motor pool and he collected trucking stories. On that convoy in 1919 Lieutenant

Colonel Dwight Eisenhower went along even though he was a tank corps officer; went along as an observer. They had around fifty trucks and were to follow the Lincoln Highway from Washington D. C. to San Francisco. Of course the Lincoln Highway was at that time mainly an idea on paper, just mainly a line drawn across American. They sure had trouble but they made it while averaging about fifty eight miles per day. They had a couple of tractors to pull trucks, cars, ambulances, and such out of mud, rivers, and ditches. Among the trucks were Mack and Dodge." He pat a fender of the big yellow Dodge.

"I don't wonder that. But, say; no Liberty trucks?"

"Sure, there were a few Liberty trucks. Those trucks were fitted with big tanks to carry fuel." Louie rubbed his head. "Now I wonder if old 'I like Ike' doesn't regard the roads us loggers use as luxury routes compared to roads used by that army convoy of 1919. Boy, I'd sure like to get him aboard this big yellow beast here."

"I'd think tires were improved more than roads over the years. That convoy was all on hard rubber tires, Helio said, really rough! That's just like they were when they chased after old Poncho Villa and throughout World War One. If not for pneumatic tires, I wonder if even Mack and Dodge could survive the roads we truckers with logs travel upon."

"Yes, and with tires covered at ten to twenty ply or so of casing and tread. I'd say you're right."

"We'll get at your logs this afternoon. That's why we stopped in; figuring you could use a check in the mail now and then."

"There are two families in the world; the have and the havenots, so the man wrote. I'm afraid we're more the latter, but we keep on chugging."

"When thou art in Rome, do as they do at Rome; see there, I've managed to use one of your sayings from that Don Quixote book. We, too, keep on chugging, hoping to get somewhere. No baby for us yet on the way; or at least she hasn't said so, but I noticed she eyed your Rose with hungry eyes."

"We're looking forward to the blessed addition. It's maybe made Dosia hungry for some tiny feet, like Sid's Maxine. They were here when Rose announced. She grabbed Sid and said 'Dear, we gotta get on home.' Now she's announced so now we await news from Wesley and Jo, from Dan and Wynona, and, of course, you folks."

"As God wills, but we're pinching pennies these days, sweating the purchase of eight new Coopers for the semi trailer. Helio knew they were getting thin but we didn't write him they were showing cord. Our folks aren't wallowing in dough, either. So we thought we'd meet that bill. As well, they're paying on two tractors and the Fruehauf semi trailer along with the house. Hearing you guys had trucking for us has sure made Christmas in January. Those good lookers on the semi trailer now are really pre-war tires we got for five apiece, but the guy said we shouldn't expect much longevity from them."

They'd strolled back to Del's rig as they chatted. Louie kicked a tire. "Kick good as new, and you're worried?"

"I think tires go out faster on hot pavement like down south. Three trips there shouldn't be too bad on them seeing's it's winter. We'll load the logs a little light but guess at what you owe us. Keep a watch on us so we don't cheat you."

"No, you figure it your way. I'll just help keep watch of the tires. Deal?"

"You have it, Pard. You boys have a big crew nowadays?"

"No, we just added a bible-slapper to replace you."

"A what?"

"Slap, I call him sometimes, but his name is really Lester Day Blanes from Battle Creek. He's a seminary trained and ordained preacher but he works with us. Good worker. Shares leadership with Wesley when I'm away. He wears BVDs. With his shirt off, one can tell there're BVDs as the things are one-piece. Slap claims to be a relative of one of the BVD inventors."

"My dad has taken to the same kind of underwear. My ma-in-law said Bradley, Voorhies, and Day invented BVD underwear back in 1915. Dad said it's more comfortable than other unders because it made of a light cotton fabric; not knit like other underwear. Ma-in-law said the fabric's called nainsook."

"Well, being one piece is what troubles me. One'd have to work fast in an outhouse emergency. The top part, however, is sleeveless and resembles a tee or other summer shirt. Slap went swimming in his; the legs go a quarter, or so, down his thighs."

"Good man despite the unders though, I'll guess."

"He's at home in the woods, anybody can tell. Good man. Once in a while he and I go at it."

"Get mad?"

"No, we debate. He has some corny ways, to my thinking. Plan to eat Wesley's cooking at breakfast. You'll meet old Slap. I had him whipped on that calling a human an ape thirty and forty years before Darwin. Not Darwin's idea at all nor was it Darwin's belief."

In the house, Dosia hurried toward a whistling teakettle. Nearing the house, Louie and Del heard the whistle. Joseph Block invented that pretty sounding pot back in 1921. Around here it means that instant coffee is served. We think it's a little cheaper than perked as we don't waste so much by pouring it down the drain." The shrill whistle put a rush to their feet. Louie grabbed the teakettle. "She saved S@H Green Stamps enough to get it."

Rosie entered the kitchen from the laundry area. "Sheet're in," she said, "and darn that whistle. Louie, I just can't come a charging any more."

Just then Dosia's call from the kitchen stove popped their heads toward her. "How could we have missed you?" Louie wanted to know, as he eyed Dosia.

"Miss me and you miss brunch," she joked. "That whistle startled me so I missed the griddle when I flipped a pancake. Still that shrieking pot, Louie. The pancake rolled to behind the stove!"

To the men's surprise, brunch that day was actually to be made hardy by the addition of the pancakes, Rose discerning that her guests had skipped breakfast. Del grinned now at seeing Dosia back at the griddle flipping cakes. "My kind of brunch," Louie said.

"Wow! I'll say, mine too."

"Won't this much brunch throw a monkey wrench into lunch?" Louie wanted to know, his eye on Rose.

"Eat slow, pilgrim, and you won't even know you skipped lunch." She suddenly paled and brought a cupped hand over her mouth. Spinning, she hurdled toward the bathroom.

"Shoot," Louie said.

"Again," Dosia said. "Second time since we came here. Cooking, I've heard, brings on the trouble. Morning sickness, it's called. Louie, I'll be in to cook breakfast tomorrow, okay? Other meals, too, when I can. That morning sickness, I've heard, shouldn't last this far into her term."

"Sure, but tomorrow, we'd planned to all of us eat Wesley's cooking. We've a cook shack now that we can tow around to different work sites. The glorious thing is constructed of four sections that we tow separately then join them all together in a row at the new cook site." He turned his head to include Del. "One of those pre-constructed aspen jobs dad's company makes; and three sections of it form into our eating room. But now, Dosia, there's always other meals you're welcome to cook any day."

His head swung back and forth between Rose and Dosia, his eyed settling upon his wife. "Really, is the sickness supposed to be over?"

"Dear, I sure wish it was over, but my doc says not to be alarmed just yet as the baby's doing fine."

"I'll ask aunt Edith about it. She'd know. Meantime, Louie, I'll sit down with Rosie to figure out a schedule. Hopefully, she'll get over morning sickness sooner that way. Louie, that tea kettle really is a nuisance just at this time."

Louie nodded his agreement, "I'll decapitate it directly, sure enough." He spoke then to Del. "Speaking of monkey wrench," Louie said, "like in the expression I just used a sec ago. You know what they are?"

"Adjustable wrench. What's up? I'm sure you know that. We carry several sizes in the Mack"

"Well, it's a funny thing that Nathan told about around Christmas. Sid's and us managed to get down to the college to see him; visited with him right in a dairy barn while he milked cows. He didn't know about causing trouble with a monkey wrench. We're both looking to see where that adage came from, but as to the monkey wrench, itself. It was invented by a guy named Charles Moncky in 1858. Spelled M-o-n-c-k-y but pronounced like a monkey."

Dosia arrived with a platter of pancakes. "Let's all sit down," she said. "Let's say a little prayer."

Louie obliged, even included a request for Rosie's wellbeing and for Del's tires, and a thanks for yelling teakettles and for the monkey wrench. "Amen."

"Say, Louie, I just thought of something my ma-in-law said about the monkey wrench when they bought extra so both trucks had a set. She said they are used in industry and in a labor-management dispute a monkey wrench would just happen to fall into the pulleys here or there. It sure monkeyed up production."

"Strange that such should just happen to happen, but now it does make since. I'll consult with Anna Mae pretty often after this."

"Speaking of strange things, or surprising things," Del spoke around a savor of syrupy pancake. "We'd thought all of the steam train engines are gone. Boy, I sure miss them chugging up the Ellington grade. One day just driving along with a load of aircraft parts and old cars, we had our window's open to enjoy a southwestern winter when a Whoooot! came right in our windows. Snapped our heads, bent our necks but we couldn't see where to look. I drove along and Dosia had her head out the window of the Diamond-T until she popped back in and said 'It sounds ahead,' then I punched the gas and we scooted. Just in time. Some sight, I'll tell you. Smoke pouring up. It gave me gooseflesh at seeing that beautiful Atchison, Topeka, and Santa Fe engine steaming past pulling a string of freight cars."

"Still a steamer, hey? I'm glad they're not all gone. Diamond-T, you said?"

"Yup."

"Honeymoon trip," Dosia came into the conversation. "We traded with a nice man, his Diamond-T for our Mack. Our trip from Oklahoma to California and then east back to Texas was our honeymoon trip. We cooked outside everyday, except here in Michigan, of course. Didn't ever get rained on or snowed on, and everyday we cooked outside. Wesley will be proud when he hears about the cooking." She stopped, and rubbed across her forehead. "Perhaps not, now that Wesley's gone inside with his cooking; that cook shack, I mean."

"Oh he's always glad to hear good reports to do with his cooking." His eyes took them in. "Honeymoon, huh? How big's that Diamond-T inside?"

Her eyes lit up, and a gentle grin creased Del's face. "Wonderfully snug," she said. "Not enough room in it for us and our larder so Del put that in his seat behind the steering wheel at night. We'd stop at towns to buy blocks of ice. Once we had nearly our whole larder packed with Mississippi catfish. Cooked and stored with the ice, we ate some everyday, eating the last of it in Tillageville."

"Big mess of catfish, I'd think. Del catch any?"

"No," Del said. "She did it all, but she only caught one fish."

Louie grinned at Dosia. "One?"

"A man named Cherokee helped land it and to cook it. He said it'd weigh around thirty pounds."

"Del tell you about a pounce we did on my Uncle Leonard Coffee? We were kids then, and Nathan, Joe, and Wheaty - now called Sid - were in on it too. Right here at Perch Lake. Recall that Del?"

"Sure, I thought all about it when she landed that fish. About the size of the fisherman, er, woman, seemed like. I just wish it could've been real for Leonard."

"Well he went to his grave still with that record fish on his mind. Any big fish I hear about reminds me of Uncle Leonard. Dosia, you're sure lucky to have a record fish already."

"I'm real proud. Cherokee snapped some pictures. They should be in our mail when we get home. He says that he'd not seen a catfish bigger, but he'd heard tales that'd make my fish seem like a minnow."

"Shisst! Now be quiet or you'll have Uncle Leonard thrusting right from his grave over at Solon Center cemetery to hike right to that big river." Suddenly he again looked serious, asking; "Is there a town of Jordan or West Jordan? I've wondered why the one is called East Jordan; kind of strange."

"There's the Jordan River that runs through. East Jordan is on the northeast end of it, but I didn't ask why the town's East Jordan. Actually, I believe that through the town the river flows north."

"Town history'd be an interesting topic for somebody in old age. I think I'll look forward to it." Louie rubbed his head. "River history, too, maybe. You know about the Nile River. Well, it starts out as two rivers. The Blue Nile is in Ethiopia and in the country of Sudan it joins the White Nile to become the Nile River everyone's heard about. Now why would they've named them a blue and a white river? Now the Jordan River I'd bet was named after the Jordan River of the Bible, likely by somebody like our Mr. Slap might do. The Israelites crossed the Jordan, another one of those hold back the water deals so they could just walk across as if on land, and they faced Jericho, the first city they had to conquer with Joshua in command. So folks the ilk of slap would likely name a river Jordan if they came onto one not already named."

"I look forward to meeting your Slap, er, Reverend Lester Day Blanes."

"Yup, tomorrow morning."

"Del, I'll stay here with Rosie while you load the logs; pick me up here."

"Okay."

CHAPTER SEVEN

In the late afternoon the couple pulled in at Anna Mae and Helio C. Outhe's house. They both strained their eyes and craned their necks as they pulled to a stop, each expecting to see the folks even knowing they were at present located somewhere in the great northwest. Del felt like a burglar when her key fit and the door swung open. They walked inside on tiptoe. "Hello!" she'd called foolishly.

"I feel the same," Del said. "But we're the only ones home, dear."

"Y . . . Yes, sure, of course." She held a package of hamburger under one arm, nearly dropping it at seeing the dining room table covered with mail. "You start the meat cooking and the macaroni and onions while I sort out letters and bills." He was stirring in fried onions, canned tomatoes, and catsup when she arrived with a grand smile on her face and a half dozen letters. There's a little package on that table from Cherokee. And a package arrived from The Davy Crocket National Forest." She waited quietly, waited to catch his eye."

"Huh? What?"

"You need to guess the content of that package."

"Uh, well, from David Crocket Forest, my guess is they sent us more earthworms."

"Wrong. Here, I'll give you a clue." She crushed her tummy to him, her waist tight against him and ground back and forth. "Can you guess?"

"Wow, keep trying." He held her close. "I'm sure I'll sparkplug with it after a long while."

"Oh, I'll bet you will." She began grinding into him with an up-down motion accomplished by repeated bending of her knees with her waist pressed to him. "Now, can you guess?"

"Yes, yippee! To heck with macaroni goulash, I'm going to be too busy to eat it right away." He swept her off her feet and into his arms, toting her as if heading for the nuptial threshold of a wedding day.

"No, wait, the belt buckle."

"Huh?" He stood with her in his arms.

"Mr. Diamond-T sent me my belt and belt buckle. I'd left it in his truck. Remember, I pushed it behind the mattress in the sleeper of the Diamond-T. He found it under the mattress."

"That guy is sure smart, knowing just what it'd lead to."

"Put me down for now. You may take the fool thing off later. Right now, its goulash and letters." Returned to her feet, and handing the letters to him, she said, "The oldest are on top. Read them aloud while I set the table. Oh, good, you found coffee too."

"And condensed milk." He dragged the kettle of macaroni goulash from the burner. "What'll we do with our time while this stuff gets cool enough to eat?" She caught his ogle of her big pearly belt buckle and environs.

She grinned. "Read Momma's letters from the top, the oldest is on top."

"Oh, that. Er, well, okay." He began reading from the top of Momma Anna Mae's letters. She told of their trip west and that everything went as planned. She rode with Helio on most of the grocery runs, delivering to small stores up and down the coast. They'd made a rental housekeeping cabin their home. Semi trailer tires weren't mentioned until the third letter. That letter contained a check in the amount of forty dollars to use toward tires. "I wish they hadn't sent that," he said seriously. "I'd hoped not to be a bother. After all, they're loaning the whole rig and a house. We should be sending them."

"Hush. They want to help."

"Let's say that we have enough, or will have by spring; that we've purchased the used tires for the Lufkin. Don't say how much."

"Okay, but I'm sure they want to help."

"Sure, I know." He was into the fourth letter as they sat down to eat. "Oh, wow," he was excited, "here goes." He read about his father-in-law's first day in a forest guiding a big Hayes, that part of the letter written by Helio. "I came out with gross of 90,000 pounds, big stack of fir logs, and a bulldozer was used to ease me down several of the hills. It sure felt good to clinch my butt to a real truck seat."

"His what? Clinch?"

"An expression he uses when the going is especially challenging. Dear, he's having the time of his life! That's what he means."

"Good, then I'm agreed, let's not bother them about the tires."

The remaining letters held family news and that Anna Mae was helping in a dispatcher's office and that she'd landed a second part time job; that of writing and selling some advertising in publications offered at truck stops. "They both sound real contented," she said.

"I am, too," he said. "And this goulash looks to be excellent. Let's hurry on with the eating." She was opening the most recent letter.

"By now you will be back to the house and it will be your headquarters. I've worried that one or more of our letters may be lost. The letter you're reading is my/our number six. Do you have a count on yours? We plan to leave here in early March. Papa has applied for hauling uranium ore at Lake Athabasca, Saskatchewan, Del knows where, to fill in a little time before Sid and Louie have, hopefully, excelsior bolts to haul. Or any hauls, actually, as we're trying to remain quite local once back in Michigan. So don't write here after the last week of February. We're pleased you're home from California and Texas. Your adventures sound happy and exciting, as have been ours, but I look forward to seeing you and to feeling our old bed wrapped around Helio and me again."

The house lights coming on that evening served as a beacon in a storm, attracting relatives right and left. They'd just seated before the television when Grandma Ella Platt tapped their door. Entering she said, "Grandpa Delibar's coming too. Den and Naddy're helping him with his wheel chair. How have you been? You look lovely." She and Dosia hugged.

Grandpa Delibar called: "Hey, me too." His arms rose feebly, painfully in reach of hers.

She smacked a wet one to his forehead and then fell to a bear hug by mother-in-law Naddy Platt. Den Platt, always a bit shy, reached to pat his daughter-in-law's back before turning to grip his son's hand. "Long time, no see. Good trip?"

"Wonderful. Dad I'd not guessed before I saw Helio's Mack truck that day that I'd become a continental wayfarer. Sure some lively country out there and a host of marvelous folks."

"Staying in a while?"

"A few more trips to make to Oklahoma and a few rather local ones or just little jaunts out of state our dispatcher is drumming up. The most may all be here in Michigan; at least one load for Delton Watkins, that to the Upper Peninsula, and several hauls for Louie and Sid. Our dispatcher mentioned a possible load to the Salt Lake, Utah area to a place called Copperton. If that works out it'll be a good trip for our tires."

"Interesting how names change; Sid, Louie, and Del now rather than Wheaty, Peanny, and Danny but I'm getting used to your grownup names. Delton Watkins doing okay, is he? And what's the load to that Copperton?"

"She said only there're starting to restore some town to attract tourists when Eisenhower's new roads get built."

"Oh, well, we could use new roads, even right around here, huh?"

"Sure, but Louie's laughing about such as that. Louie thinks that old 'I like Ike' will be a time, if ever, getting around to fixing the roads we all need to travel to and from work." They took seats at the table that held the mail accumulation. Noting the order of the table, Del figured that Grandpa Clarence had a hand in it as the mail was arranged by dates and with Anna Mae and Helio's mail laid out in lines separate from Dosia's and his.

His mind suddenly returned to his dad's query about Delt.

"As to Delt Watkins, he's staying on the wagon and is a good business man; salesman especially. Their pre-constructed buildings are beginning to sell well. They make dozens of adaptations using mainly standardized components, walls, and such, and so are assembling anything from hunting cabins, cook shacks, to play houses, even to a dentist's office and a hotdog stand. Delt's sure interested, too, in that Copperton development."

"Sure came on well, hasn't he?"

"It's just hard to believe he's the same guy I met years ago on railroad tracks near our driveway. I'd placed a penny to be flattened by a freight train and he was down on his hands and knees the same as me hunting for it. He's come a long ways alright."

Papa Den suddenly jumped to his feet. "Whoops," he called, reaching to support his dad who was near the television, and tilting toward it.

Ella was on hand to steady the wheelchair as they settled him into it. Dosia held the front door open and was startled there by Clydis and Clarence Groner. All eyes had been to Grandpa Delibar until the Groner's hello reeled them.

"Well, hi."

"Gee, er, well, come in."

"We'll be back," Den said as he, Naddy, and Grandma Ella began the short wheelchair ride across the street to the Platt home.

Clarence stood holding a large bowl, its contents hidden by a towel.

"King Arthur Whole Wheat Flour" he explained. "Helio bought several bags of it when he and Anna Mae were honeymooning out east. Norwich, Vermont, since 1790 is written on the bags along with a recipe for bread; like here." He flipped the towel aside, revealing a large lump of rising dough.

"That's the last of our Vermont flour supply," Grandma Clydis said. "We were about to form it into loaves when we saw your lights were on. Welcome home. We thought it'd be grand to bake it here while we chatted."

"Gosh, yes," Dosia chorused with Del. With her arm around Grandma Clydis, she led into the kitchen. Soon, with the bread plumping in loaf pans, they settled with Postum, condensed milk, and sugar around the kitchen table but hadn't sipped before Naddy and Den returned. The group settled around the big oaken kitchen table content to hear of the young couples' adventures.

To catch Grandpa Clarence up on Indians, Del began reporting on conversations they'd had; mentioning the code talkers, the Chickasaw, and with the mention of Cherokee, Dosia's comment pierced the air: "The pictures!"

She rushed from the kitchen. From out of the dining room, they heard, "Here they are!" Darting back into the kitchen, she tossed the Cherokee package to Grandpa Clarence. "Open please; gather around everybody."

"Trick photography," Clarence passed a photograph to Papa Den. "Real clever, that Cherokee."

The photographs passed along for all to see. "Ain't fake," Naddy said. "Why you kids caught the biggest fish in the river!"

"Mississippi. And there's just the one fish, no fake. Dosia caught it. Cherokee thought a thirty pounder."

"My word!" Grandpa Clarence studied, smacking his lips.

"Yes. Cherokee helped me land it or it would've broken my line. He said he'd not seen a bigger catfish but he'd heard that my thirty pound specimen was but a minnow compared to the tales he's heard."

"Gosh, where along the Mississippi?" His chair pushed back in concert with Papa Den's. Both of them saying: "Let me at 'um!"

"I can show you on a map; in Missouri, in a little cove off of the main river. We were at a truck stop ten, fifteen, miles or so below the Trail of Tears Park. Cherokee is a ranger there."

"He's a real Cherokee, born in Oklahoma. He said that at times he's shed tears thinking of his people's suffering. Tending their park is an honor, he said."

"You have any of that bait left? What'd you use?"

"Earthworms reared at a worm farm near Lufkin, Texas; raised by a ranger there in the Davy Crockett National Forest."

"Well, by gum," Papa Den said. "Daughter, if you're by there again, I want some of those worms." He stood from his chair. Naddy caught his eye.

"Work day tomorrow."

"It's late for us, too." Clydis stifled a yawn. "May we come at breakfast to sample the bread? Dosia, that should come out at eight-thirty. Go ahead and eat on it."

"Can't. We've a date to breakfast with Louie and Sid and their crews at their cook shack."

"Gee, say, that's right," Del plowed fingers through his hair. "Thought of that bread will haunt me all day. We'll lay into some of it as soon as we return here from the Coopersville saw mill."

"What time?"

"Near dark; like today. We'll load after breakfast then haul the load into the mill. It was near dark today, but maybe sooner tomorrow as we'll load earlier. Could be a couple hours earlier, I hope, so's the bread won't be lonely."

"I know how it is with fresh bread," Clarence said. "You eat some. I know you'll have to eat some to keep from going loco, but not all of it, please. We'll notice your lights and be right over tomorrow evening to help with the remaining bread."

"It's a date."

* * *

The cook shack in the woods west of Yelrom was the first example Del and Dosia had seen of the new building technique practiced by Delt Watkins' group. In building the structures the center sections of aspen logs were cut into rafters, trim boards, and slabbing boards, leaving four rounded slabs of wood, each with a flat surfaced reverse side. The slabbing boards were used to nail the rounded slabs together, producing an outer surface that resembled a log cabin, and with flat inner surfaces suitable for wallboard, if desired. The cook shack had no wallboard to conceal the construction technique. Wesley had festooned the walls with nails that held his cook pots, pans, and utensils. Other nails were driven handy for hanging coats and hats.

To eat, one grabbed a plate and went to a counter, there helping oneself to pancakes, eggs, bacon, biscuits, and pilot bread. On a help-yourself bases, one procured silverware, napkins, cups, coffee and makings, along with butter, oleomargarine, syrup, jam, jelly, milk, and else which altogether crowded the center of each table. Each of two tables seated twelve persons. Dosia, Rosie, Jo, Wynona, and Maxine were seated together with Rosie occupying an end seat. She was handy for a quick departure should her tummy suddenly rebel. Dosia sat beside Del and across from Sid. Louie sat beside Sid and across from Lester Day Blanes. Blanes, everyone knew, was that notorious Mr. Slap.

"Well, Slap. What's new with you?"

"Another day before the end. I've been these many evenings and weekends traveling the roads trying to bring people to God before it's too late. And I'm telling you again and with loudness for all to hear; the world is about to end."

"Oh now, you're kidding." Louie's tone was soothing.

"Television and atomic energy are the final clue, especially the bombs." Lester rose into preaching poise as he continued: "Humans have no more to gain of the earth so must make ready for the return of Christ."

Suddenly upset, Louie slammed his fork, rose in his seat, and laid into Lester Blanes, saying, "Slap, you ignorant beast." His nose was a foot from Lester's. "Such irresponsibly ignorant prattle is what drives the youth, and all others, but especially the youth, away from religion, away from any chance they might gain the grace of God in Heaven. I wish you could see that."

"Romans 8:32," Lester calmly quoted: ". . . won't god, who gave us Christ, also give us everything else?" Louie settled back but with his forehead crinkled, and his eyes questioned Lester. "Well, he has," Lester said. "We have everything, even the means to our damnation and to the death of Earth itself. Through television we're exhibiting death of mind. Atomic holocaust threatens death of all people and of the earth."

Louie said, "He who gave us everything, you say. Well, He included ability in all of that. He gave us the ability to figure everything out, or, at least the ability to figure out methods for trying to figure everything out."

"We can't know more, our minds won't take it," Reverend Lester Day

Blanes vehemently averred. "You, we, can't know everything, can't know more."

"We can too know more, and no, of course, we can't know everything. Have you not read Plato's Aristocracy."

"God's Word is the only reading anyone needs."

"You are a lover and adherent of the Dark Ages, that's your trouble. Well, Slap, that's ostrich country, a place where one buries one's head in fear of knowledge, buries the head in futile escape."

"I'd guess your Mr. Plato wasn't Christian or I may have heard of him."

"Plato wrote of an aristocracy that would raise Plato, the philosopher, to the highest possible pinnacle from where he could converse with God, thus learning all of the answers, that is, he would learn the why and the how of everything."

"And you call me ridiculous? He couldn't know the true way to heaven. Why, the way into God's presence is written for all to see. We shouldn't try to learn of some other way. It's wasteful and there isn't time. In God's Word, the end of the earth is described."

"A bird in hand is worth two in the bush. Man can't know it all, but God expects us to try. My friend Nathan is a Christian and a biologist. Mind you, he says he's not met any biologist who isn't religious. The more a scientist, or anyone, finds out about the intricacies and workings of nature, the more God is understood and appreciated."

"My friend, spend that time with the Word. There's no salvation through work in a research laboratory."

"That laboratory is as Godly a place as any other, even these woods or this cook shack Nothing and no place is without God. God is the brain of the universe and all within it. So, Rev, hide your head in the sand if that comforts you, but don't bellow at me or anyone contemplating the how and why of things. We must learn all we can before we give up this life. The more we learn of His works, the more we recognize the wonderful beauty of residing in heaven in the presence of God, the Being of all beings who knows with precision the how and the why of it all."

"The important why and how are answered in the same verse spoken by our Lord. I want to post John 14:6 on the wall over there." He nodded toward the wall opposite an entry door. Jesus said, 'I am the way, the truth, and the life: no one cometh unto the Father, but by me.' I've paraphrased it a little bit for clarity. I want everyone to understand that our time is short, our time is now, that there is a way, the only way, but we must hurry."

"Sure, I agree as to the way. A word to the wise is enough. That verse is a wonderful thing to hang on the wall. That wall, I hope you notice is something new, that is just figured out; new knowledge of the how of something. That wall answers the how to utilize scrub wood, aspen in this case; to make an excellent product of it, even producing a durable, handsome wall and a place to hang your Bible verse."

Throughout Louie and Lester's discussion the ladies and the other patrons heard little but each other, as their attention had been to eating and to visiting their own topics. Louie and Lester, however when an unspoken truce quit their debate, looked upon their empty plates with derision, feeling yet hunger because they couldn't recall the food. Louie studied his dirtied plate, evidence that he must've eaten. Slap looked up from a study of his own soiled plate. "Did her again, didn't we?"

"Yeah. Well, there's pie yet. Let's grab a slice then get the chain saws into that silver maple copse."

* * *

Instead of an early arrival home on that day they'd celebrated the cook shack breakfast with Sid and Louie's crews, Del and Dosia pulled in at their house just as dark was thickening. Two automobiles were tucked into the driveway as they pulled the rig in parallel to the curb. Lights were on in the house and figures were seen moving about.

"Why, it's Aunt Edith," Dosia said, her expression merry.

"Yes and the big car's Grandpa and Grandma Groner's."

Just at that moment a third car pulled in, stopping nose on nose with the Mack. Uncle Harold James climbed out.

"G'evening. Pleased to see you're back north."

"Hauled to Coopersville today and then a load of aspen to Bruin City. Good to see you again; and we see Aunt Edith inside. Separate cars, what's up?" They were by that time approaching the front door of the house.

"I'm just from Gabe's garage," Harold said. "This old clunker needed some tweaking before we gave it to you."

"Us?" The front door swung open in time for them to pass right on into the house without altering their paces.

Holding the door for them, Aunt Edith said, "Yes, for you. Joe and Parrot have finally sprung for their yearned-for Power Glide Chevy. We thought you could use some extra wheels. As you know, Anna Mae's old Ford is no longer dependable, but your brother-in-law, Gabe, is coming to tow it to his garage, hoping to have it perky and well when your folks return from Oregon."

"Gee thanks," Dosia hugged Aunt Edith. "Great, that'll be a pleasant surprise for Momma. And today a spare car would've saved Del a run to Perch Lake with the truck. I spent the day there with Rosie, Louie's wife; she's expecting."

"That dear. We met her last winter when they were down wondering how to contact you."

"She alright?" Grandma Clydis moved in for a hug and peck with Dosia.

"Yes," she returned a peck to Grandma Clydis' cheek, "but morning sickness. I want to be there every day that I can to help until that subsides." She turned to include Aunt Edith and Uncle Harold. "Thank you again. The car for us is God sent. Momma, too, will be as pleased, I'm sure."

"Wish I'd thought of it sooner," Grandpa Clarence said, "and as to morning sickness, it seems to be a bane on the beauty of God's gift of a child. I'm surprised Genesis didn't mention it. Praying on it may help. God'll will its cessation in due time. Yet another of God's gifts is home baked bread like I've just pulled from the warming oven."

"Great, Grandpa! Get to slicing. I near broke speed records getting home today. I'm glad the roads aren't slippery."

"We've had a slippery gooey winter up here until just lately, but don't be fooled. This still is Michigan and March is coming. You've noticed they haven't pulled in those barrels.

"I'm always glad to see those barrels. Helio said that in slippery weather it's best to have two men in the cab. I think I'll just have to stay off the roads when it's real icy. I can't see Dosia out there throwing sand under my truck wheels from those barrels. Grandpa, why don't you learn to drive the Mack enough for the two of us to make the hills?"

"You'd be better off if I hurled the sand. Call me if you need me. We could talk of Indians as we cruise along. I hate to say it, Del, but there just could be more Michigan winter left to us."

"Speaking of cold weather, was the temp here in the house about right when you arrived home? With three grandpas minding the house, it seems that one sets the thermostat just so's another can change it."

"We didn't notice the temp so it's about right. I hear you're putting in new ceilings in your house."

"Called a false ceiling; actually they're lowering them from ten feet to seven and a half. It'll be easier to heat."

"Oh, Grandpa, I've had a notion about high ceilings. Are they high so that smoke gets trapped up there out of one's eyes and lungs? That's what I heard."

"Smoke could accumulate up there, alright, but in the summer the old timers would open the lower pane of windows on the coolest side of the house – from on a porch or if not, then open lower windows on the north. Cool comes in and chases the heat up to the ceiling where it flows out through the top of windows; lower the top pane of windows to let out heat, you see."

"Yes," she touched her forehead. "But why do you want to change that arrangement?"

"Central air conditioning, like your grandma Clydis' father had installed in here. We all thought he was a bit loony at the time."

"In the truck is where I'd like air conditioning. In summer one can nearly cook in a truck cab."

"I've heard that air conditioning can reduce miles per gallon."

"I wouldn't worry with diesel only eighteen cents a gallon."

"A lot of hauling to do is there?"

"I sure know it, or, at least, Sid and Louie and Delt know it. I'm going to haul like mad to give them paychecks before the March lion again buries their logs."

"Ready," Dosia called.

Talking around stuffed mouths in savor of the warm, butter melting, homemade whole wheat bread slowed chat briefly; until Uncle Harold said, "Speaking of that hurrying you were talking of, Del. I've warned your Aunt Edith, that fireball Edith that we know, that the county sheriff's department is trying to clamp down on speeding. They've been ticketing all winter because of accidents; sighting that 'too fast for conditions' counts as speeding."

"Family, I'm sorry," Grandma Clydis said. She pat her lips with a napkin. "It was me that set them out with their enthusiasm to nab speeders. Before Christmas I ran across an old newspaper article. It came to the library as packing around a shipment of books, an article about speeding; that is, and of the first speeder car driver. Like a dunce, and for a joke, I sent it to the Leadford Register office as a Letter to the Editor. Something like, in 'August, 1904 a man was arrested for speeding in Newport, Rhode Island. A Judge Darius there gave a speeding ticket to the man whose speed was 15 mph. About a week later the same man was arrested for speeding;

again doing 15 mph. Judge Darius jailed the guy, delivering the first jail sentence for auto speeding in the United States of America.'"

"You know, just lucky, I guess, I did see a patrol car parked in pounce position when I pulled from Coopersville. I was just on my way and hadn't had time to climb the gears to be speeding. I did speed, though, after that on a rush to get a load of aspen logs into Bruin City. Delt's shop is sawing like mad crazy to be ready to fill orders for their new type of building."

"Dear, the tires; please be thoughtful of that."

"Tires? You got trouble? Say, you did mention tires a bit earlier."

"Money. We're saving for a new set of Coopers for the semi trailer. A traffic ticket would sure be a waste of the money we're saving for the tires. We're doing that instead of fretting Papa Helio about the tires."

"But Papa knows about needing tires," Dosia said. "And the folks sent some money toward them. I'm going to write our thanks and to say we've purchased a set of used tires for now, tires with lots of tread. The folks may need the money as much or more than we do."

"That's with payments on a house, two trucks and a semi trailer," Del said. "Besides, they've loaned us a truck and semi trailer and a whole house, for corn's sake. They're sure doing enough."

"They're still in Oregon?"

"Yes. He's off road trucking, his favorite kind of work, hauling loads of logs out of the deep timber; high pay, dangerous work, but he'll haul there only while various other truckers are taking vacations. He's applied for the same situation in Saskatchewan, Canada. There to haul uranium ore to fill vacation gaps of the other ore truckers."

"Sid and Louie's logs mainly go to Coopersville, huh?"

"Yes, their scrub wood, but when they come onto a log with furniture wood, that's what they call a quality log, it goes to one of several different band saw mills; one's at Stanwood. They have a recycled military Dodge truck now and a heavy lowboy trailer. Often a single furniture log or two is what they run into, so I'll seldom haul logs to other than Coopersville. Aspen's the same way, hardly ever a Mack load, except like today."

"Delt needing a lot of aspen, is he?"

"Yes, aspen that wasn't cut earlier because it was too big to form into excelsior bolts. I had a full load of big stuff for Delt today. He needs a paycheck once in a while, too; his from selling those buildings."

"Have you eaten in that restaurant near the saw mill in Coopersville?" Aunt Edith had joined into the conversation. "Your Grandma and Grandpa Groner ate there just a few days ago."

"No, we squirt right on back."

"We recognized Mrs. Biloxey Perkins running the place," Grandma Clydis said. "She didn't recognize us so we thought we'd wait until later to let her know who we are."

"Oh?" Del looked keenly at Grandma Clydis, and wondered what was up.

"Grandpa Delibar," Uncle Harold said, "related a set-to Dosia and you had with Ronnie Perkins out in the Coopersville mill yard."

"Oh." Del held a puzzled expression, wondering what plan was in the wind. "I thought we'd taken care of that situation."

"You do recall Big Harley Perkins from the Ellington two-room school days?" Del nodded his recognition. "Well, he's a brother to Ronnie Perkins. Alliance Perkins, called All, is their father. Ronnie attended a private school near Coopersville. She worked in that restaurant near the saw mill while Ronnie attended. But school or not, Ronnie was with his mother every day. We've heard that Big Harley killed a box elder bug with a blast from a twelve-gage shotgun," Aunt Edith explained, "in the living room of the Perkins' home here at Ellington. Loxey, that's the name pinned to her uniform, and Ronnie stayed in Coopersville full time after that."

"All Perkins drives to Coopersville every weekend," Uncle Harold took over the conversation, "to be with his wife and son. Big Harley still lives with his dad here at Ellington. They get along fine, we hear, even to his joining his father each payday at Carley's bar and pool hall. They get drunk at other times too, we've heard. Drunk for special occasions, like when All and Big Harley went on that mad rampage through the woods blasting off shotguns. Remember that? It was in the woods behind your folk's place; trying to bag a black panther."

"Yes, I heard about that. I was real little on that day Big Harley blasted a dead alley cat that my brother Ward'd already shot. At school I heard Big Harley bragging he'd shot it; killed that black panther, he claimed."

"Yes, so you have that family relationships and behavior straightened out now, do you?"

"Sure."

Grandma Clydis said, "Do you see Ronnie Perkins each time at the mill?"

"Yes, usually, but he now works over at the debarking machine, not near the trucks unloading."

"Does he ogle Dosia?"

"Since we've been back north, Dosia hasn't gone to the mill with me. She's been helping Rosie."

"Good." She reached to touch Dosia. "Dosia, please don't go near that mill. Grandpa Clarence and I will continue eating at the restaurant, hopefully to gather information that might ease our minds about Ronnie Perkins."

"To be blunt," Uncle Harold said, "Ronnie is stupid like his brother and father. Good reliable workers, though. We were shocked to hear that Ronnie has a dangerous attitude while his brother and father are quite harmless; well unless black panther hunting."

"However we can't forget that it was Big Harley who injured Nathan that time. In a rage he twisted the boy's neck nearly off. Nathan still has pain from that. The Perkins boys do, I believe, have a mean streak. Even after he injured Nathan, he and cousin Joe, and their friend Wheaty Watkins, now called Sid, tried to befriend Big Harley Perkins, in an effort to get around his mean streak. Big Harley responded somewhat positively to kindness. It seemed to calm him down a little. Back then we were thinking Big Harley's behavior stemmed from his being lonely. Please let us feel out the situation before you go near that Ronnie. We'll keep you posted on what we find out."

"We saw Ronnie that day we were there," Grandpa Clarence said, "getting into a dark blue and cream, really sparkling, Ford Crown Victoria. Nice car, like I said; neat, clean. You might mention his well-kept car as a means to divert his attention from clobbering you, but get that near him only at a last resort, okay?"

"Yes, but I suspect he'll always be over at the debarking, some hundred yards away from where I unload, but I'll be careful."

Del suddenly tried to stifle a yawn. "A hard work day can bring on fatigue," Grandpa Clarence said. "But a funny thing, I've been struggling to hide my yawning as well, and I manage to not work at all. Best we call it a day."

"Heavy day tomorrow, Del?"

"Trucking like mad for Sid and Louie. Trying to get ahead on it before midweek when we load cast iron products at East Jordan. The iron stuff, road building components, we'll haul into the Ardmore, Oklahoma area; right about down to the Texas border."

"When's that trip to Utah?"

"I'll ask Papa Helio about it. He's talked on installing a turbo to boost power before we tackle mountains like out west. I'll ask him if there's a low altitude route to Copperton before we decide definitely on a run to Utah.

CHAPTER EIGHT

A few days later, and with thoughts of the fresh baked bread finally at ebb, and with Rosie's morning sickness still bothering, they pulled in at East Jordan. Having backed the Lufkin to the loading dock they hurried along to the restaurant, stumbling in at the rear door. Still bent against the cold wind, they clattered into seats well away from the big plate glass front windows. "Good morning – Hey, I know you people. Stayed south too long, I see."

"Here to load cast iron road components, thank you. We're headed back into that south."

"We've been warm up here, believe me, but you heard the breeze and thought it cold, cold, cold this morning, now didn't you?"

"Oh?" Dosia looked startled. "Really! Not cold?"

"Just bracing. I like a bracing breeze. You folks stuff in a breakfast special then go on out to the sidewalk. You'll see, a mere bracing breeze is all."

"The special sounds good to us. Business been brisk, has it?"

"At times, but other days are lonely, and I wonder the why of it all."

"No beau a-tapping your door?" Dosia popped her eyes to her husband, her poise warning him of infraction.

"Jacqueline, I'll apologize for him. Dear, none of your business."

"Not so." He stood his ground. "Jacqueline, if there was a beau in the wings my family's plan wouldn't work. Say no."

She grinned. "No. No beau . . . and ding blast it." The last phrase had a sad note to it. She walked away toward the kitchen, she with her broad beam anchoring a seafarer's gait.

She brought their coffee. "What plan?"

"Well, it may not work out at all. First place you'd need to give up bracing breezes; in fact you'd be denied the sight of big water altogether. Instead you'd be immersed in swelter and you'd be wreathed in diesel fumes in lieu of lake-freshened air, but the food you serve here would also be ideal for that other place."

"Hold it, pilgrim." Dosia held his arm. "Just what are you jawing about?"

"Grandma and Grandpa Groner stopped in last night before you'd returned from Rosie's. That restaurant near the Coopersville saw mill is for sale. They talked with Loxey in there. She has to sell because she can't keep up. She needs help but cannot afford help. She's been seeking a partner but hasn't found one. The grand folks asked that I review in my mind all the eateries I've been to as a trucker, thinking on a likely prospect they could approach to find help, or a partner, for Loxey. Meantime, they asked Loxey to take down her 'For Sale' sign; to give them a chance to look around."

Jacqueline looked to be in shock. "Why me? Why, we've just met, you folks and me, sure. I mean; not them."

"Our Aunt Edith called this morning; you were in the shower, dear. She'd heard us speak of Jacqueline and suggested that I ask."

"Why, you stinker. You didn't even let me in on it."

"I wasn't sure, but when I saw Jacqueline just now, then I knew."

"Wait here," Jacqueline said, her face now with a grin as broad as her beam in spread. "Here, I'll bring your food, but wait here. I've a couple of telephone calls to make."

They'd finished breakfast and were growing antsy when Jacqueline burst in at the front door. "I'll find it. Coopersville, you said. I just got some off days next week, vacation days I've lined up. Thanks. I'll look in on that Loxey."

"I don't get it," Dosia complained as he set the Mack on course for Ardmore, "I cannot see Aunt Edith's plan." Her pretty hand bumped her forehead. She peered across at Del. "It is a plan, huh? Some idea she has, and with the whole family involved?"

"You know Aunt Edith. Her plans work out well even if others may be baffled. She and her friend Maggie sure rescued you back then and I'm eternally grateful." He reached to pat her thigh.

"Those two; and with Grandma Clydis too, when I met them, I knew I was to be alright. The doctor and the nurses tried hard to help me, but those dear ladies had the touch that I needed."

"You bet, all the way from a street waif in Paris to adopted daughter;

and now my wife. Those ladies knew what they were about, alright, and so did Grandpa Clarence and Uncle Harold, to say nothing of brothers and cousins, that's why I decided to work along with Aunt Edith, and the others, on this restaurant caper."

"I'm with you, but I'm truly anxious to know the details and to know who they're trying to help. Jacqueline? I don't get the picture. They don't even know her. Why, they haven't even met."

Discussion of Aunt Edith's plan surfaced from time to time throughout the trip south and resumed soon after their time at Ardmore with the road crew foreman and his buddy, Police Chief Allen. The Ardmore pair had the money on hand to pay in cash for the load down. The foreman'd stood proudly while the chief counted it into Dosia's hand. They'd heard by radio that snow was returning to blanket Michigan, enough of it and with drifting to bury Louie and Sid's logs. "Guys, snow's so deep back home that we can't haul for an outfit up there for a time. That means that we'll haul the rest of the cast iron assortment promptly down to you."

"No problem, old son. We've cash on hand to cover."

Batting northwest wind under a gray sky, their mood was gray as well for they hauled empty clear to Peoria. Gunning out of Peoria with a Caterpillar loader and a bulldozer chained on board, their opal mood swung to glitter. Glad they were for the load. Later that day, however, they were just into buffeting snow when an outside tire of a tandem dual on the right hand side blew apart! In her mirror Dosia caught the splatter of pieces and a puff of blue-white smoke. "Trouble! Smoke!"

Del brought the Mack down, looking for a haven, ultimately rolling into a Kroger parking lot on the edge of a town. The wonderful deep crisp tread of a recently bought used tire was ninety percent missing, and likely decorated the road a few miles back. They'd not before seen a tire ruined in just the manner displayed before them. "Sidewall failure," Del muttered. "I've not seen this before."

With determination propping his eyelids full up and with Dosia chattering about any topic she could think up, Del drove well into the night to make up time. They were cuddled asleep in the cab when daybreak showered the idling Mack. Snow lay deep on the road and half way up the windshield. Dosia rolled her window, pushing snow out of the way as the pane came down. Del'd left his window open a crack and snow had whitened his feet. Looking about, they were gratefully beckoned by truck stop neon.

Each with a duffle of freshening paraphernalia, including clean clothing, they dashed across to the building, stamping snow free of their boots and brogans as they entered. It was the last of their extra clothing. "Clothes to wash, we'll need a laundry."

Conveniently, their next tire met waterloo with that wash shop in view ahead. Inside, Dosia read Reader's Digest while the washer sloshed and the dryer rumbled and tumbled. Outside Del labored at a task now familiar to him. They left northward with Del already into his fresh-washed Levi jeans and munching a hamburger. As though God was watching, she'd found a stand selling burgers at five for a dollar. Their two dollar lunch was ingesting with abandon as Del sent the Mack on the trip's ending run into Michigan:

One hundred twenty to go for Tillageville.

Their eyes beheld the next dawning as they were backing to the dock at East Jordan. Sleepy eyed day shift dock men were just emerging from automobiles. Actually needing sleep more than breakfast, they trudged with disinterest to the restaurant. At the rear door a waft of frying sausage perked that latent interest. "Good morning," she called from the kitchen's service window. "Special's coming. How was the trip?"

"Snowy roads and some tire trouble, but cash on the barrel head." She arrived with coffee, cream, and sugar.

"I told that Loxey down there at Coopersville that she had a deal. I'd been offered a partnership here, but here is lonely at times then impossibly busy on any day that I'm sweaty-hot and dead tired. Bidding for a steady clientele, I said to her I'd buy in. They may have to close here, that I'm feeling miserable about, but I've saved and saved and the setup down there appears more to my liking."

"We'll soon be doing our last trip south from East Jordan, but we haul often into Coopersville. Hope to see you there."

Two more of the good looking deep treaded used tires had shredded into tire purgatory by the time they'd finished the Ardmore runs. Each dual of the Lufkin now consisted of an old Texan deep treaded used tire paired with a badly worn other tire. Hope rode on every mile toward spring. In desperation Del ordered the eight new Coopers, being able to place about a third down on them, trusting they'd be able to meet the final bill. But if they couldn't meet it they'd readied their minds to run with as many new tires as they could.

* * *

On a Saturday morning, and with Del and Dosia plunging north along sloppy slush-thrown roads, Loxey Perkins looked with a smile as the restaurant door opened, clanging the bright brass door bell. Loxey, looking from the kitchen, was pleased to see her new acquaintances had returned. Grandpa Clarence, Grandma Clydis and Uncle Harold and Aunt Edith crowded near the bell ringing door and knocked muddied slush free of their boots. Hanging outer wraps on handy wall pegs, they responded to Loxey's greeting with an apt description of the weather, finishing with ". . . warmer anyway."

"We were expecting to see this nice abode bulged with customers this morning, guessing it too miserable to work outside around the mill," Harold said. "Don't they come over here to warm up?"

"This place booms at breakfast where pancake, egg, home fries, and sausage hold sway. I've yet to serve a single Tony The Tiger nor any compadre of his. Lunch favorites always hinge around instant mashed potatoes or pasta. Of course I always post what special we've prepared." Their eyes followed her gaze to the chalk board which listed the day's lunch special.

"We, that's with Jacqueline and me by telephone, keep thinking of ways to have more customers between meals and at night. At night, the younger crowd, you see." She set coffee and makings before them, the pot centering the polished round-topped table. Amid a jovial scramble for cream, sugar, cups, and spoons, Aunt Edith poured. "We'd hoped to meet your son," Aunt Edith said over her shoulder. "Doesn't he lunch or coffee break in here with you?"

"Sometimes, but not enough of the men take coffee breaks in here. Coffee breaks are a thing we'll expand into. I'm surprised you know of him. He comes in, but usually he doesn't take a break before noon." She stood ready with a Ticonderoga No. 2 lead pencil poised over her order pad. "What will you have?"

Clarence didn't turn from his scan of the specials written on the wall-mounted chalkboard. "Special number one for me?"

"For all of us," Clydis said, "and over easy eggs."

"Our nephew-in-law and niece, that's Del and Dosia Platt, spoke of Ronnie," Edith said. "They haul in here frequently with logs; a big green truck with a large chromed grill."

"Sure, I've seen the truck; not them, though."

"They may be south right now with a load of road construction stuff. Warm there in Oklahoma, but I'll bet they'll batter snow and slop most of the way home. Snow's too heavy here to load logs, so they've been taking loads of gray iron products south." Loxey listened while she was receding toward the kitchen's order window.

"Hey," she said spinning around, their order still in her hand. "Now, I hope this isn't trouble." She took a step back toward them. "If it's about the time Ronnie was injured?" She noticed she still held their order. Turning to place it onto a hook for the cook, herself in this case, she said over her shoulder. "Ronnie said that he deserved it."

"Oh? We hope that is all peacefully settled."

"The saw mill boss seemed suspicious of Ronnie's explanation so he's moved him to a different job, different location; over at debarking. Please, I hope there's not more trouble."

"Come and sit with us, your only customers."

Looking spooky, she sat down, sat stiffly a moment, and then rubbed a hand over her mouth. "I think she shouldn't come here anymore."

"Oh, we've wondered, has he had trouble like this before?"

"No, not that I've heard about, but that time I took him to a hospital so other times, I may not've heard about. He's really a good boy, but not smart. He's a good worker, like his dad and brother."

"So we've heard. Do All and Harley come often?"

"All comes weekly, but Harley, hardly ever. We've always kept the boys some apart, but they like each other; get along well. All says Harley's found a gal."

"Gee, that's swell."

"Girls don't take to our boys, so I'm glad for Harley."

"No gal afoot for Ronnie, huh?"

"Some gal better hurry before he gets old like Harley."

"Twenty-eight, that's Harley, it's a good age to wed."

"Sure. We're all rooting for him. Seems Ronnie'd benefit maybe if there were more lady customers."

"Seldom any women. Usually just guys." Suddenly a smile sweetened her face. Her customers caught the broad smile, each instinctively knowing she'd suddenly thought of Jacqueline.

* * *

Louie, Sid, and Delt contracted with Helio and Del for trucking during the coming summer of 1957. Helio signed on his x-designated line while still in the uranium ore fields of Saskatchewan, attaching a note stating they'd be home around the first of April. Del opened the mail from Helio while sitting with his friends in Wesley's cook shack, signing his own name in an appropriate blank. "Helio'll be here around April 1." A heaped spoon of scalloped potatoes interrupted his talking a moment. "Our dispatcher's found a load of furniture using that company's closed semi. We'll run furniture to Chicago and glue, varnish and such back to the plant in Grand Rapids. The Lufkin'll be set in to the loading area near that tin can on a stick if you get time and a chance to load it."

It was a lucky break that Dolly Reams, their dispatcher, found the Chicago runs for them, including their use of that furniture company's semi trailer. The deal would spare the weary tires of the Lufkin. "I see your plan," Louie said. "But Dad has two, or so, loads to the Upper Peninsula, hoping you can get that done before April. Best leave your semi trailer backed in at his dock. They'll load and tarp it; ready for when you get back. We heard from Helio. He talked with a dispatcher that knew about the Utah area around Salt Lake City and Copperton. He recommended we ship pre-constructed buildings by rail as three or more trips by truck would be required and not enough time for youins to do it anyway. So a train would be best. Dad's getting that Copperton order ready and you'll be hauling loads to Grand Rapids where we'll load freight cars."

"Sure, there's no problem with that. Helio, along with me, is glad that your dad's pre-constructed buildings are catching on. You'll be a dad yourself by then, huh?"

"Likely. Rose and Maxine are painting the nursery room pinkly and Sid and Maxine's bluely, betting that a baby bottle held by a string over their tummy when they were flat on the floor at a baby shower has correctly determined the sex of child in each case." Sid and Del gaped at Louie.

"Well," Louie said, "I also asked old Slap to pray some sense into that bottle. He said he'd try."

Sid asked if Dosia'd announced yet. "We'd like to see a clean sweep of Rose, Maxine, Jo, Wynona, and Dosia, getting the business on the road all to once, you see."

"She's yet mum on it but she's set aside her regular magazines for baby reading, that's stuff by Dr. Spock and she reads over and over a pamphlet about that La Leche League."

"Our wives, too. You'd think breast feeding was the usual, and not necessary to have a whole league about it."

"That league's no pain to me. Me, I'm fretted over that pile of Good Housekeeping mags she's passed on to Maxine," Sid put in. "Lot of stuff in there for a wife to want, stuff we can ill afford."

"My mother-in-law said those mags are like catalog shopping, mainly just to get ideas for when times are better."

Sid reached for his hat and gloves. "Well Louie, let's have at it. Could be those better times are near."

Del, too, slid back from his cleaned plate. "I'll back the semi trailer in at Delt's. We're off for Chicago. Couple of runs there intermixed with Delt's loads, and then to your logs if by then they're uncovered."

In Chicago, while the furniture was unloaded, Dosia picked up a day old newspaper. Back in the cab, she thumbed the pages, finally settling on an item by a fledgling columnist named Ann Landers. He climbed aboard and sat on his hands to warm them, glancing over at her. "What, do they have a baby page?"

"No, but the Ann Landers column was interesting. Another writes here too; his about equal rights for people of all races. It's already going on two years, he wrote, since Rosa Parks refused to give up her bus seat to a white man. He said also, and it really surprised me, that Mrs. Parks may have moved to Detroit."

He flexed his fingers then placed a hand on the steering wheel, the other on the shift lever. "She's made a tough decision, all right; like with our tires. A possible life or death situation, I mean. With this trip we'll have enough for half of the Coopers. The inside tire of each dual will be new."

She folded the paper. "Good, I'll call Cooper at the next truck stop to set it up. See if they can mount them soon, maybe like before we deliver a second load for Delt."

Following the quick squirt into the Upper Peninsula for Delt, they cruised into Chicago on another haul with the furniture company semi trailer. Meanwhile the Cooper Company located south of Grand Rapids mounted four new Coopers. On the next trip for Delt the Lufkin wore a beautiful new tire paired with a weak one on each dual. They followed that second trip for Delt with yet another squirt into Chicago. By that time they were feeling atop their woes and ready for a rest. That Chicago trip would've aimed them toward a day of snooze and slumber at home, but dispatcher Dolly Reams telephoned: "I've another Delt load for the Upper Peninsula. After Delt's load, I've a load of brake drums from the East Jordan Iron Works, Inc, there're bound for Detroit."

"We'll truck the load into the Upper Peninsula and will load the drums on our way back. Tell them we'll be in there by tomorrow afternoon. Thanks, Dolly."

That load for Delt into the Michigan Upper Peninsula was light weight and was borne mainly by the husky larger-diameter new tires, sparing the thinned tires. In contemplation of the load of brake drums, their foreheads were in corrugation. Gingerly, they backed to the loading dock at the foundry. They watched the new Coopers sag as crate after crate of the drums were shuttled aboard. They pulled from the foundry with around sixty thousand pounds resting upon the new Coopers and the baldies and the old Texan well-treaded. They rolled into Detroit, breathing a sigh of relief having backed into the loading dock of a Ford Company warehouse. With the trailer duals humming a rhapsody in concert with the Thermaldyne purring sweetly, they sailed along toward home from Detroit with justifiable confidence: The tires held. By golly, the tires held!

"Hey, we're near East Lansing."

"Golly, you're right." He studied his wristwatch. "We could make it to that barn during Nathan's milking cows." She pulled the map into her lap.

"At the next highway, cut down to Route 43. We'll be right on time."

* * *

Squatting beside a cow, Nathan looked up at the sound of his name. "Well, howdy, howdy."

She stood with a brogan resting against the white-painted wall behind her. "Hi, I've not before seen milking. Does it take a long time?"

"About three minutes per cow. I get sometimes a minute between cows. Keep talking, it's okay." He pulled a set of cups from his cow, reached to unplug a regulator and draped the regulator hose over his shoulder, next emerging from the cow with a silvery stainless steel container of milk. In a bucket smelling of chlorine, he dipped the set of cups. He dumped the contents of the milk container into a strainer. Milk was heard draining into a standard ten gallon milk can as he grabbed his supply cart, drawing it to abreast the next cow. From another bucket he drew a wet soapy cloth. Kneeling beside the cow, he began to wash her udder. He plugged the regulator into the DeLaval overhead vacuum line. His cow was dripping milk onto the floor before he could install the cups. "Be just a few minutes. I can't take a break until after old leaky here."

He dashed back a couple of steps to remove equipage from a cow that, like all of the other cows, had a large plastic tag dangling from a loose-fitting belt around her neck. Her tag read 108. He took care of milk and materials from old leaky, then said, "Break time. No rush now. We must milk the leakiest cows first then we can loaf along a little more."

"Why the leaking?"

"Oh, like in people, I've heard. Sometimes just the thought or just some sound or sight can cause milk to let down; to be ejected, it's called in people."

Dosia couldn't help but touch her forearms to her chest, as the tingle there seemed almost to overwhelm her with giggles. She held a straight face. "That one cow, that 107 had a lot of milk, or was that from two?"

He pointed. "You've seen that cow with the 107 neck tag. She gives two to three times as much as cow 108. Surprisingly, they are twins, identical. This whole barn is full of twins. Of the pair, one is treated differently. Cow 107 was fed an especially rich grain and supplements diet while she was dry. Her twin sister 108 was treated as dry cows are traditionally treated. You can see the difference."

After a minute spent on record keeping, he was leading their way to an office. "Herd Manager" was lettered on the door.

"All the cows in this barn are in one experiment or another. It's to help farmers make sound management decisions or to help figure out a problem or problems one can have with a dairy operation."

He handed Dosia a photograph as they entered the office.

Inside were a desk and some worn wooden chairs and a couch. The couch was obviously a worn-out job discarded from some lucky living room. He directed his guests to the couch. "Our finest seating," he joked. "The manager donated it; said there'd be a replacement for it on a future day at his wife's discretion."

"Who is she?" She held the photograph for Del to see.

"Luisa Plantieri. I wanted to say about her on my visit last fall but I hadn't found her yet. We met at registration and I tried to remember her name. I don't pronounce it correctly, but I'm closer now than I was then. I thought I'd go nuts calling dorms trying to ask for her. Finally I got it close enough for a housemother to connect us. She's from the Alsace-Lorraine region of France. I've had a time trying to speak French, but she's, of course fluent in English, but her name, her last name especially, is pronounced very French-like. We plan to marry. I'll telephone her now. When she gets here, you ladies can chat while Del and I finish chores."

He sat on the edge of the desk to make the call. Upon his hanging the receiver, Del said, "You'll need me as best man."

"Gosh, Del, I'm sorry but the time press here is atrocious. So I grabbed the first of my brothers that I saw. Ward and family stopped in one day about a week ago."

"Well, it's good you're covered on that." Del's grin exuded forgiveness.

"Thanks. For bride's maid, we decided to collar the first pretty French lass we ran across." Dosia sat up straighter on the couch. She reached and took Del's hand. Her grin was for Nathan. They chatted a few minutes longer with each brother trying to catch up news of the other. Hurried footsteps were heard approaching the office door. Nathan gave a wink just as the door opened and Luisa swept into the room.

She was slender at five foot three and one hundred fifteen pounds. Her shoulder length light brown wavy hair was pinned back on each side by a lavender colored barrette. Her smile was at once captivating. Dosia jumped to her feet and the pretties hugged. "I'm Dosia. We are so very pleased. You are so lovely."

"You are perfect. I'm so lucky. Will you be my bride's maid?"

"Yes, oh, yes. We are the two luckiest French belles in the world, each having landed a boy of the Platt family."

The ladies fell to energetic conversation, hardly noticing when the boys returned to the cows. "The Alsace-Lorraine area, if I heard Nathan correctly. Is that right, Luisa?"

"Yes, near the Rhine River." Luisa went on to explain, "The Rhine River empties into the North Sea at Rotterdam of Holland. It's a prime immigration route. In the 1870s, Germany annexed Alsace and Lorraine, separate provinces then. In World War I they returned to France as Alsace-Lorraine, a single province. In World War II Germany grabbed the region anew, but only to give it back in 1945. By then my family had arrived in America."

"Was it dangerous when you left?"

"The war was in Europe, but we sailed from Holland to England before England became as war torn. We went to Canada and crossed into the United States at Detroit. By the time I was in high school we were U. S. citizens. How about you?"

"I was a Paris street waif. Members of Del's family and a dear friend of the family rescued me in time to become an American teenager. I've always loved Del."

"I can see why. Say, can you eat with us? It'll be at the campus snack bar because Nathan works there a couple hours a day."

"Sounds wonderful. We're hamburger nuts. Del will be delighted."

Out among the cows, Nathan had just invited Del to dine at the campus snack bar. "I get a discount there as part of my pay. Luisa often meets me there. Sometimes during the morning milking, she arrives here at the barn. I really love her, Del. Around Christmas time Sid and Louie and their wives stopped and I hinted that marrying in the Yelrom woods would be fun, but, of course, I didn't know then if she would say yes. A while after their visit, I dared to ask her. I wrote Sid and Louie about wedding plans. Reverend Slap will marry us in Wesley's cook shack."

"Wonderful location; really, it's perfect."

Meanwhile, inside the office, Luisa asked, "Is there a Mr. Slap? Sometimes, Nathan jokes."

"Yes, he's a dear man, the Reverend Lester Day Blanes. He's related to the D part of BVD; D is for Day. BVDs are a type of men's underwear. Pastor Lester Day Blanes works for the brothers, Louie and Sid Watkins. The Watkins brothers are long-time friends of Nathan and Del. There's a quaint building in the Yelrom woods called Wesley's cook shack, as Wesley is the cook. Del and I often use the cute little guest cabin near the cook shack when we're hauling logs or excelsior bolts for Louie and Sid. Pastor Blanes seems to like Slap as a nickname, but Louie is the only one I've heard calling him that. It's some joke between the pastor and Louie. They often debate one issue or another; both men are bright."

"I get giddy thinking about being there."

"Me, too, even as we've been there a lot. On a day soon, you'll be there with us."

In the barn Nathan stood from one of the last of the cows. "I'll let Sid and Louie know our wedding date as soon as we know it."

Del picked up one side of the ten gallon milk can, wondering how that Nathan by himself usually carried the cans to the milk room. Recalling a neck injury Nathan suffered in grade school, Del asked, "Your neck okay now?"

"It hurts a little most of the time and a tad more with each milk can or some other clumsy hoist, but not as bad as back then. Harley Perkins still around is he?"

"We see his brother now-a-days. Works at a saw mill where we haul to. Dumping this can of milk, this about does it, does it?"

"Last of the milk cows. I've some shovel work to do for the cows over there before we can go."

"Oh," Del looked over at the row of cows. "They're already milked?"

"Those aren't milk cows. Each of them has a portal installed in her side. Test agents can be introduced there or samples taken for testing in the laboratory."

"Amazing."

"Yes, come along. Half of these cows are drunk. Alcohol is being tested in their diet. Contented cows, they say give more milk. Odd experiment because these cows aren't milkers but I think it's to test alcohol metabolism or tolerance. I'm anyway leery of the alcohol logic. I don't see that contented and drunk are synonyms I won't claim that cows have religion yet keeping them drunk, or even just promoting the consumption of alcohol bothers me. It's as though consuming alcohol's a good thing to do. It just doesn't seem a Christian thing to do. I'd rather they did a different experiment. I've heard that cows milked by women produce more than those milked by men. Playing music also seems to be beneficial. We keep Lansing radio on all the time here because if we shut it off it'd add a variable to the experiments; so either on or off, they said, so we choose on."

"Oh, now what?" Nathan tugged at the scoop shovel that a cow stood upon. "86, now darn you, please move!" He placed his shoulder against her hip and pushed hard, nearly lifting her into the air. He strained, holding a steady pressure. The cow looked around at him as though laughing. Finally she lifted a foot and he whipped the scoop free. Del leaned against the white washed wall behind his puffing brother and that dearly amusing cow number 86. "Go ahead and laugh," Nathan chuckled. "You should see um when we need to place them on the scales." Del burst out with peals of jubilee!

"Each cow is weighed each Tuesday morning. Gosh, that's a hard day around here!" The wall again served to support Del's jubilee.

Nathan headed toward a down stairway while Del interrupted the sound of giggling sweeties as he popped back into the office. "Nathan's showering." That news sent the ladies into peals.

"We're sorry, Del," Luisa finally could say. "Poor, Nathan. We peeked at you guys from the doorway here. Those cows' actions such as you saw, or some other amusement, happens daily to my Nathan. On Tuesday six men are employed to keep each poor cow on the scales."

"Up on it, huh?"

"No, just on it. The scales is built into the floor. You just walked on it getting to this office." Del stepped back to the alleyway he'd followed to get to the office. The ladies rejoined their discussion of daily campus life.

Del stood on the scales rubbing his head as Nathan approached.

"Both funny and sad," his brother remarked. "Dairy science staggers on."

The girls had just time enough to slow their visit back down to a walk before Nathan and Del returned. Nathan was dressed in tan slacks, a lavender shirt, and penny loafers.

Dinner was hamburgers, potato chips, and chocolate malteds. "We're lucky they serve malteds, huh, brother? I recall you've always favored them."

"You bet. You know Del I've never shopped at a Walgreen's store. They've been in business since 1901 and I don't even know where even one Walgreen's is located. One must credit them for introducing the chocolate malted drink in 1921. Dumb me, I didn't discover the malted, however, until I was in high school."

"Well, eating with you in that eatery down by the Caners Ball Park is where I was introduced to them, I think." He turned to Luisa: "How about you, Sis?"

"Sis? Gee thanks, Brother. We'll make that official as soon as we can. Malted milk, huh? You bet. It was served on our first date in this snack bar." She reached to place a hand on Nathan's forearm. "I often eat here with Nathan. We get together when and where we can."

At the close of dinner, Nathan began his job of bussing dishes. "He works incredible hours," she said. "After work here he'll study and rest until three-thirty in the morning when he returns to the cows. He mentioned, too, that he'd like us to attend church so I pray that soon he'll have time so that we can." They were able to catch him with a nod and wave as they were leaving. Luisa walked with them to the truck. "It'll be soon, we hope, when we wed. We've agreed that if necessary it can be on a weekend day between morning and evening milking. The honeymoon will wait until he can get free of the cows for a longer period."

In the truck she said, "He's sure a lucky guy, finding Luisa. I think she wants to attend church with him, but she isn't angry seeing as that he can't."

"I'd think she could attend."

"She wouldn't without him. They're a team; like us. Together as much as possible, not separate. Praise God, dear, we are our own church together, but with children I'd like us to go to regular church."

"Sure, we can. As kids we went to church, but Melanie and Nathan really worked hard at it; verses and songs and such, I mean. They both got saved and Melanie got baptized. Come to think, I guess they nearly all got saved and baptized ahead of me. I'm saved but not in church; just between Jesus and me. I'm saved somewhat, I think, like the man on the cross next to Jesus. Nathan, I do recall, was saved in church but didn't want to get baptized. Louie told me one time why Nathan got saved but Louie and I were too young when he did it so that we don't actually remember just when he did it. Nathan was only about seven, or so."

"So young?"

"Louie said it was because Nathan could read. Even before kindergarten, he could read so by the second grade he'd read nearly every book in the school; a one-room school to the eight grade."

"He seems to know a lot; like you."

"Well, more like Louie, but also Nathan always took to science stuff. He liked bugs and such right along with airplanes. He knew all about the inside of chickens before he began raising those caponette birds for the market. Louie said Nathan said he was very confused when he began listening to sermons. It seems that much of what he knew, according to the preachers and the ameners, was a pack of atheistic lies. Nathan concluded that God, not preachers, knew the answers, the how and why of everything. He wants to figure out all that he can while on earth then in heaven find out the real how and why or to see how right he was. That's why he got saved; so he could one day be in heaven immersed in the answers."

"I see that, but ameners I don't see about."

"Coined by Louie or Nathan. Nathan studied it. My dad is an amener, like most dads in our church. It bothered Nathan that no matter how ridiculous were the preachers' stated notion or opinion, the ameners would amen it. He figured out that amening was induced by the preacher by his pattern of speech or his pauses, and their amening triggered the preacher to call forth even more amening. The ameners apparently aren't even listening. That's obvious, Louie said, as happened in a Baptist church near Yelrom. They had a preacher, a real bible slapper, who howled relentlessly against the teachings of biological science. He sure drew a heap of amens. Well, that preacher was called to serve a different church. The new preacher came in chucked full of good news and enthusiasm. He preached that evolution is true and, you guessed it, the ameners amened right along with his every word, his opinions, and to all else of his sacred revelations."

"All ameners are like that?"

"No, some are genuine. The genuine amens, Louie said, seem to interrupt the preacher, or seem to come as a surprise to the preacher. I don't know that I can tell the difference. I didn't listen to sermons after hearing a certain one. In Sunday school our favorite song was red and yellow black and white, they are precious in His sight. Those colors, I knew, referred to the various races of humans. I liked the song even knowing that there are no red people, never have been. Native Americans are not red. But the other colors sort of represented the races. Well, to my surprise, that day's sermon was against blacks. The sermon was so pathetically stupid yet the ameners were in high gear. So I guess I just turned off the whole business, no more sermons for me. But Nathan listened carefully to every sermon and he doesn't agree with preachers who limit the wholeness of God."

"I think I know, he thinks God is of science as much as of any other thing. I agree."

"Yes, me too. Nathan told me one day that nobody, including no scientist, can discover any thing unless it is already there. There, because God is there, God is the how and why of everything. What one discovers is already present because God has originated everything whether an object, a process, an idea, or a fact. The scientists can only make discoveries, discoveries that always magnify the magnificence and omnificence of God. That's why Nathan says he's never met a biologist that wasn't religious. Especially true among scientists, and especially true of biological scientists he says, because biologists deal with the greatest miracle of all, that miracle is life itself, of having life in the first place. He said that that miracle, like all miracles, humans may never understand. Even more reason, he said, to be in heaven some day. That's the other great miracle, Nathan says, and I agree, that by accepting Jesus we are assured of eternal life with Jesus."

"You sure have a complicated brother but I like my man better. Del, please, lets do our best to keep our day to day, our moment to moment simple."

"You got it, sweetie."

* * *

Del and Dosia made some local hauls to abide the time for the snow to melt. They made a run with sheet metal from Detroit to a plant in southern Michigan that stamped out automobile fenders and hoods. Another run was with sheet metal from Gary, Indiana to a stamping plant south of Bruin City, Michigan. That plant manufactured poultry rearing equipment. They worked back into hauling logs but found them too buried in snow to load with even a modicum of efficiency. They wished folks would hurry with more orders for Delt's pre-constructed buildings. His crew had been busy all winter. They'd constructed nearly one hundred of the pre-constructed aspen 'log' buildings. Del and Helio were contracted to haul pre-constructed cabins to central dealerships dealing in riverside accommodations and lakeside cabins and who provided living quarters for hunting camps. The dealerships had expressed a desire to stock up on the units. All hoped that those orders would be coming in. "Would be,' however, wasn't paying the bills while the snow was deep. It seemed that many buyers needed sunshine on their toes as a stimulus for ordering. Meanwhile the train cars to be loaded with pre-constructed units for Copperton were in at Grand Rapids and soon they'd be hauling to those cars.

A sigh of relief escaped Dosia as she listened at the telephone. Dispatcher Dolly'd caught them at home, telling them of a load of mahogany Duncan Phyfe bedroom furniture to ship from Grand Rapids to St Clair Shores, Michigan. The next day at the St Clair Shores furniture store Dosia commented to the proprietor, "Very pretty. It's the first we've seen of such furniture."

"Mahogany, he said, "is the true cologne of furniture wood, the very essence of furniture beauty."

"Cologne, huh?"

"Yes, my comparison. Cologne was a scent first produced in Cologne, Germany, my ancestral homeland. The world is blessed by fragrance as furniture is blessed by mahogany."

"That's neat, and, does all Duncan Phyfe furniture have the lyre shapes, swags, plumes, and leaves? Very pretty." She touched with her fingers. "Where does mahogany come from?"

"The furniture quality mahogany comes from South America; from a type of evergreen tree. There's mahogany in the US also but it's shrub-like, I took notice of it while visiting in Texas and in Oregon. The beautiful designs we see here," he flowed his hand smoothly along a headboard. "These designs are typical Duncan Phyfe all right. Our customers want to see some combinations of Phyfe's basic elements in every piece of his furniture. The headboards are especially cherished. The wood is hard and durable yet I'm surprised they shipped with you under canvas. It came through all right. Even though all shipments are enclosed in corrugated cardboard, usually they're carried in a covered semi trailer with steel walls."

"They said that was the usual but your order was special and no inclement weather was in the offing. I'm glad we were privileged to see such furniture."

"Thank you. The deep reddish-brown color is especially popular here because of Chris Craft. You've heard of Chris Craft runabouts?"

"Uh, no, I'm sorry. Boats, do you mean? Oh, wait. Chris Craft cabin cruisers we saw on Lake Charlevoix. Are they runabouts?"

"No, those crafts you've seen on Lake Charlevoix, they're a grade or two up from a runabout in size. It's like this furniture being a grade up in beauty from the average. Real special, I mean. My son works at Chris Craft over at Algonac. That's on the St Clair River." Her smile told him she didn't have a mind picture of the river. "That's the river that flows between Lake Huron and Lake St. Clair. Those Chris Craft cabin cruisers that you saw likely would've left from Algonac and sailed up through Lake Huron to the Strait of Mackinaw and through the Soo locks into Lake Michigan and on into Lake Charlevoix. Chris Craft makes several kinds of boats, the runabout being a recent new type. My son says they're making a lot of them to be powered by that Wisconsin Evinrude outboard engine. It'll get power boating down to the level of the common man, he says."

Del had been flowing his hand along the smooth beauty of a headboard while listening to the proprietor's recital. The 'common man' grabbed his attention. Common, to his mind meant 'most folks,' like himself. "They'd put those runabouts through the locks?"

"Oh, well they could, but I wouldn't think so; too slow for so many."

"They'd likely truck them, huh?" Dosia caught the gleam in her husband's eye and she read 'light load' in that gleam.

"Where is this Chris Craft factory?"

"Hug the bay on up past the air base and keep on hugging it right on till you get to the river and there she'll be."

"The runabouts will be easy on tires," Dosia said. His grin told her she was right on track with the comment.

"So let's mosey on to Chris Craft for a visit."

They strolled into the plant and were met by a white collar man. "We've recently fallen in love with mahogany wood," Del said. "We're truckers and just carried a load of mahogany bedroom furniture to Lake Clair Shores. The proprietor there suggested we get a look at some very pretty runabouts that may require some transportation."

"Indeed? Do you mean to say that nobody sent for you?" The truckers grinned and nodded. "Follow me," the white collar said.

In an office decorated with models of the numerous Chris Craft products, suddenly Del clicked his fingers." "Say, how about those PT boats used in the war?"

"No, we didn't build PT boats. The boats, however, used some mahogany so I'm pleased you associated us with them. I served on PT boats during the war and wanted to be near real special boats forever after. I'd guess that enthusiasm led to my landing this job. After visiting a few minutes they landed a deal for several hauls, the hauls to be coordinated through dispatcher Dolly Reams. Dolly would contact either Del or Helio for hauls to Holland, Muskegon, Grand Haven, South Haven, Benton Harbor, Michigan City, Gary, and other towns along Lake Michigan and on into Chicago. "We feel very good about the runabouts," the white collar said, "perhaps the best idea since we began back in 1922. When Christopher Smith started this company he planned to be the biggest boat builder in the world. The runabouts just may get us there, as they'll open a huge market. Just about any average workman will be able to afford a runabout."

"I'm pleased there's a market," Del said, "and that Chris Craft is at the helm."

"Well, yes, and that helm's a spot that can itch one's pants, I'll say. To stay competitive we'll need to copy old Henry Ford's technique for assembly. Assembly line, I mean, and mahogany is not cheap wood. There may need to be well planned changes along the way. We also fret that room to expand our plant here is limited and may fall short of our ambition to be the largest small boat company in the world."

"Another fellow we haul for has been in the excelsior business for years. Now it seems that plastics may replace excelsior as a packing material."

"You're right on, young man. Plastics! And wouldn't you know old Henry Ford pioneered there as well. He made soybeans into plastic and largely used that to form an entire car. Cabin cruiser and yacht owners will likely hold to mahogany because they can more afford it, but for the common man, some form of plastic, but with some real mahogany incorporated, may someday take the sales to the record height we're dreaming about. Meantime mahogany runabouts powered by Evinrude outboards will put power boating in reach of the common man, hopefully, and some green in your piggy bank."

"Green for our piggy bank," she mused as they began the homeward roll. "I wonder if those banks were made originally from pig iron. I'd bet Nathan would know."

"Yes, he and Louie looked into that. From p-y-g-g, Louie said, and Nathan said that was the name of a certain type of clay used in making kitchen pottery. It's like a cookie jar is today but then it'd be called a pyggy jar or p-y-g-g-y jar; or, I suppose pyg was pronounced like p-i-g, pig. So the pottery shops began molding the pots into the shape of a pig; thus, the piggy bank." The pair of truckers remained starry-eyed for a time, their minds to bulging pyggys, but as the home distance shortened, concern began to center upon hauls for Louie and Sid, and for Delton Watkins.

* * *

Delt's outfit in conjunction with Louie and Sid's crews had accumulated thousands of board feet of building material in filling the Copperton, Utah order. Additionally, their cutting produced still another forest commodity, pulpwood. Pulpwood needed for paper production, pulpwood in direct competition with Canada, the largest foreign supplier of pulpwood. Louie scratched his head. "Dad, where do we take this stuff?"

"Well, a paper company. I've heard about one over at Muskegon and one in Kalamazoo. Tell Del to contact his dispatcher. His dispatcher'll tell him also that the train cars are in at Grand Rapids. Son, we're done pre-constructing. It's time to load this stuff and send it on to Utah. Del can't haul your logs with the snow still on them, huh? Your next pay check'll be from me. Okay?"

"Well, rain is predicted. That rain'll likely melt the snow off our logs, but not soon. Sid and I need paychecks real soon. From you'd be fine."

* * *

Del and Dosia slept contentedly to the drum of rain upon their roof, dreaming of a snow free assault on logs for Louie and Sid. At daybreak, "Oh, no!" Peaking from his blankets, Del could see tree limbs cruelly sagged at the bedroom window. From the living room window they saw that a heavy mantle of ice everywhere bowed trees and brush. Their eyes crept to the Mack and stared, they could see the truck frozen to the street by an unwelcome mantle of ice!

The street in front of their house was a glare and was being sprinkled by a powder of snow as they peered. "Dear, do you recall Papa Helio saying anything about chains for the Mack?"

"He has none, I'm sure."

Silently they sat at breakfast until startled into action by the telephone's jangle. "Hello, Del here."

He recognized dispatcher Dolly's voice.

"Del, er ... How's the weather there? The train cars are in at Grand

Rapids. Check with the yard foreman. I just heard there's ice in Grand Rapids. Are you clear? Can you haul today?"

"Lots of ice here, but we plan to haul to the train cars. I have the yard foreman's number. I guess I haven't heard why is it we're hauling to Grand Rapids?"

"The yard's kept clear in the winter, guaranteed, so Delt Watkins decided to ship from there."

"Thanks, Dolly. I'm sure glad it'll be available on this slicky day. We'll get at it and maybe it'll rain some yet; get the ice off and maybe even get the snow off those logs."

Hanging the receiver, he looked across at Dosia. "I hope Grandpa Clarence wasn't joking about going along so he could throw sand ahead of the truck's rear tires. I'll need help on the hills. Those barrels have a mix of sand and salt in them." He touched a thoughtful finger to his chin; "Maybe it'd be best if he could drive the Mack."

Grandpa Clarence Groner picked up the clattering telephone. "Grandpa, I ..."

"Hey, Del, I thought it'd be you. I have truck driving experience, did you know? I was the first guy at the paper mill to learn to drive a Grabowski Power Wagon. About in 1906, that was. The paper mill, eventually bought several more and put Pal Toberton in charge of them, but first the mill asked me to teach Pal how to drive one."

"Oh?"

"Yes, well, in a few minutes Pal could drive better than me so that ended my sojourn as a truck driver instructor. I just wanted you to know that you're not dealing with a total amateur here."

"Huh? Er ..."

"Just joking, what's up?"

"Well, old tutor. I'll simply check you out on high range third gear and set you at it whilst I toss the salty sand; okay."

"You know, through the years I've enjoyed tossing snow. I've developed a fling for it and I'll gladly adapt my fling to salty sand tossing. I even have little skid chains attached to my work boots. Del, you start chipping away at the Mack. I'll be along directly."

"Dosia'll be along with us all the way up to Louie's, taking care of Rose as she's still combating morning sickness."

"Sure thing. And your grandma's fussing at me to bring her along too. See you in a bit.'

Grandpa Clarence and Grandma Clydis arrived by a horse and

buckboard. Del and Dosia looked up from tapping ice from the Mack. Having sages for grandparents, they saw, was paying off. Grandpa Clarence toted a stepladder and a steaming teakettle of water. Other steaming kettles were seen in the buckboard. They each had furnace damper chain wired to their L. L. Bean boots. The pair moved gingerly toward the ice-shrouded Mack with Clarence stabbing the ladder firmly to the slippery way in time with Grandma Clydis' scurry forward. In a dozen ladder stabs and scurries they were at the Mack. She gripped the stepladder as firmly as she did her husband's leg while he stretched to melt ice from the windshield and side windows. In half an hour Grandma Clydis departed with the buckboard and Dosia settled warmly between Del and Clarence in the cab. Finding a shoe factory parking lot with scant cars parked, Del pulled in to check on Grandpa Clarence's truck driving skills.

Their loads of Pre-Constructed buildings would be tall but light weight loads and Del guessed that high range third gear would be the most useful for Clarence. The pull north from Leadford involved several rather abrupt hills before a gradual two-mile-long ascent that landed them on the brink of Porter Hollow. "Stop here, Grandpa. Let's study the situation."

"Hey, Del, how's it going?" The shout startled Del and he cranked down his window.

"Well, I declare, Dan Francis, and with your companion, that old Nancy mule. What brings you to this idyllic declivity?"

"Nancy and me and Wynona, and two teams of horses have moved in here at the hollow. Me and Wynona, we rent the house and I get paid pretty good for boarding the livestock. It was Louie's idea to get up a crew to man this valley. Sid's getting a crew, too, to cover that huge hill south of Leadford and to help down at the Grand River; at the base of that steep hill just before the river bridge, you know. That'll cover the worst of the icy hills all the way to the boxcars sided at Grand Rapids for the Copperton order. Sid and Louie worked out the arrangements with the county road department. We're keeping the hill sanded on each side of this valley, as you see, and are able to do some pulling now and then but only cars so far. You'll be our first truck, if you need us."

"Gotcha pard. I teamed with a driver here that dates back to 1906, or so. You and Grandpa Clarence have made my day, pard."

"Some of the crew here drove down from the Bruin City area; no ice up there."

"Gotcha." While closing his window, Del looked over at Clarence.

Grandpa Clarence nodded. He checked to see that he had high range third then brought up the engine speed and eased out the clutch. The Mack moved smoothly into Porter Hollow, picking up speed as the rig descended. Momentum powered the rig partly up the far side of the valley where upon getting a nod from Del, Grandpa Clarence gently eased his toe against the accelerator peddle. The big green Mack easily topped the grade to the flat that carried them into Ryanton.

The ice storm hadn't reached north of Ryanton. They'd planned that Dosia would be left at the corner some few hundred yards from Rose Watkins' home because ice would impede an easy turn around in her yard, but with the way free of ice Grandpa swung speedily in at the home of Louie and Rose.

Rose leaned from the kitchen doorway. "Hi Dosia, come in. I can't wait to display Louie's gift. It's his tribute to Jane Russell; and to me, of course."

Dosia planted a moist one to her husband's cheek and another to his temple. "Be careful, Sweety. I love you." She slid from the truck at the driver's door, it being held for her by Grandpa Clarence. He walked with her around to the other truck door. She pecked his cheek and turned toward Rose. "Jane Russell," she called to Rose. "Did you say? Rose I can't imagine."

She began her explanation while leading her friend into the house. "Louie stopped to see what Aunt Edith telephoned him about. It was about my birthday so I didn't pry. Well, Aunt Edith told him about a store in Kalamazoo dealing in maternity apparel. So Louie and Sid stopped in there after making a run with pulpwood. They have a huge trailer now to pull with the Yellow Beast. That's their new army surplus four-wheel drive truck – painted bright yellow, you've seen it. Well, I couldn't guess they'd buy Jane Russell brassieres for Maxine and me." She was unbuttoning her blouse as she talked and now swung it free in a swooping display of her Jane Russell. My other bras I've had to lengthen by hooking safety pins together in a chain. That chain was to three safety pins in length. Maxine loaned her Jane Russell to me also, as she's not too large yet."

"I guess Louie surly loves you to compare you to a movie star, huh?"

"I'm thrilled, of course. Louie said that Howard Hughes, that famous flyer, designed the bra especially for Jane Russell. Louie said she's bigger than even Marilyn Monroe. I guess I'm pretty special. I'm ready for that La Leche League, alright."

"I, too, look forward to that league." The table was set with teacups and cookies. Dosia poured the tea and they began sipping and continued talking.

"Louie's going to stop in at the Grand Rapids library today because he's likened me to Theta Bara. She did a movie where she was Salome. She danced around while supposedly removing seven veils. King Herod, Salome's stepfather, so liked her performance that he granted her a wish. She wished for the head of John the Baptist. Louie saw a movie about that story. You know he has a dint for rooting out the facts. Anyway, I did wish for a better brassiere arrangement and Louie says I'm a tolerable dancer.

So he gave you a gift. Nice guy, that Louie. You seem well today, are you?"

"I realize I'm chattering like a magpie. No morning sickness yet today and I'm dressed in a Jane Russell apparel. Can life be better?"

"I'm pleased; and how is Maxine getting along?"

"She's wondering if she isn't more than a month behind me. She's not ready for the Jane Russell and she hasn't been morning sick." Rose touched her forehead and nodded at her friend. "Say, can you help me a moment. The time has come." She pulled open a closet door. "Help me with this bric-a-brac stand." She tugged at an ornate shelving unit.

"Oh, an étagère, it's called in French. Very nice. How sweet of Louie."

"It's what?"

"That's an astute translation from the French. The French word refers to the confusion of items to be displayed; a handy place for items of all kinds."

"He brought it home one day last week. I said we'd use it to celebrate my first day without spitting up. I really like it. I'm putting baby things on it for now, sentimentality of all kinds later."

* * *

While the ladies chatted, Grandpa Clarence and Del settled the empty Lufkin in at Delt's dock to be loaded with the first of many loads to be hauled to Grand Rapids. In a little while Louie joined in with the hauling. Delt's crew loaded Louie and Sid's large new trailer that was hitched behind the Yellow Beast. In late afternoon, Del and Grandpa Clarence, with Grandpa Clarence at the wheel, crested the steep hill that led down to the bridge over the Grand River. With the steep hill partially deiced, the way ahead consisted of four gravel ruts to comfort traffic on the uphill and the down hill runs. The ruts were rather ice free but ice gleamed meanly over the remaining roadway. Del had had no trouble on the hill with previous loads and wanted to give Grandpa a turn that'd be something to brag about.

This being his first turn at hauling a load, Grandpa Clarence halted the rig at the brink and they looked down at the Grand River Bridge. The other hills they'd encountered on their way were pictures of the one that loomed before Grandpa's eyes except for one thing; the bridge! The bridge at the foot of the hill prompted his gentle words: "They ought to call this the Lorelei Bridge," he said. "It's like being lured to one's doom. If this river was called the Rhine instead of the Grand, I'd bet that'd be the name for this bridge."

Del knew Grandpa would decline his offer when he said, "I'll take it, Grandpa."

"Oh, it don't look too bad, huh?"

"Well, the ice is pretty much off the roadway where our tires must travel, but do keep attention to your mirrors. Be ready to apply braking to the trailer if it looks to be coming around the truck. That'd be like a trick of Lorelei's, to not only lure us but to make sure we entered the river."

"Here we go." Grandpa released the foot brake pedal and touched the accelerator. His glancing to his mirrors diverted his attention from looking forward. Suddenly the truck shifted position to ride along the ice rill beside the tire ruts. Looking back, Grandpa mistakenly saw that the trailer piled high with pre-constructed buildings was, indeed, coming around to the right of the truck. He shouted, "Jackknife! Jackknife!"

"No, Grandpa, we're okay! Hold steady. Ease in some trailer brake. Keep steady and aim for the tire ruts that cross the bridge." But the loaded Lufkin, to follow the truck, shifted to the frictionless surface and the towering stack of pre-constructed buildings gained steadily on the Mack. Seeing that a jackknife was to occur, Sid and his crew and the county road crew scattered at a dead run, each man hoping to not encounter the sideways rig as it slid toward the bridge. "Stomp the gas, Grandpa! Claw for the tire ruts on the bridge!

Del was as scared as was Grandpa. The bridge loomed ahead as though Lorelei beckoned. With inches to spare, the rig careened over the bridge and although partially crosswise of the road, Grandpa brought the willing big green Mack with its loaded to the sky Lufkin to a chattering halt.

Silence.

They both sat there. They each felt drained.

"Whew," Grandpa's voice was unsteady, "Del, my entire underwear's wetted with sweat that feels like grease or some other, but I guess we beat that mean old Lorelei, but no more. Hills nor bridges, or not, I'd rather you took this load on in."

Del patted Grandpa's shoulder. "You did alright, you old trucker. My seat feels a might greasy too, but I couldn't have done better at saving the situation."

"Del, get over here and drive this thing. I still hold that I'm best at salty sand tossing."

Long after dark that evening the tired men gathered at Del and Dosia's home. Earlier, Grandma Clydis, wearing her skid chains and toting a pair of loafers, had walked over to the house and set to work preparing soup and sandwiches. Grandma Clydis had called Dosia and Rose. They said, "okay" when Grandma invited them down. "The men all plan to meet here at your place, Dosia, dear, after they've finished the loads. I'll see you two in a little while. Rose, no morning sickness is God sent news. So we'll celebrate."

"Good, we'll be in on the tales and a lot less lonely and anxious. I'll call Maxine, see if she wants to come."

The two ladies soon joined Grandma Clydis at food preparation. "Maxine decided not to come. She's behind on mending Sid's socks and Carhartts."

In a while Grandpa Clarence entered ahead of Del and began at once shedding damp layers of clothing. "Dear, see if Del has a dry shirt for me. I'm sloshing in my own perspiration."

"Oh, my gosh, dear, you've been all day in your brand new Arrow shirt." She tugged at it, finally drawing it up over his head.

She held the garment at arm's length, looking it over. "It looks like it'll do up fine. Arrow's been making shirts since 1851. I shouldn't have been alarmed."

"Well, now I'm shivering."

Dosia charged up with a big flannel plaid shirt of Del's. "Dear," Grandma said, "you slip this on and get onto that couch. Dosia, we'll need blankets. This old fool's worn himself to a frazzle."

Sid and Louie pulled to the curb with the Yellow Beast just as Dosia answered the telephone: "They're just pulling up. Wait, I'll get Sid." From the front door, she called "Sid, Maxine's on the phone."

As Sid hung the receiver, he asked Grandma Clydis "Is there such a thing as evening sickness?"

"Sid, I haven't heard of it. What's up?"

"Like Rose, but in the evening. I want to get on home." In a minute Sid streaked out with the Yellow Beast and its big clattering trailer. Beside him in the seat was a sack full of sandwiches and a thermos of coffee. The Yellow Beast tore along U.S. 131, its light beams boring steady for home and to his mate.

In the kitchen around a kettle of chicken soup, hot coffee, hot chocolate, and a heap of sandwiches, conversation settled around Rose fitting perfectly into her Jane Russell. "Louie, what about Theta Bara caused you to think of Jane Russell?"

Louie held up a finger while he chewed and swallowed a generous sandwich of peanut butter and jelly. "I can't keep up with her dancing; that twist, you've seen. So I've likened my Rose to Salome who was played by Theta Bara. Theta Bara, I saw in the paper about a year ago when she died. Today I had just a moment to stop at the library where I'd requested a search to see why she's called the Vamp Theta Bara. Its because she was a vampire in a film. I've been feeling sorry for Rose sort of not able to twist so well lately so for a gift I bought her that Jane Russell, actually a bric-a-brac shelf, too."

"Well, now perhaps without that sickness I'll feel like a twist, dear."

"Gee, I don't know. A logger can't get too limbered up because a logger to be worth his salt should always be hurting someplace, legs or back. But, dear, you get a notion, I'll go along; do my best."

"You know, in the Bible books of Matthew and Mark, some other maiden danced that dance. I don't recall reading about Salome in there."

"But, Grandma Clydis, that part about the head of poor John the Baptist was in there. Maybe Hollywood got a little carried away with the rest of the story."

"Isn't that John the guy who baptized Christ?"

"Yes, that's in the Bible so that's true."

"Say, Louie, I'd been planning our trip to Utah, that's before Delt decided to ship by rail, and, guess what I found. I found West Jordan."

"Now, Dosia, didn't I say there should be one? Utah is west of Michigan so it makes sense, West Jordan and East Jordan. Where'd you find it?

"About twenty south of Salt Lake City, and a tad north of Copperton. I'm not sure Copperton's actually a town anymore. It's the site of the largest dug pit in America, possibly in the world. It's an open pit copper mine. The size of the mine destroyed a few towns, but Copperton was built to house workers, so maybe it's actually still there. It was our dispatcher who found out the most about it. She said that because workers came from all over the world, many different nationalities of folks still live in the area."

"I wonder if we shouldn't head out, Louie."

"I was thinking just that; perhaps to catch up with Sid."

"Drive our car," Dosia said. "Say, isn't Sid's and your truck some sort of war jeep? Only bigger, of course."

"No, Willys invented the jeep. I think General Eisenhower said the jeep was the most important vehicle of the war, but Sid said to me, 'Perhaps, but I'd like to see one out do our Yellow Beast.' I suspect a lot of companies built vehicles for the war. Ours is made by Dodge."

Grandma, what should we do about Grandpa? He's sound asleep on the couch."

The group gathered at the couch. "Louie, help me lift this front edge. It'll click into a bed."

Grandpa didn't stir during the jostle to convert the couch into a bed. "Dosia, I walked over, but I think he's too tired to walk home. Let's let him stay here the night, and with me cuddled to him to keep him warm."

* * *

Maxine's trouble was the flu. She recovered quickly and was soon helping Wesley with the cooking at the cook shack near Yelrom and of ordering it up in preparation for a bustling summer season, for suddenly sunshine had broken through, winter had leaped into spring overnight. Orders came in by the fistful! Twenty-four hours a day were not enough. The loggers began falling trees like dominos. The young truckers were staggering.

Dosia and Del were certainly glad to see Helio and Anna Mae roll in from Saskatchewan.

"Papa Helio, if you'd pick up the present load form Delt Watkins' outfit, maybe I can get a few loads of logs hauled for Louie and Sid. There are other hauls coming up all the while, too, that Dolly recommends we take; keep our head in the door for any possible load, she said. That assures a future. Expect a call from her at anytime to haul runabout boats from Algonac. She tries to get a haul for us in the Detroit direction and then we load the boats and head for the Lake Michigan shore."

"She's right. Didn't I say to always get along with your dispatcher? That means taking advice, as well. That Dolly has a good head on her. I'm glad she's coordinating the boats. If a run comes up to go to Holland, Michigan, your ma-in-law'd like to ride along so I'll take it. Holland is home office for Life Savers candy, Squirt pop, and Beech-nut gum, stuff she's including in her book about trucking."

"Oh please, no." In the kitchen, Momma Anna Mae'd looked up from her stirring of Charley Tuna into a mix of lettuce and salad dressing. She waved the spoon. "Dear, please live here with us." The kitchen wail came to the ears of the men.

Helio and Del shrugged and they motioned with empty palms.

Upon entering the kitchen they heard, "No, Momma, not a tent this time." Dosia had just straightened from pulling baked fish sticks from the oven. "We'll be in a log cabin."

Momma still held a worried expression. Del said, "You bet, Momma. It'll be located close to Wesley's cook shack."

"Cook shack?"

"Sid and Louie aren't camping out anymore. They've constructed buildings of good aspen wood, buildings like Papa Helio and we'll be hauling."

She still was spooky. "Way out in the middle of nowhere?"

"Not like in British Columbia, the Yukon, and Alaska, where you were rambling for years. You were a long ways from Brillo pads, Hush Puppies, and instant potatoes. Momma, didn't you stay in cabins; or even in tents?"

"Momma, come and see; say tomorrow morning" Del urged. "We'll all have a Wesley breakfast in that cook shack with Louie and Sid and their crews."

"I'm sure looking forward," Papa Helio said. He placed an arm around Anna Mae and he pecked her cheek.

"I'm getting old, I guess," she said. "I just don't want to live rough anymore; Dosia either."

"We won't be, Momma. No worries. Come and see."

"I'll set it up this afternoon," Del said. "And Papa, I'll be sure Wesley cracks out his stash of pilot bread."

"Great. I'll look forward. God smiles upon us. You say Delt's load's ready?"

"Cabins for the Upper Peninsula. We're all glad, glad, glad you're back. The Lufkin'll be stacked it's full forty feet and likely more tied atop, but it's a light load, no less, so the tires will have an easy time. Each inside dual is new but paired with either a badly worn tire or a good looking used tire. The load's for Copper Harbor. Me and Dosia'll be loading your Fruehauf with logs from down near Bruin City; load for the Coopersville saw mill.

The log location is marked on the county map; tin can on a stick, as usual, if later you need to haul from there. They managed to drag a load's worth from the woods with a winch. Louie and Sid own a surplus Army Dodge now with a winch that'd yank a tank. Of course now with the snow relenting, they may not need to use it."

"It'll remind me of back home. They'll always find ways to need it. We had some of them big Dodges on Rte. 2. Fellow'd get off sometimes into mire, thawed permafrost and like that, really like quick sand. About had to swim out to 'um then winch 'um free. Dodge could do her, all right."

Rapping at the front door snapped everyone's attention. Del was positioned to see who: "Aunt Edith." He hurried to the door. All eyes studied as Aunt Edith and Grandma Clydis strolled in.

"Hi. We've lately been to that restaurant, the one with Loxey and now Jacqueline, but didn't bring it up during that icy mess. I think Loxey's dreaming that something could develop between Jacqueline and Ronnie, just as we hoped. Still we just wonder if such could happen; or if something bad could happen."

"Del, what do you think?"

"He scared us bad, his grabbing Dosia, but Jacqueline's a lot bigger a girl."

"What's this about?" Anna Mae looked about ready to burst and Helio had clinched a fist. "Who did? What monster touched her! "

"I'll break his back end," Helio said.

"No, Papa, wait. Del and I handled him. Sent him to a hospital. He's stayed away since."

"Loxey said for you to stay away from the mill," Aunt Edith said. "She means just for now. Soon, if all goes well, he'll be okay."

"Del, we don't want her near that mill!" Helio was really hot. "Please stay away. Ask Louie and Sid if a different mill would do."

"Please, let's calm down so we can talk. Dosia, put on a pot of Sanka."

"Sure, Grandma. There's some of the bread left, too; and some of the sandwiches." She was relieved that Grandma Clydis had spoken. Smiling, she said, "Papa Helio, come help me with the table." She took his arm, saying, "We're in good hands, Papa. Come. Come, help me." She tugged his sleeve and he trotted along like a puppy.

He really did feel like a puppy, a puppy in the embrace of a loving caretaker, yet his forehead was crinkled, demanding that no harm befall his precious.

Dosia felt wonderful. Loving wonderful hands, they were her family. As they sat down together at the table she felt secure in their embrace. She felt strong and ready to face any giant. Just let her in on the plan. She'd do her best because she was a part of them. Proudly she sat with her family at table.

"Aunt Edith, what went on there?"

"Big Harley Perkins has a gal, so Loxey said. I said that some gal better hurry and land Ronnie before he gets old like Harley. She said twenty-eight is a good age to wed. We said, sure, we're all rooting for him. Then one of us asked if Ronnie would benefit by more lady customers."

"Suddenly a smile sweetened her face," Grandma Clydis went on to say, "and we knew her thinking was in concert with ours."

"You mean Jacqueline?" Dosia touched her chin. "I wonder."

"The customers are mainly men, workmen from the mill and neighborhood. I think Loxey's wanting her to choose Ronnie."

"Jacqueline's also trying to think up ways to expand the clientele to include women. To draw in families, you see, but Loxey's not as eager on that idea."

"She has ideas mainly for those two, we're sure."

"So it's important that we get Jacqueline and Ronnie together. We want you to help us get them together; that is Ronnie and Jacqueline, er, like, uh, innocent like."

"Likely he eats all his meals there." Helio had settled down enough to whet an interest in the developing game.

"Yes, Helio, but would that be special enough? Just as his waitress, do we mean?"

"Special, huh?" Del rose to the occasion. Grandpa Delibar sure felt special that day we all surprised him with a birthday party. I thought then that everybody, and I do mean everybody, even I don't know if Grandma Ella ever had one, just everybody should have at least one happy birthday party. A surprise one, the better."

"Birthday?"

"Yes," Del said, "When's his birthday?"

"She said that Jacqueline's due to start full time tomorrow. Should we get her in on it?"

Grandma, you said you'd like to get them together 'innocent like.' Well, I'm for a sledgehammer approach, er, or an axe handle, say. That is figuratively speaking, of course. But let her in on it, yes. You bet, let her in and encourage her to largely plan the whole affair. Dosia will agree that

Jacqueline's sure hungry for a mate and is worried as to her future. I'd bet Ronnie is too. What can we lose by trying?"

"Sure, that's it; what can we lose?"

CHAPTER NINE

Helio trucked the load of pre-constructed buildings into the Upper Peninsula. He followed that with two loads of pulpwood to Muskegon. In Muskegon a paper mill manager said that cargo ship deliveries on the Great Lakes were often slowed up during winter. "Winter's a good time to check on us; we're usually good for a load or two. And to be honest, truck deliveries are often cheaper for us at our mill. Ships here are unloaded by hand, adding to our overhead. Check with us from now on. Michigan wood is as good as Canadian." Helio told the boys about it at Wesley's breakfast, finishing with a surprise query: "Can you come to a birthday party?" Helio packed in a large chunk of pilot bread and began to chew.

"Huh? Er, why sure, where? Someone in pulpwood, is it? At that Muskegon mill, is it?" Louie rubbed his head. "Party, huh; birthday, you said?" Helio chewed rapidly, his eyes twinkling.

Finally clearing his maw of pilot bread, he could say: "No, not that mill." He belched from behind a cupped hand. "It's Dosia's in-law relatives behind it. Party is for gents into logs and saw mills, guys who know that Ronnie Perkins."

Sid sat aside his fork and joined into the conversation. "Met him once, but don't know him but by reputation. Del and Dosia near killed him and he deserved it."

"Yeah, he's the guy. I still'd like to break his back end. No excuse, no forgiving what he tried with our little girl. Send me off to Timbuktu, please, if you would with a load of anything. For corn sakes, I don't want to go to a party for that guy."

"Why us?"

"Del, Dosia, and his whole family's in on it. They've done such before, along with Maggie, that baseball player"

"Why her; you mean that Grand Rapids Caner?"

"Yes, to help Dosia back then, she was in on it big, but I hadn't heard on this one. They saved Dosia back then when her case seemed hopeless. Then praise God she was ours and then Del's, too, so Anna Mae wants to go along on a birthday party. I'm still mad at the guy and I think she is too, but we know how Edith and Clydis are. Their plans work out, I know. That restaurant near the Coopersville saw mill is run by Loxey Perkins. She's the wife of All Perkins and mother to Big Harley Perkins, whom Edith said you'd know."

"Big Harley Perkins, now there's a corn head. He in on it? Big Harley near killed Nathan once."

"Ronnie Perkins is his younger brother, raised separate from Harley to give him a better start. Harley doesn't know about the party. She bought a house then converted it to that restaurant. Still umpteen payments to make, but she's having trouble making it, only clearing four hundred dollars each month."

"That's not bad dough," Louie said, and she's beefing?"

"She buys groceries some for that All and Big Harley 'cause often they drink up too much of their pay checks. When the gang gets there, that's morning, noon, and night, she can't keep up nor can she afford to hire help 'cause it'd be full time help, of course. So she looked for a partnership with someone. Del and his have found her one."

"Oh, well, that's good, huh?"

"She's that Jacqueline from East Jordan. Del and Dosia found her."

Sid and Louie moved to the edge of their seats. The Reverend Lester Slap Blanes, seated beside Louie, also leaned into the discussion. "I'm going to that party."

"Slap, you don't even know the guy. You should stay here in charge of my crew while we're gone."

"Wesley'd do that. I may be needed at that party."

"Well, sure. Go. But what do you know? You keeping something from us?"

"Nothing, but it sounds like a marriage is planned."

"At the party? How do you know?

"Del told about Jacqueline. She's pining to find her a guy. Likely Edith and them have realized that and are planning to find her a hubby. I want to be there to offer my services." He looked toward a wall of the cook shack.

"That verse there. I'll make another sign just like it for their present. I'm making another one already for Nathan and Luisa's wedding."

"You sure there's time enough? What with the world to end at any minute, like you've been telling, you'd best go ahead and get them saved, not take time to hurry them to the altar of marriage."

"Nathan and Luisa're already saved. I just gotta work on the two others. Being saved urgently counts, of course, but I just feel God has called me to officiate over the whole affair; that's both the wedding and the saving there at Coopersville."

* * *

Jacqueline carried leaflets around to businesses in the Coopersville area advertising their a.m. and p.m. coffee break specials and that bringing your own eats is acceptable; "We'll fill out your empty spaces," their ad promised, "round out your homegrown fare, slosh your innards with imported Brazilian java that'll set you back to work with a grin." Now the place boomed at breakfast, forenoon coffee break, lunch, afternoon coffee break, and at supper and the ladies began a campaign to catch the evening crowd of moon eyed and starry eyed along with the lonely, the weary, and the hopeful. Edith James contacted fourth estate reporters, including those of Grand Rapids, Coopersville, Leadford, and Smartaway, the press that would also carry prominent "Cozy Cafe" advertisements.

Ronnie Perkins continued taking his meals at the restaurant and took note of all the changes around the restaurant. He truly noticed Jacqueline, his mom's new business partner, but was careful not to say a word to her. He wanted to, he wished he could, but was afraid.

No girl had ever liked him. Even one who acted like a man, even to handling heavy log chains; that one who wore heavy brogans and levis, that one nigh killed him with a pike pole. No girl had ever liked him. But that new girl, that Jacqueline, that was a lot of girl, a whole big lot of girl! He wished, and he daydreamed, and he tossed at night, but he wouldn't touch her. No Ma'am! He wished he could speak but knew that if he did, she'd go away. Go away. They all did, all before. If he didn't speak then she would not go away and he could see her, dream of her, dream about that whole big lot of girl!

One day Ronnie Perkins strode cautiously in for an a.m. coffee break. He carried an apple.

"Apple a day, kind sir," Jacqueline greeted, "is supposed to keep you hale and healthy." She poised with her No.2 pencil tipped to her order pad, but her eyes took in the grand specimen. "May I round you out with home baked wholegrain cinnamon rolls and creamy Brazilian java?" Boy, he's some hunk; her muse brought a pleasing grin to her face.

His eyes followed her every move, his heart dancing and fluttering as the broad beam advanced toward the order window, the beam transforming to a delicious swagger as she approached that window.

She turned from the window and met his eyes.

Sweat popped onto his forehead. His apple tore in two in his wringing hands and he sat with a half of apple in each hand, bringing both simultaneously to his mouth. The half-apples crashed there and one went flying, bounding toward her.

She leaned forward to retrieve it for him. Heavy breasts pulled the cotton dress firmly to her apron bib and opened an avenue of desire nearly to her navel.

His gasp snapped her to attention to where the half of apple bobbled and fell again to the brick-patterned linoleum. "Oh, I'm sorry! Clumsy old me."

"No mind," he rose in his chair, stretching to trim in his rotund belly. "I'd like another roll instead," but his eyes shouted a clear opine; I'd sure like it be you. Suddenly he paled and sank deep into his seat. He had spoken. Oh, My! Oh, my, now she'd go away!

"Sure, on the house. You're Ronnie, huh? I've been hoping to visit with you."

He held a worried expression, expecting her to hurry away. "Me?" His eyes bugged. "Yeah, well, uh, well, yeah, I work over at debarking. Loxey's my mom."

"Sure, I guessed. She's pointed out your pretty car. You take good care of it." So he'd likely take good care of me, she thought. "I'm buying in here with your mom; partners, you see."

"Yeah, I heard. It is good to have you," his words were a breathy whisper and he looked about to crawl under the table. Sweat yet popped. He was having the most frightening day of his life; but the grandest! She's not going away!

"Be right here with your java."

"Yeah." His eyes locked to her. He bit into his half apple and his jaws began a work in cadence with her loin-throbbing gait as she moved toward the kitchen order window.

He burrowed into his half apple, the cinnamon rolls, and the creamy

Brazilian. His mind was in near panic by the time he could rush from that Cozy Cafe.

At supper that day the James family of Harold, Edith, and eight-year-old Hulda Clydis Sunshine took seats at a table near to the kitchen. "Hi!" Loxey greeted them through the order window, and received a grin and a wave. "She's on her way."

Jacqueline passed by with a loaded tray of burgers, fries, and Cokes. Returning momentarily to take their order, she was surprised to see Edith already at the order window and that Harold was seated alone. Her glance caught Sunshine over at the jukebox just as Harold said, "Special number three all around; Sanka java with cream for us and grape soda for Sunshine. As you see, Edith's over confabulating with your pard."

"Oh," she said, jotting on the pad, "I thought for a jiff we'd gained a waitress. Be a minute."

Marty Robbins began charging the air with 'A White Sport Coat and a Pink Carnation' as Sunshine Hulda danced back to her chair. "I want grape."

"Ordered. Say, sweety, isn't there another song? That's not the message we want to hear in here right now."

"Oh, why?" Worry crinkled her sweet young brow.

"All dressed up for the dance, I mean, that's a song about a messed up date and we want a successful date to occur."

"Oh, when?" She leaned close to Papa, already at age eight she was anxious to partake of any adventure promulgated by Momma.

"We think on a Thursday afternoon some time soon."

As she resumed her seat, Momma Edith elaborated her husband's reply. "Yes, a Thursday. They're opening another room to the restaurant and will initiate it with his birthday party." She sat a chilled grape soda before her darling. "Sunshine, is 'Tammy' on that machine?" She handed her daughter a couple of quarters.

Sunshine slurped the top inch from the delicious beverage. "I'll see."

"His birthday's on a Thursday in two weeks," she heard her mom say while scampering as a lightening bug toward the flashing juke machine.

Tammy, from the movie 'Tammy and the Bachelor,' soon pulsated the air. "Sunshine," Papa said, "would you mind on that Thursday afternoon skipping school? There's to be a birthday party here and we'd want you to run the juke box and maybe a record player."

"Gosh, yes!" She'd become as bouncy as a kangaroo. "What do I do?" She hopped beside her chair. "Let's get started!"

"We'll have a list to play from the music box, dear, and 'April Love' from our selections if the juke doesn't have it."

"I'll see." She stepped back from the table.

"No, wait. Let's eat then go there and prepare our list together."

"Oh." She slumped behind her grape soda.

"Oh, darn," Momma said. "Let's go over there right now. Let's get started."

* * *

During the time that others planned and began preparation for the birthday party Del and Dosia'd hauled loads of aspen logs to Delt's mill and factory and Helio'd made runs to Muskegon and Kalamazoo with pulp wood. Both trucks had then set to transporting scrub logs to Coopersville and furniture logs to a band saw mill at Stanwood. One day both trucks were loaded sky high and traveling in convoy along Highway 131. Helio led the huge duo into a calm shady woodlot near Yelrom. Helio and Del jumped from the trucks and dashed into a small 'log' cabin. Dosia and Anna Mae strolled on into Wesley's cook shack.

In Wesley's tiny kitchen at one end of the cook shack the Reverend Lester Slap Day Blanes knelt in solemn prayer. Nathan and Luisa were seated with bowed heads on a bench facing Pastor Blanes. Dosia walked quietly to the front and sat beside Ward Platt, the best man. Dosia was dressed in a calico Dolly Varden with lace ruffle at the neckline and on the short sleeves. Her attire was a match for Luisa's.

Ward was dressed in tan slacks, a sport shirt, and suit jacket, his attire a match for Nathan's. Dosia, in telephone conversation with Luisa, discovered that Nathan had no money for wedding attire, like what others may deem appropriate. Dosia had taken over coordination of the wedding outfits.

Anna Mae took a seat with Doreena and Brandy, Ward Platt's wife and daughter. Anna Mae had so much wanted an elaborate church wedding and reception for Dosia. As if this was the day of that longed for wedding, Anna Mae was dressed to the nines. Gossamer gowned in delicate organdy, she was pleased to see that Doreena and Brandy were spiffily dressed in matching outfits that were a credit to her organdy. She sat comfortably with them. Looking to the front of the cook shack they saw that Reverend Lester Day Blanes had finished his blessing. Blanes rose to his feet, his eye on the wind-up wall clock. Taking his action as a signal, Luisa and Dosia walked down the aisle to the rear of the room and left the building.

Slap Blanes again looked at the clock. "Er, uh, it is – " Helio and Del rushed into the room, claiming seats held for them by Louie and Sid. The cook shack was packed and as many guests were seated outside. A side panel was raised for their convenience in viewing the proceedings. "Er, yes, it is time."

Where Sunshine Hulda Clydis James ever had found a wind-up record player was any one's guess except Grandpa Clarence's. Luisa and Dosia entered the room at the rear. Up front, Nathan and Ward turned to look along the aisle, their eyes straining for a first glimpse of the beauties. Grandpa nodded to signal Hulda Sunshine. Sunshine carefully positioned the needle and flicked the switch 'On'.

The audience stood listening to the familiar revered notes of Mendelssohn's 1843 Wedding March. The pretty ladies walked slowly up the aisle.

Up front Nathan took her hand.

Reverend Lester Day Blanes began, "Dearly beloved . . . "

* * *

Helio and Anna Mae tripped three times to the Lake Michigan shore with the Fruehauf stacked with Chris Craft runabouts, each with an Evinrude engine wrapped in cardboard and stored in the hull. They were busy with the boats, wanting to deliver them and yet get in needed hauls for Louie and Sid, too busy in actuality to visit and gawk around in Holland, but on their third trip Anna Mae put her foot down. "Dear, we'd just be a minute in each factory; just for Beech-nut gum, Squirt pop, and Life Savers candy." She held a map of the city for him to see and one finger pointed to the nearest of the desired factories. "Just a few minutes in each one. After all they're in my book." She rustled the map.

"She's lined up enough trucking for a couple of more trucks, dear. Can't leave so much for Dosia and Del. Let's come back in the fall." He swung the rig onto a bee line headed for a lakeshore boat dealers. "Qooh, now what!" The red Reo plunged to a stop. "What's up? What, what, what?"

She was delighted – "A parade." She clapped her hands. "Oh, I do love a parade."

He shifted into reverse and studied his mirrors. "Darn, burn it, no go."

"What's that? Am I seeing what my eyes behold?" She opened her cab door and stood on the running board. Look, dear, look. A Beech-nut vehicle, like the Thermos-mobile of old."

He hopped onto his own running board. "Sure is; why they've built a car into a Beech-nut-mobile."

"Hey, look at that darling paper mache chicken."

"Yeah, advertising Zealand. Lot of eggs boxed around there."

"What's Gallus gallus?"

"Kind of egg maybe." They were hooked by then, trucking forgotten.

"Hey, old husband, are we committing a Casus belli?"

"What? Where do you see it?" He stood tip toed, craning his neck. "I don't see it."

"Remember, I put that in my book about Pearl Harbor; using an event to justify one's doing something. Like going to war or like seeing a parade provoked our bugging out."

"An excuse, huh? Yep, we're guilty."

"With this parade dragging by we'll need to overnight here in town."

"You get the mind bogglingest darned ideas."

"It's like that Mae West movie we watched up at Northway Village, recall?"

"'My Little Chickadee?'"

"No."

"'She Done Him Wrong?'"

"Nope, guess again. There's one left."

"Oh, now I'm scared. We saw 'I'm No Angel.'" He peered across the cab roof at her. Suddenly her wink melted him. "Oh, no. Not starting again. Dear, you're too old. I'll need to try a trick like that flapping Henry VIII if I want a natural."

"Old Henry did that beheading stuff because he wanted a son. I just want a babe in the house. I dearly miss Dosia even as I'm very happy for her and Del."

"I know darling. I know. We can adopt again. Try for a boy if we want."

"Yes, well, let's try again first."

Between unloading the boats and visiting three factories, Helio was ready to plop into any motel bed they could find. They found none. His eyes blinking, he poured out the road to Grand Rapids. They were hardly on the way when a huge mache chicken caught his eye. "There's that chicken."

"Oh joy, and a restaurant and motel nearby."

"Eats first."

Just into the driveway, they saw a man approach the chicken – and the Gallus gallus sign. She leaned from her window. "Kind sir, please tell us the meaning of Gallus gallus."

The man grinned. "Grabbed you, too, did it? Boss's idea. It means chicken. That's the science name for chicken, er, really it's for an early chicken. That's the bird that all the chickens were developed from. My boss went to college so now, he says, how would anybody know that? So now I have to tell everybody so's they'll know about the origin of the modern chicken that the boss learned about at college."

"China, I'd bet that original chicken was found in China."

"India is where, and a few was in southern Asia. It was sure an important discovery, you'll admit. Why, the chicken is by far the most abundant bird on this earth and a large lot of them are around here." He pointed to a large factory-type building. "That's our egg packing plant. Pack them with our name; also Kroger's, Borden's, you name it."

"How may one tell them apart?"

"Huh? Well, we just change the cartons."

"Eggs are the same?"

"Of course, but not all the same price, of course."

"Of course. We're here for that restaurant and motel."

"Good choices. My boss runs them, too. He'll be the one with the Gallus gallus pictured on his shirt."

Mr. Gallus gallus was the first person to catch the eye as they entered the restaurant. He seated them and reserved a room for them in the Chicken Roost motel.

"They selected 'old hen' from the menu and it was delivered with salad, dumpling gravy, mashed potatoes, biscuits, and mixed vegetables." They'd just about finished the meal when Mr. Gallus gallus returned.

"Truckers, I hear."

"Yup. I hear you're a college man."

He grinned. "Sure am."

"Why the red chicken? Do you raise red chickens?"

"No, that's Gallus gallus, the original chicken. It was a red jungle fowl that folks in India captured and had soon domesticated."

"Now we know the origin of today's chicken; most interesting. I've written a couple of books so I'm intrigued by information such as that. How about other things, say, like cows? Do you know?"

"Right up my line. I wrote a paper on just such as that. Iraq is prestigious in agricultural history. Iraq had sheep by 9000 and they raised grain there in 6750 b. c. All the dates I give you are b. c. dates. In 5000 Iraq had cattle, cows and beef, you see; and they also had pigs and goats by 5000. The pigs were found in what is now the Kurds part of Iraq and the goats were found in Jericho which is actually part of Jordan, but right there in that part of the world, I mean."

They missed Mr. Gallus gallus at breakfast but saw him wave from the egg packing plant loading dock. Helio sounded the air horns as they pulled away.

* * *

The truckers returned to a determined assail on Louie and Sid's logs, hoping to gain for them much needed paychecks. But alas, only a dent of progress had been accomplished for Louie and Sid before Delt Watkins received an urgent telephone call. A fellow wanting, rush, rush, to put in a row of housekeeping cabins handy to Iron Mountain, Michigan. "He said that it's a fast developing tourist area."

Dispatcher Dolly Reams managed to catch Del and Dosia loading at Delt's. "There's also a load available in Garden, Michigan. That's down off Highway 2, below Garden Junction. When can you get it?"

"We're to scoot back to the Upper Peninsula, Iron Mountain. We'll catch Garden on the rebound. Explain where Garden's located."

"Good going. Garden, Michigan, you'll see, is located on M-183, in Michigan's Garden Peninsula 17 miles above Fayette. Coming into the town, you might see slag heaps not as yet grown over. Slag is residue from Iron smelting but there's no smelter there. You look for an old unpainted warehouse. At the warehouse see an old gent named Bixby Ferrous."

"Got it covered. Thanks, Dolly. We're rolling."

She played the gear shift game a couple of times on their way north on Highway 131, calling each shift correctly on several up shifts, and even on low to high range shifts. On deciding when to down shift, she wasn't as accurate. Especially she was a bit baffled when high to low range was involved in a down shift yet Del was highly impressed, doubting that he could do better himself at calling the shifts while another shifted. The Mack had a lift tab on the shifting lever for shifting into high or conversely into low range. There were five shifts ahead in the main transmission but the five could be ranged to ten shifts up, or down, by incorporating the low range function. "Dear, you should really try driving sometime."

"Explain again."

"In a higher gear put the clutch in then lift the little lever to shift into low range of the next higher gear. In low range and if you want to go to high range, pull up the lever while the clutch's in then complete the shift so that shift is into higher range."

"Oh, sure," she said. She playfully bumped his shoulder. "My man does the hard stuff." She knew he was tired and dreaded that she couldn't visualize the moves he'd described. Long after sundown on several recent occasions he'd loaded at the tin can on a stick location, trying to work in extra log hauls, therefore, extra pay checks for Louie, Sid, and the truckers. She kept up the gear shift game for quite a while. Her aim was not necessarily to equip herself but to keep her hubby alert. Finally satisfied that he'd not nod right away, she opened a Reader's Digest at her ribbon. After several hours, they'd rolled some one hundred thirty miles into the trip. Dosia had her nose deep into a Reader's Digest. Suddenly excited, Del said, "Well looky, looky here."

Reader's Digest went flying as she grabbed the map and her spiral bound notebook. "I'm ready this time. She scanned her notes then stabbed the map with her finger. "See here? Boyne Mountain, elevation 1,120 feet."

He'd slowed the truck and was peering through the windshield. "That'd be above sea level," he remarked wondrously. "Old Boyne here is sticking up, I'd say, five to six hundred feet right before our eyes."

She still had her finger on the map. "It's sure amazing, and we're only twenty or so to the east of East Jordan."

He kept peeking out at Boyne Mountain until they were too far past it. He glanced at her map point. "Amazing isn't it, that much difference in topography from there to here?"

"I do believe Michigan's the prettiest state."

"You bet." He added throttle; "It's around sixty to the ferry at the Straits of Mackinac." She found her place in Reader's Digest.

She lowered the magazine and looked his way. "Dear, the tires."

He eased off a little, "Yep."

She'd hardly read another word before she called, "Ticket! Ticket! Dear we need the tires."

Sheepishly, he let off on the throttle, "You're right." She'd cautioned before that traffic tickets wouldn't buy tires.

"Hungry?"

"Sure." She passed a hamburger sandwich.

He chewed, his rhythm timed to his thinking: The Lufkin was carrying a towering load of pre-constructed buildings that were chained on securely. However, beneath the trailer bed and the load, the Lufkin itself rode on iffy tires. Each set of duals consisted of a new Cooper paired with a badly worn tire or with a good treaded Old Texas they'd purchased from Mr. Diamond-T. He chewed, he fretted, wondering if they'd make it through to the purchase of the other four much needed Coopers.

They rolled on until as if by magic the Straits ferry loomed before them.

Off the ferry, he accelerated along Highway 2, continuing on the roll to Iron Mountain. She touched his bicep. "Dear, no rush. It'll be after dark anyway before we reach Iron Mountain."

They did take note of Garden Junction, the turn off Route 2 that led down to the town of Garden where on the morrow they'd load anew, but cruised on as the night was falling. It was pitch dark when they cruised into the town of Iron Mountain. Morning found them tangled together on the seat of the Mack.

They were parked on the roadside in front of a cafe, their rig nearly hiding the place. The sign on the front announced the Chin Up Cafe. A light came on in the Chin Up. Dosia dug for her hairbrush. Entering the small cafe, a man called to them from the kitchen, "Bacon's over; eggs and pancakes are on the way. Egg over easy, okay?"

"Yes. Don't rush," she said. "We'll be a minute."

"Toss on a couple of whole wheat toasts with that you've mentioned, please; and reg coffee, cream, and sugar."

"I got ya."

Shortly, they returned, both looking shiny-skinned and still sleepy-eyed but in fresh clothing, and with him clean shaven. They reached to cuddle chilled hands around hot cups. Lips extended, they enjoyed that first over-hot sip. "Aaah, good, just what we needed."

He arrived with the order and then sat at a nearby table with his own cup of inky black elixir. He said, "Good coffee brings your chin up. Get it, Chin Up? Chin Up Cafe."

"Grand," she said.

He began humming a tune between sips. She caught the tune. "Fever?"

"Er, yeah, sorry."

"Peggy Lee."

He turned in his chair to see her better. "My favorite." He nodded toward the far wall. "Hung her picture over there next to Lucille, my wife. She died."

"Sorry. Peggy Lee from here is she?"

"No. North Dakota. My favorite singer. My wife looked like her a lot, blond hair, and even the mole. I hung Lucille's picture there with Peggy Lee after Lucille died; like a shrine, I figured. Could've been sisters." He passed his hands down his cheeks, seemed also to hump his shoulders. "I hadn't heard of Peggy Lee until I came up from the mine. They didn't ever play any songs down in there."

"I'll let my papa know of you and Peggy Lee. He liked the Lady and the Tramp song and lately we found the Fever record for him. Papa's a trucker from Alaska, an Athabascan Indian. He may stop by one day with a load like out there. His truck is a red Reo. He has a radio in his truck. I'd wish trucks had record players inside. Couldn't you have a jukebox in here?"

"We had a record player but it broke."

"Some one along here is building a cabin court," Del put in.

"That'd be Jake. Along ahead a quarter mile or so. Housekeeping cabins. His cabins we hope will build up my Chin Up business as well as his tourist accommodations. I've known Jake since boyhood when we went down into the mine. We both had grand folks that came over from Germany in steerage. That's near the rudder, you know, the cheapest accommodations. Now Jake wants to offer top grade cabin accommodations.

"I clubbed Double Jack with Jake for years down in the mine boring holes for the dynamite. They'd blast away a whole lot of iron ore but dust and water, too. Wettest mine in the world. You see all these mine pictures along the walls. See that electric tram? Me and Jake's lungs began to go bad so they had us driving that electric tram; like a small, but tough, electric train locomotive, it was. We hauled miners down 400 feet into the drifts and tunnels and we top-sided millions of tons of iron ore, just me and Jake alone transported a lot of that iron ore."

"Wet, huh? They wetted out, did they? When?"

"We had the wettest mine in the world, they said. Ahead a ways, you'll see the biggest water pump in the world standing along side the road. Mostly the mines closed in the 1930's but some not till 1945. Got so the ore wasn't worth fighting the water for it." He positioned his cup on its saucer. "Say, I usually eat about now before the crowd comes in. Around a dozen for breakfast."

"Your pancakes are delicious."

"Buttermilk's the only kind I bake. Go good alright. I'll bring you some more, if you'd like."

"Sure."

"They start coming in right soon, but Jake'll be last. He's a stubby gent with a waxed handlebar mustache and an engineer's hat; striped hat, you'll see."

Soon the clientele began coming. They took seats but didn't have to order. Glenn already was preparing the usual for each. They'd settled in with their forks when at seven-thirty the door opened and Jake came in. He called, "Glenn, the usual." The others grinned as though thinking, 'Good one on Jake,' amused that he didn't know he needn't order. Jake went to a table, removed his engineer's hat and slapped presumed dust from the table and chairs. He tossed his cap onto a chair and called, "And coffee, black."

A quiet giggle snapped his head toward Dosia. "Tiniest trucker I've seen. "Glenn," he called, "get food out here for this tiniest trucker!"

She and Del both grinned their appreciation. "It's because of this here handle bar mustache," he explained, "that I'm a little later to breakfast. I need to wax it every morning then wait until it dries so it'll stay nice all day. When Glenn and I went to driving the electric tram down in the iron mine, folks begin calling me Nanook because of my stature. Stocky, short, I mean, but I was always so dirty Double Jacking that nobody actually saw me until I was cleaned up. I cleaned up when driving the tram. Well, with this mustache no one again confused me with Nanook"

"Nanook of the North." I read that a time ago. My Papa is an Alaskan and very interested in the Eskimo. Why the reference to Nanook around here?"

He'd taken a bite of pancake while she queried him. He grinned, chewed, raised his hand, and extended a finger, then swallowed. The finger came to point at his handlebar. "First, you see how my mustache keeps clean when one eats. Now, old Munn there," he pointed Munn out, "he gets food all over his mustache whenever he eats. Real messy."

"Now just a darn minute," Munn complained, coming to his feet. "Ma'am I'm wearing a Mark Twain style mustache. Granted, it gets soiled some when I eat, but I finish with coffee and that cleans it. Old Jake, now old Jake he must eat cold food all day least the wax melt and his mustache fall apart. He must even all day drink cold coffee."

"Well, tell um about Nanook, seeing as how you've grabbed the floor."

"Friends, I'm the history teacher at the school. Robert Flaherty, from right here at Iron Mountain, journeyed to the Northland and lived for a time with the Inuit, or Eskimo. He wrote a book about them, that 'Nanook of the North.' Later he returned north and made a documentary film about them. His was the first documentary film ever made and yet today stands as a model for all such films. Now," he pointed, "see that blank space on the wall where once hung the fire extinguisher. That hangs now over by the out door. You see, too, that Glenn has a shrine on the wall honoring Lucille and also Peggy Lee, who hasn't even died yet. Well, in that other blank wall space I'm to hang a shrine for Mr. Flaherty as soon as the framing is finished, and with words about him also framed."

"Bravo!"

"Wait!" Jake raised his palms. "Don't applaud him or he won't sit down."

Munn feigned annoyance at his friend Jake. "Jake, will insist I tell about mountains while I'm on my feet."

"No, railroads first," Glenn chimed in.

"No, forests first."

"Oh, yes, the Queen Mary." He turned to look right at Del and Dosia. "Folks, it's possible to work international history right in with local. You'd believe that in 1936 Escanaba, Michigan, right here in the UP and you likely drove right through there getting here. Well, in 1936 Escanaba sold 100,000 sq feet of bird's eye maple to England to use in constructing the Queen Mary luxury liner. I'm proud to include such as that in my lectures."

"Yeah, so now the railroads," someone called.

"As to railroads, then," Munn said, "and just because Jake and Glenn drove an electric tram during their mining days and they'd want that mentioned. But not so much about railroads as about railroad gauge. You know, the distance between the rails of a railroad track is four feet and eight and one half inches. That distance is standard gauge. That's also the gauge of automotive wheels and is the gauge also of a Roman chariot. I do include interesting side lights when I teach. That distance is actually the width of the horses that pulled the chariot. It's been standard gauge ever since the Romans."

"And HOMES," Jake acted annoyed. "I know you want to tell that before you'd think to discuss the mountains."

"Sure, Jake, now you listen. Folks, I also include handy crutches when

I teach. HOMES is a mnemonic; H-O-M-E-S standing for lakes Huron, Ontario, Michigan, Erie, and Superior."

"Interesting." Del nodded his appreciation. "We arrived here last night after dark, but hoped we'd see a mountain near town and maybe a cliff. I'd heard of an escarpment, the Niagara Escarpment. Can you tell me, Mr. Munn, if Niagara, Wisconsin is located on a cliff and are there cliffs near Iron Mountain, and is there an actual Iron Mountain?"

"No, there's no mountain named Iron Mountain, the town, only, is called Iron Mountain, but you'll see Pine Mountain nearby. It sticks up there around two hundred twenty-three feet. Its elevation is 1523 feet but the town of Iron Mountain rests at, I recall, 1300 feet above sea level. The town of Iron Mountain actually lies a few hundred feet higher above sea level than does that Niagara, Wisconsin. An escarpment; geology is, by the way, a type of history and right up my alley. An escarpment is an elevated layer of rock, but not necessarily visible as a cliff. The Niagara Escarpment is an elevated layer of limestone rock topped by a layer of dolomite so large in area that it lies in a vast horseshoe shape around nearly the whole of HOMES. At Niagara Falls, I mean that magnificent Niagara Falls out east, the escarpment or layer of limestone rock can be seen as the water falls over it. Dolomite doesn't erode away as fast as pure limestone will erode so Niagara Falls will still last a long long time There are a lot of waterfalls here in the Upper Peninsula you can find on a map, likely in association with the escarpment. Even more spectacular falls can be seen over in Ontario where rivers fall over the escarpment from higher up." He stood poised on the ball of his feet, confident he could clearly field most any question.

"And the mountains," Jake said, "I know you're reluctant to discuss them."

"Which?"

"The biggest, for corn's sake."

"Sure." He cleared his throat. "Michigan's tallest mountains are Arvon at 1979 feet and Curwood at 1978 feet. They're located within the Huron Mountains. Those Huron Mountains are located north of here and along the south shore of Lake Superior." He didn't look at Jake. Jake looked about ready to jump up from his breakfast. "Well, good day, friends. It's off to work I go."

Jake jumped to his feet, hollering, "Wait!" Munn waved to the group through the cafe window as he was already out the door.

"You'd leave my relatives out!" Jake called after. "Well, I'll tell um myself then," Jake's voice was still raised an octave when he resumed with the truckers. "He's always leaving my important history clean out. Leaves that all up to me." Calmed by his own declaration, he began:

"My friends," he stood as tall as he could beside his chair, "my middle name is Caleb. Caleb and Joshua are middle names of many men of our family. It's to do with those Huron Mountains that that Munn knows darn well all about. You do recall that Caleb and Joshua are named in the Bible. Moses and Aaron sent them and many others into Canaan to spy and the others brought back false reports so the Israelites refused to enter Canaan but God had sent Joshua and Caleb, who'd told the truth, and they went in and led the conquest of Canaan.

"Well, our family names of Caleb and Joshua happened back when site surveying was underway here in the Upper Peninsula. The boss sent boys into the mountains to scout around. Well the first ones who came out said there weren't any tall mountains in there to survey. It seems it was cold weather and they wanted to go home so they lied. When my kin came out they said yes there's tall mountains in there to survey. Most of the crew had gone on home because they believed the liars, but the boss believed my kin. So in they went. Those who didn't go in got fired, you bet. The boss was so proud of my kin he named them Caleb and Joshua right on the spot and they led the way in to survey those mountains." He stood beside his half eaten breakfast, shaking his head in a gesture of 'yes' and with a grin raising his handlebar. "Yes sir, that's all true. That Munn sure does leave interesting history right out of his classes."

"Interesting alright," Del said, "why, we didn't learn a thing interesting back when I had history class. Another interesting thing that should be a part of history class is what my friend Louie told me about was how cold it can get. I'd asked him about the Niagara Escarpment but he thought I meant out at Niagara Falls. He said Niagara Falls froze solid in the winter of 1911 and he thought also in 1932. What are the winters like around here?"

"Cold, but not too uncomfortable; but the snow can build up real deep; it does a time or two in every winter."

"Hang history on events of interest like the dates of important weather events," Dosia said, "and I should think the history of songs should be taught, too."

"Sure," Jake and Glenn chorused their delight at having acquired a new conspirator, or two. "Which?"

"Katherine Lee Bates wrote 'O Beautiful for Spacious Skies' as a poem after she climbed Pike's Peak. The poem was published and then she wrote several versions of it and tried them to music, trying for a song, she was. Finally the song became 'America the Beautiful,' and a runner up for our National Anthem."

"Sure, I would've studied that."

"What other song, should we?"

"Time," Del interrupted. "We must get unloaded as we're due in at Garden as soon as we can."

"My crew's not coming to unload until nine o'clock," Jake countered.

"Good, we've time," she said. "Our National Anthem, 'The Star Spangled Banner' has a long history associated with it; not just the story of that lawyer, Francis Scott Key who wrote it. Poncho Villa of Mexico even figures into it. Old Poncho attacked America, at Columbus, New Mexico, you recall; back in 1916. General Blackjack Pershing went after Poncho Villa in that Punitive Expedition. General Pershing liked the Star Spangled Banner and his band played it everyday.

"It happened that President Woodrow Wilson heard the song and proposed it to congress as the National Anthem. In World War I when General Pershing and our American Doughboys arrived in France – I'm from France so I really like this story. Well, the French played The Star Spangled Banner, thinking that it was the National Anthem of the United States, but it wasn't. No, it wasn't. That's because our congress was still debating it. They debated it during the terms of four presidents, finally passing the bill in 1931, while Herbert Hoover was president. That's just before F.D.R., as you know. So the debate went on while Woodrow Wilson, Warren Harding, Calvin Coolidge, and Herbert Hoover were presidents."

"Now that's history I'd have studied," Jake declared.

"It's like Will Rogers said," Glenn opined, "about aging. 'If you want to slow up the process of aging,' he said, 'turn it over to congress.'"

"Say, can you folks stay a while? Say till the next breakfast? We could explain to old Munn how he should be doing it."

"Gosh, wish we could, but really, we are due in at Garden."

CHAPTER TEN

Leaving Iron Mountain, Del crossed the Menominee River for a swing through Niagara, Wisconsin where they passed along a cliff, the face of the escarpment. They swung back across the river for a view of Pine Mountain and of the iron mine where Glenn and Jake had clubbed Double Jack and had driven the electric tram. "This could become a tourist area," she said, "if folks could hear Munn, Jake, Glenn and the others talking; and see these interesting sites, as well."

"Interesting, alright. You see a route shorter than Route 2?"

Dosia moved a finger along the map that she held crumpled in her lap. "It's about a hundred to go to Garden Corners. Looks like 2's our best bet." He glanced her way and caught a soft smile, an expression he'd not noticed before that very morning at the breakfast just past. Could she've enjoyed it so much?

"What's up? You okay? You alright?"

"Yes, okay." She smoothed the map with her lovely hands. "We'll be in the Hiawatha National Forest about half of the way." She looked keenly at Del. "Was Hiawatha a real person?" He thought: It's the usual thing she does, to ask questions like that to keep us awake; but that slight smile?

Deciding to mull over her new smile at a later time, he answered her query about Hiawatha. "Yes, he was a real person, but not in Longfellow's poem." Is that it? Is she musing over Longfellow? "Longfellow used the name of Hiawatha for his hero in The Song of Hiawatha, but the real Hiawatha lived long before that." Del continued to take peeks at her. "He organized an Iroquois confederacy of . . . uh, we'd better ask Grandpa Clarence."

"Well, real or not, I like Longfellow's Hiawatha and I wonder if there's a monument or some such." Again, that shy, starry-eyed smile! "I don't see any marked on this map but this Hiawatha forest looks to me like it reaches north clear to Lake Superior." She still held her finger to the map, but looked inquisitively at him. "Del, did you know? There's a town up near Superior, at the north end of Hiawatha's forest, a town named Christmas." Now her smile was radiant.

"Oh? Way out of our way, I'd think, huh?"

"Sure, but someday."

"Sure, maybe."

"We could go there with our child."

His chest locked up as though his heart was too big to fit there. "Really! Our child!" In slowing the truck, he shifted down and set all eighteen wheels to griping tarmac. The rig came to a stop on the narrow road shoulder. "Really!"

His hand shot out, reaching her abdomen.

"Silly, you can't feel yet."

"Praise God, are you sure?"

"No, not sure, but what should have occurred if it was going to – didn't. I'm praying, really praying." Tears trickled down her cheeks. "Del, how I do love you."

He blinked furiously but was futile in stemming his tears. "Better quit trucking, huh?" By then, she had his hanky. He passed a shirt sleeve across his face and the damp sleeve came to rest across her shoulders.

She moved into his arms, cuddling close. "No, likely I'll be trucking a while longer. I'll ask Aunt Edith, but I read to keep on with whatever there is to do is the best thing to do."

"Praise the Lord."

"Del, lets keep it our secret for a while, a month or two, until I'm sure. Just our own wonderful secret."

"Sure thing, dear, our own wonderful secret."

"A while back, I asked Megan about La Leche; that League, you know. She said to experience every moment possible with our child. She was overjoyed, she said, to have them nurse." Her arm crossed over her breasts and shivers cruised to her shoulders. "Oh, Del, I want to!"

The truck rolled back onto the tarmac and the Thermaldyne sang their praises up through the shifts, settling to a steady hum in high range fifth. They sat quietly as if each was to daydream the whole hundred miles to Garden, but after a while she said, "Del, I like Hi for a name for our boy."

"Hiawatha?"

"Hi, but I don't know what it's a nickname for."

"We'll have time to study on it." She quieted again, and began paging the spiral notebook. In a moment he noticed her busy with a pencil. Suddenly the pencil waved through the air. "We have it. Dear, we have it. The money Jake gave us made the amount needed for the rest of the tires for the Lufkin."

"Praise God."

"While in East Jordan, I'll put a call to Cooper. Just think the money from Garden can go toward outfitting a nursery. It's a wonder they haven't already started on the nursery. They're trying again, I can tell, but I don't think she can so we'd better move in with the folks."

"Yes, they'd want that." He pat her thigh. "Momma wants the patter of little feet in the house."

"But let's plan to buy or build as soon as possible, right after the patter of little feet, huh? I want a lifetime together. I mean us and the kids."

"Sure."

* * *

During the previous night while Del and Dosia'd cuddled in the cab of the Mack in wait of sunrise, brisk activity was underway at the Cozy Cafe in Coopersville. Jacqueline had worked shamelessly toward Ronnie's surprise birthday party. Equally shameless, Loxey'd worked beside her wonderful partner. That evening they'd told Ronnie that inventory was being conducted and that he must stay away. "Don't come into the Cozy Cafe."

Ronnie had driven his dark blue and cream Ford Crown Victoria into downtown for an oil change. Upon returning home he sat deeply into his upholstered chair, but wasn't enjoying any of the television programs. Waiting impatiently for professional wrestling, he chewed on potato chips and sipped Pepsi. Suddenly the big lot of girl came vividly to mind. He'd dared to speak with her several times yet she hadn't gone away. His pants began to feel uncomfortably tight what with his sitting deeply in his big upholstered La-Z-Boy. She'd been nice to him ever since that first day when his apple had torn in half and she'd leaned to retrieve half of - - Wow!

Potato chips scattered. Thrusting up from the chair, he smacked the Pepsi onto the coffee table. Professional wrestling might not have been good that night anyway. He'd just go to bed. At the door that separated the house portion of the building from the Cozy Cafe he paused and reached the door knob, muttering, "Just a darn peek." His thoughts were to that whole big lot of girl. He turned from the door. His big hands went anxiously to his belt buckle. He rushed toward his bedroom.

Had he opened the way into the Cozy the door to the new room would have stood open and he'd have seen that she was decorating a three layer spice cake.

Looking from the cake, Jacqueline thrilled to see that Red, orange, green, and blue crepe paper ribbon decorated the room. Party plates and napkins were at rest upon the tables. She turned from the cake in final survey of the room, noting that preparation was complete. They could lock the new room now and let it simmer until the party.

Their preparation complete, Loxey entered the house. Just inside the door, Loxey stopped. She leaned back against the door to the Cozy. She stood wondrous as to what greater hunger caused Ronnie to scattered rather than to eat his chips? And what thirst could be so great in him that he'd forgone his Pepsi, his favorite drink? She reached her fan, a treasured family heirloom made of a turkey wing, and stood gently fanning away the perspiration she'd accrued from the birthday room preparation, and from the scene before her. The fan came to a stop. She continued her peer past the fan to the coffee table with the scattered chips and the neglected Pepsi. Loxey grinned as a vision of Jacqueline cruised her mind.

Outside the restaurant, Jacqueline squeezed into her weary old Dodge, her thoughts to her efficiency apartment. She'd be alone in the night - - "For now!"

* * *

With thoughts far from that soon to come birthday party, the Mack continued along Route 2. At the town of Escanaba, Del turned north on a skirt of Little Bay de Noc. He scanned the trees as they cruised along, the while wondering what a birds eye maple looked like. Being near the Lake Michigan shore, he noted that deciduous trees were predominate, but with a sparse population of evergreens mixed in. Where would the bird's eye have been standing?

They turned east and followed a rather straight run of nearly twenty miles through forests of hardwood trees, bringing the Mack to Garden Corners. Swinging south onto M-183, they made an eight mile skirt of Big Bay de Noc, cruising half way down the Garden Peninsula before sighting the town of Garden. They began a scan, his to the left and hers to the right, trying to identify slag heaps. "Better also try seeing an old warehouse," he advised.

"Or an old rusted gent named Bixby Ferrous," she quipped. "Hey, dear, look ahead. Let's ask him." As she spoke the man hurled what resembled a pie plate. Pulling to a stop, they watched a distant gent dash then deftly catch the plate. Judging by his bell bottom jeans and white tee shirt, the near man was an old salt. "Hey, Mr. Sailor, can you tell us where to see slag heaps or an old warehouse or a Bixby Ferrous?" The gent in the distance wore an expensive-looking shirt and she guessed he'd not be a sailor. Her eyes continued to follow Mr. Shirt as he loosed the plate. The plate came as true as an arrow of Robin Hood and the near man turned in time for the plate to career off his shoulder and into the side mirror of the Mack. She watched its flutter into the grass. "What is that thing?"

"A Flyin' Saucer. Lars owns it. Brought it here from Connecticut. The slag heaps all grew over, the warehouse collapsed the rest of the way just yesterday, and I'm Bix Ferrous. At your service ma'am. You here to load pigs?"

"Pigs?" She looked across at Del.

He shrugged. "Pigs, pig iron, whatever he has, I guess."

"Yes, sure, we guess, pigs. I'm Dosia, and my man's Del Platt."

Bix heaved the Flyin' Saucer back toward Lars. "I sent for Lars, my nephew, to come from Connecticut. The Wham-O Manufacturing Company sold him the Flyin" Saucer. The Frisbee Pie Company noticed that people played with the pie plates, threw them all around. So they had Wham-O make some just to sell as toys." He held his hands as a megaphone, and hollered, "Lars, bring that here."

He climbed onto the truck running board, held to the window frame and leaned into the cab. "Ahead there to that pickup." Dosia reared back as far as she could in her seat but was spattered by his speech. "Turn right there."

"Yup, just in front of the pickup." Del yanked his head aside and turned to nose on nose with Lars who'd hopped onto that side running board. "It's down in there."

During the previous night while they snoozed tangled together on the seat of the big green Mack, she'd roused him to say, "If we take time to haul the load from Garden we may not have time to get to the birthday party."

"And you want to go?"

"If we got there we might be too sleepy to enjoy it."

"I'd stay awake just to see how Jacqueline works it."

"After we see Mr. Ferrous, we could drive empty straight on home. We owe a lot to Aunt Edith, Grandma Clydis, many others."

"Straight on through then?"

"I suppose, but let's decide it after we see Mr. Ferrous."

Now as they eased the rig down the narrow lane toward a fallen warehouse, he looked over at her just when she looked at him. Their expressions were identical. Hang the party; there's pigs to haul and we've to build a nursery.

Abreast of the pile of rubble, the Mack slowed to a stop and Bixby hopped to the ground. Dosia waved her hand, scattering the air around her nose. "Pew! Garlic!"

Lars and Bix walked on ahead. Hopping from the truck, Del and Dosia stretched their paces to catch up. They heard Bix say, "The warehouse went down and so I found the pigs."

"Pigs?" Dosia touched her chin. Del also wondered.

"Yep, hay was in the loft so I planned to order sheep and horses to eat the hay. My folks used the warehouse for a barn. They died ten years back but I kept up insurance on the buildings and property while I finished then my last ten years as a seaman on the Great Lakes. The roof leaked and the floor gave way and the whole shebang, you see, has gone belly up. Why I ever decided to be a gentleman farmer in my waning years I'll never know. You can see it's nothing but trouble."

Bix turned to Dosia. "Mrs. Platt, ma'am, those gloves are way too big for you. Here's a pair of mine. You may keep them, they're yours now. You and me need to help move debris off the pigs and a sow so your man and Lars can do what I say."

"Sure." She pushed her dainty hands into the gloves. She stood flexing her fingers while watching Del.

Curious, Del moved up to a lump of iron and pushed his fingers under its edges, but it didn't budge with his lift. Lars straddled a lump, worked his fingers well under it, braced his forearms against his squatted legs and heaved upwards using the combined strength of arms and legs, ending with the lump of iron resting on the palms of his gloved hands, and with his hands resting on his thighs. He straightened with the iron lump cradled against his belly and grinding into his expensive-looking shirt. "That's how to lift pig."

"Over here," Bix indicated with a sweep of his arm. "I want seventeen pigs laid in a row here." Del and Lars set to work. "Ma'am, Mrs. Platt, you and I must try to move rubble off the ingots so they can gather the pigs, ingots are called pigs, and you and me'll find a sow." He walked back over to the struggling men. "And I want another row of seventeen pigs right along here." He swept his arms.

Slowly Bix's project took shape. With every carry Del sought a glimpse of Dosia, wondering what to do about the baby. He didn't say anything about the baby because it was their own wonderful secret. He prayed, however, to know when to call to her to stop.

To Del's dismay she hung in there as if saying: Not me old garlic salt. I'm not resting before you do. Finally, Del and Lars stood puffing. Bix and Dosia arrived, each with a jagged chunk of cast iron. All parties were drenched in perspiration. "There, now do you see?"

"Should see pigs, huh?"

"Yes, from the iron mines the ore comes to the smelter. The iron is melted out of the ore and poured into molds to form pig iron. Look here, the chunks down the middle were the sow and along one side of the sow was attached a row of piglets, but, of course another row of piglets along the other side. They made sand molds first then poured molten iron into the molds. The molds were for a sow and pigs, don't you see? Then the breaking machine was used to chunk up the sow and to snap off all the pigs. So that's why it's called pig iron."

"Pretty heavy stuff, right?"

"Yep, a hundred pound of iron per ingot; each ingot is called a pig. Each pig weighs a hundred pounds. Even with the rust that's on some of these here, the roof leaked for years, you know; well even rusted they still weigh 100 pounds each, we figure. And each sow'd weigh, I guess, around four hundred pounds. Heavy, sure, but they loaded the pig iron onto a ship then and sailed it to a foundry. The sow, of course, they melted anew and so went on pouring pigs."

"The pigs went to a foundry like at East Jordan Iron Works, Inc?"

"Er, yup, or elsewhere; like to places that make steel. Lot cheaper to ship pig iron than to ship iron ore. At a foundry, if cast iron is wanted, pig is ready to melt down and pour into all sorts of molds. In our case here, we'll send the sows along with the pigs to the foundry. Lot of manholes and manhole covers made at that East Jordan plant I've heard."

"We trucked big loads of stuff; sewer pipe, manholes, manhole covers, sewer grates, fire hydrants, catch basins; trucked four big loads down to Oklahoma, and a lot of brake drums from East Jordan to Detroit.

Oklahoma set aside near forty-two million dollars for new roads. Mostly we unloaded in Love County near Ardmore, just above Texas."

Changing the subject, Dosia said, "Was there a mine here?" She moved her head on a wide scan of the area. "Smelters would be near mines, I'd think. Papa has asked for a job for next summer trucking ore at the Mesabi outfit in Minnesota. Would that be to a smelter?"

"That's a big open pit iron mine," Del explained, "and they use off the road trucks, so would a smelter be located right at the mine?"

"Sure, I'd think so. This pig iron here is from the Fayette smelter located south of us about seventeen miles. Ore came to it by rail, horse and wagon, and ships. A lot of mines nearby, you see? The Fayette smelter was in business 24 years, ending in 1891. It produced 229,288 tons of pig iron; that's sure a lot of pigs. Hardwood forests and limestone are needed in smelting. The hardwood ran low all over the garden peninsula and near by along the coast, so they quit smelting. The hard wood grows only close to the Great Lakes shorelines, you'll notice, so the wood got used up kind of fast. When the smelter shut down there wasn't enough pig iron left for a ship load so they stored it here in the warehouse; probably thinking they'd start smelting again when times were better.

"I've a clam bucket coming to move off the over mess and he can plop a lot of pig onto your trailer too. We'd better eat first."

Bix led the way to the Ship's Garden Restaurant. Entering right behind Dosia, he called, "Bilge!" Dosia was again plastered in aerial garlic. "Bilge, bring on a lot of heavy food for us pig loaders and the pair of pig iron truckers."

Bilge began lugging in steaks, potatoes, and vegetables. His helpers, Peg, Slew, and Dodge helped carry food along with their filling of coffee, soda, water and milk orders. Presently eight people were in position around a large table piled high with provender.

Slew tapped his glass. He cleared his throat and gave a prayer.

Bilge led off with conversation. "I see my brother out the kitchen window with his clam shell crane starting in on that over mess. Bix, I can't get over you not knowing about the pigs. It was your grand dad and mine who put it up there maybe sixty years ago rather than to ship so small a batch. When you came in here hollering about finding pig, why then I remembered all about it. Truckers, you might want an introduction. I'm called Bilge and these three are Peg, Slew, and Dodge. Along with Bix and Lars, all six of us had grand folks working in the Fayette smelter so it's an honor for us to help load that pig iron."

153

"I'm Del Platt, and my wife, Dosia. We're glad for any help; delighted I'll say. First I need boards and planks sorted from the rubble, at least forty of them to put around my semi trailer to block between the stakes. That way the pig iron will stay aboard. I'll want a solid bed of pig ingots forming an open center space where we can toss in the sow chunks. I'll need first to go pump my tires to 100 psi. They are set at 80 psi now, but the load looks to be really heavy."

Del's announcements prompted murmurs of approval: "Sure, okay. Yep, you bet."

"Now, Mrs. Platt," Bilge said, "you're not to lift an ounce of pig even as I see Bix had already treated you like a jenny mule." Answering his touch on her shoulder, she turned to his direction as he said, "Here's the key to the Ship's Garden. Please, if you'd keep us supplied with drinks and sandwiches."

Del looked carefully at his wife, wondering if her condition showed. Perhaps it showed only for some people. Bilge sure knows, else he may not've, treated her that way. Nice guy that Bixby seemed to be, obviously he couldn't tell. Anyway, he was glad their secret was still secure, believing Bilge would say nothing because he hadn't already. Del exchanged a wink with Dosia.

"Sure," Dosia agreed. "I'll keep you all stuffed; but first while I have you guys handy, I want to know why the town and peninsula are called Garden."

"Because the soil is good garden soil," Dodge said. "Like our folk before us, Peg and me raise vegetables each season for our roadside stand. Best gardens you can ever see. Our tractor and trailer, by the way, is parked out in back; a Ford tractor, so you can haul that grub on over to us after a while."

"You got it, thanks."

Del'd hurried the meal and now pushed back. "I'm off to pump my tires. Filling station near, is there?"

"Gulf." Lars set his emptied cup. "I'll ride along. I like trucks."

Dosia blew Del a kiss. She pushed back from the more than ample meal. "Bilge, I'll go and look over that kitchen."

With his eyes to the mirrors, Del backed the Mack up to the intersection by the parked pickup where he cut the Lufkin ninety degrees to make the necessary turn, ending with the Mack aimed toward down town. "Gosh, if I could do that I'd be a trucker," Lars said.

"Oh, you could. Uncle Helio, actually now my father-in-law, taught me. Had me backing all over parking lots day or night and I backed a mile along a winding road using only my mirrors. You could learn, alright, but aren't you retired?"

"Yeah, Bix and me both. His wife died, cancer, so he stayed a seaman until way past retirement age. I retired from the army then my wife died, cancer, so I'm moving here to be with Uncle Bixby. I need to go back east to get the rest of my stuff as I hurried here when he telephoned saying he had trouble with pigs. Surprised, I was, to see he met pig iron. Left ahead, see the Gulf?"

"Got it. You were in Korea then?" He turned in at Gulf and stopped with the Lufkin tandem duals in reach of the air hose.

"Yes, in supply that time. I was hit hard on Iwo Jima. They healed me up and I stayed in. If you're wounded bad enough or often enough they don't send you back into combat. Do you watch Captain Kangaroo? I do all I can and before that I'd hope to catch the man as Clarabelle the Clown. His real name is Bob Keeshan. He saved my life on Iwo. He took rounds himself doing it. That was a horrible beach where you couldn't dig foxholes. Thousands of us getting slaughtered and we couldn't see the Nips that were lobbing shells at us. Troop carriers called Amtracs were being hit. Sergeant Keeshan dragged me in behind one. He helped a lot of others. They gave him a medal, but that wasn't enough. Not anything would be enough for what he did. He really took care for his men. Watch Captain Kangaroo whenever you can. I'll be watching, too."

"Sure will." Dell detached the air hose and checked tire pressure. "That's got it, 100 psi."

"Lotta air is it?"

"A lot, all right. I usually carry only 80 psi. Papa Helio warned me to stay away from loads that'd require a 100 psi tire pressure; that is for long hauls. On around to East Jordan isn't far yet I'm hoping to complete the load with under five hundred pigs. With the sows, that'd bring my load to around fifty five or fifty six thousand pounds. The tires on the semi trailer would bare more than half of that and the rest of the load, say around 12,000 pounds or more, will be carried by the truck tires. However, that big share of the pig iron and sow weight plus the weight of the trailer itself will be on these tires I'm airing to 100psi."

"Could break, maybe; the rims?"

"Helio said he'd not heard of rims breaking but at 100 psi there's seventy thousand psi of pressure against the rims. It worries me some."

"Me too." Lars stepped back a little from the tires.

"How far can you throw a bowling ball?"

"Huh, er well, not at all far, why?'

"Seventy thousand psi is enough force to throw a bowling ball three quarters of a mile." Lars rubbed his head. "Yet it's hard to actually imagine the danger, isn't it?"

Lars stood silent a moment trying to figure the meaning of his new friend's present expression. Del seemed to be looking off at something. Lars followed the line of sight but with nothing to see. A vision of an exploding tire had gripped Del. 'Those split rims. Just thrown them away,' Mr. Diamond-T had warned. Don't try to mount a tire on one. They can maim or kill.'

"Del?"

"Huh? Er, sure a bore standing here listening to air squeeze into a tire. One more, then we're done with it."

Back at the Ship's Garden, Dosia washed every dirtied item she could find and she cleaned a counter top. She heard the familiar tune of the Mack as it arrived into the din of the clam shell at work on the over mess. Having filled the coffee urn and started coffee, she now slapped hamburger patties onto the grill. A glance outside confirmed that darkness had fallen upon the pig iron bustle at Garden. She laid out bread slices, beginning the construction of hamburger and BLT sandwiches. Somebody pounding on the restaurant door leaped her straight into the air!

She alit on a bee line through the restaurant, "I'm coming. Wait, I'm coming," and answered the front door. No one was there. Midway back to the kitchen, she heard a rattle at the back door. Dosia quickened her pace only to nearly collide with a gray haired chap who'd entered the kitchen.

"Hello. Well, who are you?"

"Dosia Platt. Who are -- "

"Mayor Tip Grainer, just in from the state capital. Where's Bilge?"

"Bilge and others, including Del Platt, my man, are loading pig iron. Didn't you see those lights?"

"I saw lights in the Ship's Garden as well; and the Ship's Garden lights were brighter. I need to see Bilge or Bixby right away. Some senators assured me they'd introduce a bill to name the Fayette smelter area as a state park. I want to be sure some pig iron is not hauled out of here, enough to show, perhaps, a sow and two piglet rows. And to select them not too rusty. Besides, I ate last in Lansing. I'm nearly starved."

Dosia affected a pose like 'The Wise Little Hen', a character momma Anna Mae told her about. Anna Mae'd read about the first ever Donald

Duck cartoon, as released in 1934 where one may've also seen the wise little hen. "I've hamburger ready," she advised him. "Raid the frig for what else. Eat, then help me. I'm sure there's no rush as there's a lot of work out there. I've decided to make some peanut butter and jelly sandwiches to go with the others."

"Peanut butter first appeared at the 1904 World's Fair at St. Louis. My folks ate some and it's been big ever since. Those pig lifters will expect it."

"Good. Help me make the sandwiches and load up. We'll get there with glorious refreshments."

"I see Peg and Dodge's tractor here in back. A trailer's hooked on."

"Great, they said to use that."

They loaded the trailer behind the gleaming like-new Ford 8N gray and red farm tractor. Dosia drove while the mayor rode upon the draw bar with his hands gripping the tractor seat and a fender. Ahead she saw the Mack being eased ahead to better advantage the clam shell crane. The truck stopped just as she pulled into its headlight beams. Del tugged the lanyard that looped down from the truck cab ceiling. With each tug pressurized air raced through the Grover air horns, blasting out a welcome for the gang to partake of rest, food, and drink. In the wake of the air horns, the Mack stood with idling Thermaldyne, its light beams a beacon showing the way.

From the patchy gloom, lighted haphazardly by lanterns, men began to stagger into the Mack beams. Two beaten to be hungry, they plopped onto the grass near the trailer of provender. To these men Florence Nightingale couldn't have been more welcome. Their moans became more pleasant when Dosia raised a man's head for the Saint Bernard who came to them in the guise of Mayor Tip.

Recalling the long hard miserable days in the Yelrom woods, Del decided to pull a stunt much as Louie would have thought to do. He sent Mayor Tip after a record player and enough extension cords. The mayor said he thought he could find some John Philip Sousa music amidst his collection.

CHAPTER ELEVEN

Some three hundred miles south of Garden, the Cozy Cafe of Coopersville had served a late afternoon steak supper in the regular portion of the restaurant. While the folks at Garden with Dosia, Del, and Mayor Trip, lay sprawled near the heap of pig iron and, by then, gingerly eating, Ronnie's guests at the Cozy Cafe were sluggish with food. Loxey deemed it time the party was spiked up a notch. She opened the door to the new party room. "This way, folks; the party begins."

Jacqueline grabbed Ronnie's hand and they seated at a corner table behind the cake. They each held an open bottle of Pepsi and their eyes reflected the candle light glimmer as Loxey lit the candles.

Eight-year-old Hulda Sunshine James kept the platters spinning from a juke box and from the record player, timing her songs to, hopefully, provide continuous music. At a nod from her Momma Edith, Hulda placed that 1893 time honored hit song, the birthday song, under the needle of the record player. Loxey banged a table knife against a water glass, gaining instant quiet. At her nod, Hulda flicked the 'on.'

Words of the birthday song ricocheted from every cranny of the room, causing Ronnie to begin pumping his lungs, making ready. At the final "you" of the song the guests chanted, "Blow. Blow." His face was lighted grotesquely from below as his exhale commenced. But he'd apparently aimed too high, his Mariah putting mere flicker to the flames.

She placed her arm across his shoulders. "Ready now, together, dear. Blow with me, on three."

At their blow the candles leaned as if pulled by the flames. The excited couple leaned forward after the candles ending with their chins nearly into the icing. "Stop!" Hulda yelled, dashing for the cake. She slid to a stop at the table. Then, looking foolish, she drifted back to the record player. Loxey and Edith began cutting and serving the cake. He opened presents during the cake's demise.

His gifts were Simoniz car wax and mostly other automobile related goodies until from a large box, he pulled a huge pair of Carhartt coveralls. Hulda's selections by then had turned to dance music. Louie guided Rose to the floor and began what he thought was a foxtrot, but after a few steps she chucked that pace, instead moving into a vigorous twist. Louie, drawn to his wife's enthusiasm, began his own gyrations. Instantly the floor was a battleground of twisting bodies.

Suddenly Sid grabbed Maxine and hurled her to safety. Ronnie had lost his grip on his big lot of girl! They both were flying, she smashing headlong onto a table shared by Groner, James, and Outhe. The table crushed amid a shower of cake orts and splattered drinks. Scrambling party denizens party-wide inadvertently completed ruination of the room. Guests began to depart save for Grandma and Grandpa Groner and Harold and Edith James, Sunshine James, and one other, the Reverend Lester Slap Day Blanes. They grouped with Loxey, Jacqueline, and Ronnie, making ready to straighten the place. "No," Loxey said, "you kids go on. This is no trouble at all."

"Wait!" the Reverend Lester Day Blanes yelled, "The saving, and the wedding!" He jumped up onto a table, scattering table service and cake crumbs. "Anyone who calls on the name of the Lord will be saved," he bawled. "That's promised in Romans 10:13. And Matthew 7 opens the door to Heaven to all who knock. Right now you must get my special pioneer wedding. In days long ago it was sometimes necessary to wed in lieu of sanctioned authority, yet by the grace of God they were wed, but conditionally. Couples then were to more officially wed when a marriage license and a pastor or other authority were at hand. Tomorrow forenoon we'll do the saving part, and that followed by the traditional marriage vows and the signing of the license. Stand before me, you two, to receive the special emergency pioneer wedding."

The ceremony was brief. Afterward she said to him, "Dear, we can go."

"Oh?"

"I'm your present."

In the crown Victoria, Ronnie drove as directed. "Ahead dear, see it? That white mail box with the pink flamingo lawn ornament beside it?"

"Yeah!"

* * *

159

By this time in the town of Garden, Dosia and Mayor Tip had held a commando raid on the nearby houses, announcing at each that extension cords were to be handed over as they were needed in the pig iron loading arena. The result was a Rube Goldberg-like conglomeration of lamps, trouble lamps, and electric cords, the most of which darkened a home or part of one or that made a radio, a television, or a reading lamp as defunct as Bixby's warehouse. Perseverance they knew to be the mother of invention, thus the pair with prideful endurance soon proclaimed a workable turntable installation. In the commanding Sousa notes the pig lifters shed their zombie stances and became marchers. Mayor Tip and Dosia's record player belted the final notes of the Stars and Stripes Forever just as Del placed the last of 507 pigs. They'd snuggled 50,700 pounds of pigs neatly onto the Lufkin.

The semi trailer's share of the pigs' weight plus around 6,000 pounds of sow along with boards and chains pressed the bed of the Lufkin. The weight of the Lufkin and all aboard it pressed against the 100 psi in each of eight semi trailer tires and upon the eight tractor Coopers. He grinned in knowing the tractor rear wheels sported eight nearly new Coopers. His mind then focused on the semi trailer tires, and he shuddered, only half of the Lufkin tires were new Coopers. The other semi trailer tires were bald, with some showing traces of cord and were in the company of ancient old Texas used tires. Chained to the Lufkin and stored in racks under the trailer bed were a few of the good treaded iffy old Texas spares they'd purchased way back in Texas. Iffy because some of those old Texas spares were displaying sidewall cracks and he wondered whether they weren't weaker than the cord-showing baldies.

Del and Dosia cuddled with blankets on air-filled sleeping mats on the floor of the Ship's Garden restaurant. They slumbered until Bilge's wake-up call.

Quickly freshening in the rest room, they slid into seats at a table to eat breakfast. Del watched with sparkling eyes as Dosia shoved her nylons into her purse. "I'm too tired right now," she explained. "I'll pull them on later."

Upon hearing her plan for the hosiery, he bolted wide awake. He'd drooled over his first glimpse of Playboy back in 1953. Since knowing his Dosia he'd dismissed the magazine as mere trivia. He wondered how vast the pull of nylon had been on guys through the years since its appearance in 1934. Thought of nylons and of placing the legs within vied with his interest in food. However, as he thought plenty – he ate plenty.

Bilge's hardy breakfast set them heavily into the Mack. In the starry sky of pre-dawn morn, they pulled from the town of Garden. Ahead there'd be a hundred mile roll homed to the Straits of Mackinac ferry.

As the sun came up, Del began fighting fatigue. His yawning was punctuated by head jerks to clear his head. She'd waited till his time of need had arrived. Opening her purse, she slowly drew her hosiery from it, and she laid them one by one upon the dashboard. Instantly, he was awake. The truck weaved along the highway, its forward speed not steady but varying several miles per hour from moment to moment as she pulled on those nylons.

He'd taken a peek at that first issue of Playboy magazine in 1953. Some friends were sneaking it around at school. The centerfold was of Marilyn Monroe in the nude. He'd thought it interesting to view but wondered just why all the hush, hush, and excitement – now he knew! That Marilyn was a toad compared to his fantastic bombshell wife. Jack Benny, one of Helio's favorite comedians, also knew love else he couldn't have selected 'Love in Bloom' for his theme song. Del felt very much in bloom, and was wide awake as she snapped her garters to the top rim of those socks.

Glancing again her way, he tried a few lines of Ben Selvin's "I Only Have Eyes For You," but gave up crooning to say, "You're a corker, you are."

She grinned.

He remained awake long after she'd shoved those legs back into her jeans. Presently they began seeing signs leading to the Straits of Mackinac ferry.

On each journey going or coming from Michigan's Upper Peninsula they'd hoped to cruise on across the new bridge which they'd watched building. At 3691 feet, the span was to be the longest suspension bridge in the world. They strained their eyes to take it in from the deck of the ferry and upon exiting the boat at Mackinaw City Dosia poked her head out her window to be thrilled anew by the colossus. Finally relenting her view, she straightened around to peer across at Del. "It's somehow grander than that bridge of the movie," she said, "even as we know the Bridge Over the River Kwai is more steeped in patriotism."

"I know, and sad, too, what with William Holden coming back to destroy it. But fortunately, patriotism doesn't die with the loss of a project. That big bugger back there," he nodded his head, "just exudes patriotism for me. Gosh! What an almighty project."

She smiled and returned his nod. "I'm sure glad we're truckers and get to see so much."

Without knowing, they'd alit from the ferry on the morning after Ronnie's birthday party and Blanes' special pioneer wedding. Del and Dosia pulled on into Mackinaw City just when in Coopersville, Reverend Blanes was doing the saving. "Should the earth end at any time you must be sure you're ready to reside in heaven beside the Master. Jesus Christ is the ticket for that wonderful adventure. My friends, what say you? Do you confess your sins?"

"Sure." Her commitment was followed by silence from Ronnie. "Hon, do you want someday to be with me and Jesus in Heaven?"

"Huh? Er, yeah."

Reverend Blanes stood with his back to the counter. The bell ringing brass cash register was beside his shoulder. Ronnie and Jacqueline faced Reverend Blanes. "Dearly beloved," he began. They repeated the vows and he declared them officially and forever "hitched." Loxey, at the cash register, rang the bell, and she passed a twenty to Reverend Lester Slap Blanes. Next Loxey rushed around the counter to the newly weds and kissed her wonderful daughter-in-law and her grinning hubby.

Outside the cafe, the couple piled into the dark blue and cream Ford Crown Victoria and Ronnie squawked out onto the route to Highway 131. "Uh, I don't know about Heaven. I've never been so far north."

She squeezed his bicep. "You'll like such a nice place. I'll be there with you. And you'll like East Jordan, too. I have some things yet to get from there. We can do that later today. Tomorrow we can leave the Crown Vic parked behind the restaurant and take the fishing boat out into the lake. You'll catch the biggest old fish."

"Yeah."

She slid her hand lightly along his forearm. Her hand came to rest over his. His hand relaxed on the ornate steering wheel. "Tonight just you and me. We'll be in our own cozy motel room."

"Yeah."

"All night."

"Yeah."

He punched the pedal. The Crown Vic barreled on up 131.

No thoughts of the birthday party or the wedding, nor of a honeymoon for Jacqueline and Ronnie, burdened the minds of the truckers. Such affairs were squashed deeply into brain crevices when she said, "Let's eat here in Mackinaw City."

"Okay, and I'm afraid I've holed these jeans."

She leaned nearly into his lap. "Oh, dear, I'm sorry I hadn't noticed." She spread shredded rust-tinted denim to observe, "Why, your thighs are shredded as well." She stayed close at his side. "Look, oh what luck, a J. C. Penny's, and ahead I see a drug store."

"The James Cash Penny store may not have jeans, but any pants will do."

"Let me off at the drug store," she said. "We need hydrogen peroxide and Noxzema. Then you drive on around the block looking for food. Pick me up at Penny's."

In front of the drug store, she hopped from the Mack. Del moseyed on down the street, his eyes and belly hungry.

He managed space enough in front of Penny's to park the rig. She dashed from Penny's and came to the driver's door. "Move over," she said. "I'm going to doctor my man right here on the street."

Eats are around the corner, a hamburger joint."

"Good, we can just stay parked here."

"Ouch."

"Hush. I wish a doctor were doing this. These are bad scrubs."

"Ouch."

"Don't mind me. Think of something else. Were the others as scrubbed?"

"Likely not. I'm sure they were tougher."

"Than my man? No way."

"Lucky I had my '43 penny."

"Your lucky zinc penny. I'm glad you had that." She pulled his tattered jeans from the floor and gleaned the zinc penny. "Good thing I didn't just discard these jeans, may have lost old lucky." Stuffing the tattered Levis behind the seat, she said, "Maybe patch them later. Dear its eenie meenie miney mo as to what will bandage these scrubs. I have a couple of clean hankies left."

"Tape?"

"None that I know about, but perhaps in the tool kit there'll be black friction tape. But no, that wouldn't be cute on my man. Shoe laces. I can tie the hankies on with shoe laces."

"Gee."

"With pretty bows. Thick brown laces tied in front would be cute." She pecked his cheek. "Or fancy would be bows to the side like at a box lunch social."

"It has to be shoe laces?"

"Yup, and tied on the side for my old fancy with his bright new jeans."

The new jeans were not Levis and so afforded room in the pant legs for his bandaged throbbing thighs, with pretty bows to the side. With the soothing Noxzema, he began feeling better and he stepped with a flourish on into the burger place.

The waitress approached with her order pad poised. "Good morning. I'm Kathleen. What will you drink?"

"Regular coffee, cream, and sugar."

"Six hamburgers with everything piled on that you can."

"And twenty strips of raw bacon."

She stopped writing. "Huh, raw bacon?" Her forehead crinkled. "Did I hear right?"

"Raw bacon."

"Raw bacon, huh?" Wanting clarification, Kathleen glanced to Del.

"Dear," - but then he remembered her condition. Louie'd said she'd likely eat strange stuff. He thought: Raw bacon sure clinches it! "Er, yes, for sure, anything she wants."

"Raw?" She didn't put her pencil to the paper. She eyed Dosia. "You sure? Why raw?"

"For bandaging." She caught Del's eye. "I learned that from Grandma Clydis. I'd get scrubbed once in a while. My skates wouldn't stay on my shoes no matter how hard I turned the key. I'd scrub knees, elbows, chin, and sometimes elsewhere. The bacon draws dirt, slivers, rust and such out of a wound. Especially it helps scrubs."

"Oh," she jotted, stabbed the dot with her pencil. "Twenty raws coming up."

They departed the burger joint with him carrying a hamburger and a half wrapped in napkins. Her napkin housed the raws. Strolling along with the Mack in sight, he suddenly spun around to see he was on the sidewalk alone.

She was just disappearing into a Mom and Pop grocery. He hurried in behind her in time to hear, "I'd like a party mix cake mix."

A grin took charge of his face. Surely next she'll order pickles, just as Sid said would happen. He'd guessed wrong on her need for raw bacon, but now surely she'd order – "Adhesive tape and cotton cloth for bandages." – Jiminy, wrong again. Is she really expecting? But why the cake?

When in the drug store earlier, Dosia'd noticed it was a combination store much like the Meijers stores down home. Returning to the counter near the cash register, the proprietor placed tape, cotton, and the cake mix on the counter. "Will this be enough cotton?"

"Yes, thank you."

"What color cake will you make?"

"Er, yellow, I think." Del, still grinning, was sure of her condition despite that she'd not ordered pickles. The cake mix alone was a new item for her. She'd always before made family recipe cake that began with two cups of Porter Hollow Mill white flour.

"You have eggs?"

"No. I'll need a dozen."

"Coming right up." Quickly she produced the eggs. "A while back," her cordiality continued, "we stocked spice cake, then we added devil's food to our shelf because that's the order they were invented. Now the new party cake mix is going like sixty. Being able to use the same mix, plus or minus egg yolk or spices and to bake a yellow cake, or a white or spice; I baked all three as if I needed pounds."

"We missed a birthday party back home so I was reminded of cake. We're truckers, and due home tomorrow."

Being wrapped in raw bacon felt bulky and strange but wasn't particularly painful. He squared away behind the wheel, and set the Mack into motion. With the sun climbing the sky, the day was quickly warming. They'd cleared the city and were climbing the gears toward cruise when they heard a loud explosion!

Their eyes bugged. He guessed: "Tire?"

"Yes, smoke's in the air behind us." Their complexion whitened.

Del brought the rig down, easing into a school yard. It was recess and several kids came running.

Del went from tire to tire on the Lufkin lightly touching each one. "Why are they smoking?"

"You kids stay back, please. The tires are hot."

"You kids, please stay back. We heard an explosion, not just air leakage."

A kid asked the obvious. "Flat, huh?"

"Yes, is there a tire store near?"

"Uncle Jesse has a gas station in Petoskey."

"He sells truck tires?"

"Yes, I think."

"Well, thanks, son. We'll stop in at Uncle Jesse's." A whistle sounded and the children tore back into the school.

"Del, I want to know what happened to the tires. Why are they hot? Why the loud explosion?"

His fingers plowed his thick brown hair. "Reciting," he said, "well, actually paraphrasing, from Papa Helio's tire notes: 'If one tire of a dual-tire installation runs under-inflated, flexion can cause enough heat for ignition; the tire can catch on fire.'"

"Oh, under-inflated." She touched her chin, not fully believing. Her words were a near whisper, saying, "Is there another sentence to Papa's notes?"

"I'm afraid so, 'If tires are seriously overloaded and/or with sustained high speed operation and/or high ambient temperature, the tires can catch on fire.' We were okay traveling in the night and early morning, but just feel that old sun now. I'd under-guessed also the size of our load. We're over my wildest guess by around a hundred and seventy-five pigs at one hundred pounds a pig and add in a number of sows. Our rig could weigh in the upper 80s to near 90,000 pounds. Lord knows the load on these tires, and He knows me the jackass."

"I know, dear, and I know my man didn't want to leave pigs behind. Not with a nursery to build." She rubbed her head, eyeing the exploded tire. "The sunny side of the Lufkin heated the most in this sun, the weakest tire exploded."

"Yes, dear, and my golly, they're all hot, some very hot." His fingers again plowed his thick dark brown hair. "I'll get the tools. We can mount a baldy or a good treaded old Texas. Er, uh, I'll mount the baldy."

He set the heavy long-handled lug wrench to a lug. Muscle bulged, sweat squirted. The lug nut turned. "Nine more to go."

He loosened all ten nuts then leaned, more like he collapsed, against the Lufkin with his hands pressed to his thighs. "Burn like cinders. Sweat in the scrubs. Really bad burning, maybe salt from the bacon."

"Stop. Oh, dear, just rest. I'll rig some shade."

She'd heard a board rattle from time to time and guessed it'd be near the cab. Working the board loose, she used it to prop a blanket and then fanned him with a Good Housekeeping magazine as he worked. He mounted the baldy. "I'll have to crawl along; maybe stop often; we must keep the tires cool all the way into Petoskey."

"About forty miles. Dear, we'll make it."

His grin was grim as he climbed the gears, topping out in high range third. After several minutes, Reader's Digest settled into her lap. She stuck her head out the window, jerked back into the truck. "There's a smell; different than before, not tires."

"Exhaust stacks. They're becoming red hot due to all the down shifting and slow pulling. Likely stuff's burning off; paint, chrome, dirt, the stacks could be crimson to their tops by now. I was beginning to catch whiffs of it myself." He smiled for her, but couldn't fool her due to his forehead showing fret lines. "I've been interested in a stop at Petoskey each time we've been through here," he said, in changing the subject. "That name, Petoskey, seems somehow to mean stones or rocks; like, say, petrified."

"No clue on the map about rocks, but the town's located on Little Traverse Bay." The map fell to her lap. "Maybe there are pretty rocks to see."

Talking helped to pass the time, yet time went slowly.

Despite their crawling along, a baldy met waterloo before they could reach Petoskey. Del decided to mount a good-treaded Old Texas. The choice was iffy, but obviously the baldies weren't able to stand the strain any better than the old Texas tires with their gutsy tread. She'd rigged the shade and fanned him while he made the tire change. Not wanting to alarm her, he waited until she turned toward the truck cab. Del placed his hands flat onto his thighs. Not fully turned toward the cab, she glimpsed his movement.

She looked back at him. "Dear, let me look again at those scrubs."

"No, sweat just got in again. They're not worse. They're a bit salty."

"We have plenty of bandages and peroxide. Maybe the bacon isn't helping. Get those pants down. I want to see the legs of my man."

The wounds were seeping fluid that drained down his legs. "Ouch!"

"Hush. Be still. What color are my garters?"

"Black."

"No they're not."

"Ouch!"

"Keep guessing until you get it right."

"Ouch!"

"These scrubs are deep. I wish a doctor could see them. Pieces of skin are missing, showing muscle, I think. A doctor could do the job right."

"Maybe use the Noxzema."

"I'm not sure. I'm just not sure!"

"Maybe soothing is the right way to go."

"Okay, Noxzema and a prayer. You pray. I pray. We pray!"

Finally they crawled into Petoskey with a strung out line of automobiles and trucks honking and racing engines behind. They limped into Jesse's Gulf.

Del sought Jesse.

Drawn to a sign advertising 'Rock Shop', Dosia walked on through the station and entered the shop.

Jesse said in answer to Del, "I had good used truck tires but they didn't sell well at all. A fellow down just past Walloon Lake is fixing up a tractor and several semi trailers. They opened a store and she runs that but he helps in there some. You can see his trailers from Walloon Lake."

"Thanks."

Del followed after Dosia. She waved him over toward the rock specimens. Coming across the shop, he took note of the hopeful storekeeper, "We wondered," he said, "if the Petoskey name has to do with rocks."

"No," the proprietor said, "the town was named after a statement by an Indian chief. Petoskey, but spelled somewhat different, is an Indian term meaning 'a pretty view.' Petoskey, we say is 'The Home of Million Dollar Sunsets,' which reflects that Indian's view of the place. There is a stone, however, called Petoskey stone. The stone is found around here. Take a look." She handed each a good sized specimen. "It became know as Petoskey stone because it was discovered for sale in Petoskey.

"It's really very pretty."

"It's a fossil coral from millions of years ago."

"We'll be back through here to buy some."

"If folk would realize that Petoskey stone is found only around here, no place else in the world, they'd not hesitate to buy some."

"Oh, we do want to buy some Petoskey stone, but today we need to buy a truck tire."

"I noticed the cafe next door to your shop is closed." Dosia said.

"I was about to open it when you walked in," she said. "Sloppy Joes are my specialty."

"Something sure smells good," Del said. He spoke from the rear of the shop. "Dear, I know we only eat in a restaurant once a day, but today I'd agree to break with tradition."

"Carry that kettle of Sloppy over to the eatery," the proprietor said, "and the first Joe's on me."

From the eatery, they crept on down the highway. That highway under the relentless sun by then was as hot as Wesley's griddle. Seeking to avert their attention from gloom and divert it to a more hospitable topic, she said, "You'd think Walloon, like the Walloon of Walloon Lake, would have to do perhaps with loons."

"Certainly I would think so, but of birds, do you think, or of people like me?"

"More like me, although I don't speak it. Walloon is a dialect spoken in France; or actually, it could be in Belgium as well. Along that border is where one could hear the Walloon dialect spoken."

"I'd bet maybe Luisa then has heard it. Alsace Lorraine Province is up that way; farther north, I'm sure, than is Paris."

"I'd guess from Paris the distance would be similar although I don't quite have the picture. I'll remember to ask Luisa about it. I see on this map, there's a Walloon Lake that is a lake, and on the shore of that lake is a town named Walloon Lake. Settled by folks of Belgium or France would be my guess."

Wham!

An Old Texas blasted to smithereens!

CHAPTER TWELVE

No more than thirty minutes had elapsed since Petoskey, twelve measly miles. Del squeezed the rig onto the road shoulder. The shoulder was of concrete as it was located for use as a turn lane into the town of Walloon Lake. Despite the ample shoulder, he set out red warning flags as the rig wasn't all that far off the main concrete. There was no air-mellowing shade on the side of the Lufkin where the shredded Old Texas was splattered. Together they rigged the blanket using pigs to hold the ends of two boards and one edge of the blanket. Stretched out upon the boards, the blanket provided some respite from old sol's blister. The blanket was short of full shade because they'd positioned it just barely clear of the concrete roadway.

Del set the big lug wrench to a stud nut. She fanned with a Good Housekeeping. Between each stud nut's triumphant loosening, he stood with the palms of his hands pressed against his ghoulish thighs. Having levered each of the ten nuts enough to loosen them, he reached for the monkey wrench. The monkey wrench was a lighter tool, and he needed reprieve. His hand met hers when he reached for the wrench. "Dear, let me; you fan."

He tried not to look as the tiny wrists and petit hands wielded the clumsy wrench. He held himself from taking it from her. He chided himself saying, it's your job you brute, but his eyes ultimately scanned away so as not to fret over her efforts. Ahead he recognized semi trailers. "With luck," he said, "there'll be a better used tire ahead there. I can see those semi-trailers Jesse told about."

"Great, the store'll be there too." She removed the last lug nut. "This town we're near is the one called Walloon Lake. The big lake by us is

Walloon Lake. It's going to be shaded here this afternoon and because of the lake there'll be a breeze. It'll be cooler. I see clouds building in the west and they'll stir a breeze. Let's pray to God and to Jesus for respite from old sol, and just fun, let's give Odin a chance too."

"Odin?"

"Odin is the father of Thor God of Thunder.

"Anyway there's help, I'm for it."

"Just rest, dear. Please, let's not be in a rush to change the tire. You just wait here in what shade there is. I'll go on down to that store to get a tire, to get help too."

He hated to see her go on alone, walking under that broiler, but she wouldn't have it any other way. He knelt in the rigged shade begging a breeze off Walloon to flow under the Lufkin and to chill him. He sat with his hands flat against his tortured thighs. Ahead down the road he watched his beautiful, wonderful, courageous wife grow smaller in the distance. He thrust himself to his feet. Lifted from his thighs, his hands felt sticky and he reached a towel from the cab. The towel removed sweat from his hands but his hands remained sticky. He looked down to see that a stain, reddish, redder than rust had oozed from his thighs, discoloring the new J. C. Penny jeans.

He grabbed the wheel with the attached Old Texas remains and moved around to the lake side of the rig. There he felt the merest whiff of a breeze and he stood with his agonizing thighs aimed hopefully into the chill a moment before turning to slide the ruin into a rack under the bed of the Lufkin. In doing so, the spilt rim mechanism came keenly to his view. The mechanism was simple. A lock ring held the rim together and the rim locked to the wheel when the tire was inflated. He dragged the split rim wheel back out of the rack.

An approaching vehicle caught his attention. Popping from behind the Mack, he thrilled at seeing Dosia in the cab of a rusted Chevy pickup. A large auburn haired woman was behind the wheel and standing upright in the bed of the pickup he espied a wonderful looking, well treaded used truck tire. Del grabbed the wheel with the split rim, that wheel still with shreds of Old Texas hanging, and he heaved it into the box of the pickup. Next he heaved in a non-split rim bearing a blown baldy.

"My husband's out on a run," Auburn said to Del from her cab window, "you can settle for the tire later." Del heaved himself into the box. As the pickup moved back toward the store, it kicked up a stirring breeze. He wished he could stand on his head to give the thighs full benefit of that breeze.

In the store he guzzled two bottles of cold pop. He filled the two bottles with icy water from the pop cooler. Carrying the bottles of cool water he left the store. Behind the store he found a cluttered shop, tools and trash abounding. As if from heaven, an electric fan was blowing, cooling the air. Del poured some cool water on his burning thighs and the moving air stilled some of the throbbing in his scrubs. Removing the split rim was easy, and he then easily removed the bead of the ruined Old Texas. "Clever mechanism, the lock ring and a split rim. Tire expansion locks the tire rim onto the wheel as the tire inflates."

His mind was rosy with a desire to mount the new good spare without using those massive pry bars. He knew he had a regular-rimmed wheel with him. Twice he rubbed his head and he started to climb into the pickup to get the other, to not use the split rim, to leave the used split rim and its wheel here in the man's trash heap like Mr. Diamond-T had cautioned that he do. Each time he looked down at his throbbing thighs his eyes lifted to study the split rim laid out on the pickup tailgate. "What have I heard about you?" His eyes bore the mechanism. "The rim supports the tire under inflation pressure, however explosive separation can occur." How? Why?

"Helio's notes," his mind reviewed: "Worse case is when there are mismatched parts." Mismatch? "Yes, especially when the components of the system are manufactured by different companies." Very dangerous with only slightly mismatched parts. Explosive separation can occur. "These parts all were together on the wheel and they held, even when the Old Texas went to glory. Explosive separation didn't occur even with maybe seventy thousand pounds of pressure per square inch on the rim!" He fingered the parts. "So you are matched parts aren't you?"

He mounted the new used tire using the split rim mechanism. "Azrael, angel of death," he chuckled. "I'm not yours today."

Split rim assemblies have been known to explode during inflation. He stood back behind the unit as it inflated. Watching the pressure gauge on the pump: 70 psi, 80, 90, more, dare I? "No!" He disengaged the air pump and rolled the mounted tire into the pickup. He poured cool water on his burning throbbing thighs. Watching, he saw the water turn brownish red as it drained down along the jean denim, but the water and fan had soothed his scrubs a bit.

At the Mack, he began installing the wheel with the split rim-mounted tire. Helio's notes: Explosive separation has been known to occur when tightening the lug nuts or even while driving along a road. Gingerly he screwed the lug nuts onto the studs. Using the monkey wrench, he snugged the nuts. He set the big long-handled lug wrench to a nut; each nut required a final vigorous yank to secure it on the wheel. He yanked the first nut. He yanked eight nuts but never ten.

Blam-t-crack! Blam and crack were simultaneous. The rim banged up under the trailer bed, it fractured and a six inch chunk assailed Del's head. At the store Dosia and Auburn had not before heard that awful sound, but they knew: "Trouble!"

"Trouble!"

Dosia's screams echoed from the hills as she tore up 131 yelling, "Del! Del!"

Del lay unconscious in that blistering sun, and with his feet mere inches from the roadway. She knelt beside her Del. The rim fragment stuck from his eye socket, shoving, or crushing, the eyeball to over behind his nose. She leaned in to kiss him and was repelled by the sight of ogre where once was her beloved husband. She fought against terror at seeing the six-inch-long, one and one quarter inch wide rim fragment that was slammed into the eye socket. Instead of an eye that horrid steel stuck from his head and an end of it bulged the temple outwards from the side his head.

She cradled his head in her lap. "Oh, God help him. Help me to know what to do!" Auburn rushed into the scene, herself too winded to speak.

She opened the door of her faithful old rusted Chevy pickup. She breathed heavily, but managed finally, "I'll get help." The old truck squawked from the scene.

Still cradling Del, she looked up hopefully at Auburn's return. Her eyes to Del and Dosia, Auburn u-turned and stopping the trusty pickup behind the Lufkin. She hopped from the cab, came to them, talking as she came: "Cops are coming. Our local ambulance is out. One's coming from East Jordan. Be a half hour, maybe forty five."

Gently she lowered her husband's head to the hard concrete. Leaping to her feet she said, "I'm taking him in." Already her hand was down into the front of her jeans.

She unsnapped her hosiery. Leaning against the truck cab she yanked off brogans and anklets. She dragged a hose free, and the other hose free. Auburn gasped as next Dosia plucked a knife from the kitchen stores behind the seat and began slashing the seat of the Mack, exposing its steel framework.

She picked up her injured husband and staggered with him toward the cab, his head dangling with that awful shrapnel obvious. Auburn steadied the head, helped Dosia push Del onto the seat of the Mack. Dosia tied one end of a hose stocking into the seat framework, drew the hose across his mouth and tied the other hose end as well into the framework. He looked like some hideous monster eating nylon. In like manner she secured Del's waist to the seat. She jerked on the anklets and hopped into her brogans, lacing them tight. Darting to the driver's-side door of the willing Mack, in a single leap she was into the cab.

The Thermaldyne shrilled, it screamed, it howled, bellowing power. Black exhaust from both stacks roared skyward and blue-white smoke poured from eight tractor Coopers. In low range low and in blinding smoke the eight tractor Coopers tore at concrete. The Mack dug out for East Jordan. Auburn stood in the smoke, her ears assailed by bellowing Thermaldyne and howling Coopers. Into the smoke came a cruiser with its siren wailing.

A few minutes before the Mack's departure, Trooper Baker, coming south on 131 received a radio call about the accident. He'd pressed the throttle and clicked on his lights and siren. Now Baker blasted through smoke. Auburn caught sight of the cruiser ahead, with its arcade of warning lights flashing, the cruiser straining to get up to the Mack, Mack and cruiser growing smaller in the distance. The partially un-mounted new used tire at that time finished its dismount, blasting into smoke, molten rubber, and tire shards. The blast plastered the grill and windshield of Baker's cruiser.

Auburn saw the cruiser waver, slewing side to side, smoke rolled from its tires. The car straightened and resumed after the hurdling juggernaut. She stood agape, wondering the fate of her new friends. Slowly her hands enfolded and positioned before her gentle face. She urgently beseeched the aid of Jesus.

Trooper Baker with all warning lights flashing streaked past that hurdling Mack. Thinking to stop the truck, he pulled in front of it and displayed his brake lights. Dosia set 88,000 pounds of Mack and cargo upon his truck lid and blasted the air horns.

She yanked, yanked and yanked the air horn lanyard. Toot! Toot! The brassy toots whammed at the head of trooper Baker while the noise of that monster pressing his trunk lid chilled his back, bugger his eyes.

Surrounded by Mack howl and horns' piercing, and with his rear-view mirror full of Mack, Baker yelled into his mike: "Don't try to stop this

Mack. Baker here. Car fourteen. I'm on 131 leading an aberrant truck. I'm nearing the tarmac to East Jordan. This truck's going on through! Clear the way! Clear the way all the way into East Jordan hospital."

"Trooper, fire chief here, coming out from Boyne Mountain. What are we up against?"

"Chief, good. It's a Mack semi truck. A tire just exploded. A little girl is driving. Injuries were reported. I believe she's on the way to East Jordan hospital."

Dosia'd made a couple of up gear shifts by that time. She had the Mack up and rolling, rolling with her man, rolling for East Jordan.

On their honeymoon trip, Jacqueline and Ronnie had that morning taken a ride around the area including a loop to get a view of Boyne Mountain. Just on their way from the mountain they were startled when a red Studebaker pickup with lights flashing and siren screaming tore past them. Expecting that the red pickup carried a fire chief, Ronnie stomped gas to his dark blue and cream Ford Crown Victoria. Ahead of them lay 131.

Ronnie was at the rear bumper of the red pickup and closing on 131 when ahead they saw the Mack peeling off the highway with every tire kicking blue white smoke and their eyes bulged as the juggernaut careened onto the tarmac to East Jordan. Jacqueline yelled, "I know that truck." They streaked across 131 in the wake of the red pickup.

"That was her driving!"

"Maybe an accident. Maybe someone's injured."

"They're on the way to East Jordan hospital but don't know the way!"

Ronnie stomped gas to his Crown Vic. He tore on past the red Studebaker, Mack, and police cruiser. He yelled, "Signal them to follow!"

They waved hands out the window, signaling follow, follow."

Dosia recognized the car and its occupants. "How could God know to send angels to guide me?"

"Trooper, the trailer's on fire, black smoke rolling, blue-white smoke as well. What's the load? What's she carrying?" Baker had no time to answer.

He saw red lights ahead. People in the blue and cream car were flashing their brake lights, waving their hands, pointing.

Dosia saw then ahead, saw the red lights flashing. She double clutched and rammed for high range first gear. The stacks turned crimson to their tops. Smoke rolled from every remaining tire of Mack and Lufkin.

She ripped into the turn. Baker, to get out of the way of car and truck plunged his cruiser down into the road ditch. The semi trailer load of pig iron slew into gravel along the tarmac sending a hail of stone into the windshield and side windows of Baker's cruiser and into the red Studebaker pickup.

Weaving crazily, the little red hurdled past Baker, Baker just coming from the ditch. Baker fell in behind little red. "I've got to stop that truck!"

Chief yelled, "What's her load?"

Siren belching, Trooper Baked charged on past the chief and the Mack. "Trooper, what's her load?" Baker again displayed stop lights and flashers to the Mack.

Dosia came right on to his trunk lid. Seeing no chance, he powered ahead of the Mack. "Can't stop her. Chief, the load's pig iron. It won't burn. What do you make of this nuisance car?"

"Tore past me. Thrill seekers, looks like. Lot of black smoke here. It's tires. Tires burning right off that thing!" Chief pulled up beside the Mack. He leaned into the view of Dosia. He waved and shouted, trying to get her attention. She jabbed a finger twice at herself then stabbed the finger down the road, down the road, ahead down the road. Little Red began to back off. An exploding tire sent molten rubber, flame and tire fragments into the front end of the red pickup, plastering grill, hood, and already shattered windshield. Through the ruined windshield he saw a mud flap burst into orange angry flame. Billowing black smoke enveloped little red.

Weaving in behind the trailer's smoke and hot flying rubber, Chief struggled to keep his pickup under control. "Trooper, she wouldn't stop for me either. Keep her way clear." Baker heard Chief gasp and moan.

The juggernaut surged onward ripping left and right, left and right around flat-road curves, repeatedly spewing aerial avalanches of ditch-side gravel and debris to pelt little red.

Before chief's eyes through the endless curves was a shower of flame and sparks that glowed as bright as sunshine. Within the huge shower of sparks there appeared four bright red columns. All four tires of that left side of tandem duals had disintegrated amid blue white smoke and on into fire belching inky black smoke, molten rubber, and tire fragments. Before him where the naked rims, those rims glowing in red hot columns. "Trooper,

I'll have to fall back. All tires gone on the left. The trailer wheels are red hot; sparking pyrotechnics everywhere."

Baker heard a moan coming from little red. In his cab Chief smacked at a smoldering limb that had poked through his shattered windshield and now was melting into his seat. He reached a fire extinguisher from the rear seat.

"Chief, you okay?"

"Some fire in here. Snuffed it with my extinguisher."

Trooper Baker squawked in behind the Crown Vic, the Vic leading him along with the big green Mack, that Mack with a child driving! Baker prayed hard, real hard, "Please, God. Oh, God, please help that child. And help Chief."

Baker turned into the left lane of the road and allowed the hurdling monster to pass, his eyes surveying the smoke-belching giant, wondering, praying. He squawked in to follow little red. "Chief, you can pull away. I'll follow!"

"I'm hanging in here!"

Ahead the Crown Vic pumped brakes, hands waving from both front windows. Ahead a stop sign meant business, the sign guarding a strait run into a lake. The lake shined hotly, like the entry into hell. Dosia clutched, tried ramming for a lower gear, ending in a gear – she knew not which. The slid every wheel, tired or tire-less, and felt the rig loosing contact with the road, aiming the cab into the ditch at her left.

Off the road now, and across a field, fence wire whipping, trees looming. She stopped braking the Mack – let God decide! She roared into a woods of aspen, scrub maple, willow, and brush, the whole shooting skyward in a rain of wood, bark, and leaves, the whole slowing the juggernaut, finally blasting the rig free and onto the roadway toward East Jordan hospital. She sensed haven for her beloved Del, for her husband, that sweety in God's hands.

Coming into East Jordan with his siren still loudly wailing, Trooper Baker was relieved to see police, fire fighters, and others holding the way clear to the hospital. Behind the Mack juggernaut, Chief also wailed his siren, and cringed at limbs flapping on to the roof of his ruined red pickup. Limbs, leaves, whole shrubs complete with roots, and with some limbs smoking flipped clear of the rig as it hurdled along the streets. Chief stayed tucked behind the juggernaut, the juggernaut being his guide ahead as vision through his shattered plastered windshield was nil. He could only hope that authorities had the way clear.

Trooper Baker in realizing the Crown Vic was leading the tortured Mack, had resolved to stay settled in behind little red. Ahead of Dosia and her barreling Mack, the Crown Vic led the way and Dosia glued her hope on that angel's chariot.

Chance had it that two familiar others heard that commotion entering town. Del's brother, Nathan, and Luisa were on the Jordan River and were approaching the dock at East Jordan. They'd made it away on a honeymoon boat trip down the swift cold river. The man had said, "At the least rush of speed, throw out the log chain; all of it. That's to slow the boat. If that's too much out, then draw in a little. Ma'am, the oars are mainly for fending off the river bank on turns and maybe to whack at brush here and there so you won't be swept into the river. She's a cold one, she is." At the sound of sirens and other sounds not recognizable by either of them, but loud sounds like roaring, yelling, and screeching simultaneously, Nathan'd grabbed the oars and pulled strongly to the dock.

Drawn toward the commotion perhaps by mere curiosity, or because of his recent stint as an army medic, they ran to their dark green 1947 Oldsmobile. The boat livery men, as expected, had parked the car under an oak tree for them. He grabbed the keys from the hiding place over a rear tire and they purred out after the commotion, already guessing they were headed toward a hospital. They hurried, they squawked turns, and with every moment the urgency mounted. Somehow, they were needed ahead.

The Crown Vic led the Mack through town. They crossed a bridge and the Vic signaled left. Unable to make the tight turns, Dorsia'd cleaved a triangle off the tip of lawn after lawn. Ahead Jacqueline said, "Last turn ahead. It's a sharp one." The Crown Vic made the turn. She craned her neck to see the Mack. Dosia climbed the curb to her right then ran the Mack up onto a lawn making match sticks of a picket fence and mashing a hedge of privet. That action stressed to the limit one of the two remaining new Coopers. That Cooper blew apart! Lufkin and the pig iron now rode on the one remaining new Cooper and on six or seven naked red hot wheel rims. Ronnie goosed the Vic after that last turn and scooted toward a straight-in to a hospital parking lot. Dosia, too, goosed that Mack.

At the far end of the parking lot Ronnie braked to a stop, his tail lights warning Dosia. The last new Cooper exploded at the edge of the parking lot just as Dosia braked. She clambered into the lot while ejecting a shower of sparks and smoke. That last Cooper was a wadded molten smoking ruin caught under a wheel rim. The rig slid on, crowding the Crown Vic, finally chattering to a stop with the load of pig iron a little past the hospital emergency door.

Chief limped in. He charged the semi trailer and set his fire extinguisher hissing at the red hot rims.

Trooper Baker pulled in. He leaped from his battered police cruiser just as Ronnie and Jacqueline walked up to the semi trailer. "Who are you," his words were spoken as a no nonsense demand.

"We're their friends," Jacqueline calmly said.

Then Ronnie's comment nearly flipper Trooper Baker, "Yeah," Ronnie said. "We're here to take care of the truck."

Inside the hospital, a gurney larruped along a corridor. A large male attendant and a short female attendant trotted along with the gurney. They'd heard of an emergency outside; trucker injured. Bursting from the hospital emergency door, they expected to see the emergency before them, at the ambulance stand, but saw nobody.

They quickly scanned the scene, espying the big green Mack through drifting smoke and stench. A child they could see had climbed half out of the truck cab. Seeing no other vehicle answering to 'trucker injured,' they trilled the gurney up to the child.

She stood with a size three brogan resting on the running board, her other foot still in the cab. One hand was on the top of the door, the other was inside grasping the rim of the steering wheel. They stood in awed silence a moment, hearing only the crimson stacks crinkling down. She met their eyes. "Help my man," she said. "He's hurt."

Traffic blocked Nathan and Luisa. They crowded the green Oldsmobile to a curb. Walking briskly along a sidewalk, they knew not where to go but guessed that ahead was a hospital. Their sidewalk led to the hospital parking lot. A crowd of folks was gathered around a dark green semi. They caught glimpses of the semi trailer and wondered as to its looking like it was going up hill yet the truck appeared to be level. Closer, they saw that all of the tires of the semi trailer were missing. A large barrel-shaped man was at the edge of the crowd. He stood with a large pyramidal-shaped woman. Both turned when they heard someone say, "Nathan, I know that truck. It's your brother Del's"

Jacqueline turned and hurried up to them. Trooper Baker joined them and immediately inquired, "Who are you?"

"I'm Del Platt's brother. Is he injured?"

Auburn of the Walloon Lake store had been blocked repeatedly while trying to follow to the hospital. Frustration moved her to jump curbs and to drive across lawns and along sidewalks, finally banging her old Chevy pickup over a curb and into the hospital parking lot. She pulled up and exited the faithful old Chevy; the cab door she left swinging. "Is he okay?" She glanced along the rig, smoke and stench still adrift. "Thank God she made it."

"She's got more guts than an elephant," Ronnie said.

"They've taken him inside. He's still alive. Dosia went in with him."

"His brother, you say." Trooper Baker was writing on a pad. "And Ma'am, who are you?"

"They stopped at my store with a flat tire. I sold them a good used one. The rim exploded. I saw you plow through the smoke. I saw your car get hit, huh? It weaved but you kept on. He called me Auburn because of my hair. Nice young couple. Too bad, this."

Jacqueline had climbed into the cab. Baker approached the cab, getting nearly backed into, bowled over, by her exit. "I have their notebook," she said. "Lots of names and telephone numbers but we'll need to know which ones to call."

"I'll accompany someone inside," Baker said.

"I want to see how my brother's doing."

"I need to know which numbers to call," Auburn said. "We can go to my store to telephone. Walloon Lake store. That'll be headquarters. The truck can be hauled there too."

"We'll take care of the truck," Jacqueline said.

Baker went into the hospital in company with Nathan, Luisa, and Auburn. The trooper still had questions to ask of Auburn and the Platt couple. Nathan walked right up to his brother's gurney-side; and was shooed back out of that emergency room. Auburn talked with Luisa and Dosia, getting the important names and numbers to call. Baker collared people as needed. Finally Auburn approached Trooper Baker. "Officer, I have the important numbers to call. Here's the number of that foundry here in town, where the load of pig iron was headed. And here's my telephone number. Headquarters will be at my Walloon Lake store. Located right where this accident occurred; store with some semi trailers along side. The truck will be there."

Baker thanked her, and waved her on her way. At a nursing station he telephoned the East Jordan foundry, telling them where to recover their pig iron. Trooper Baker noticed, as he looked from the hospital, that Ronnie was working at the Mack. He'd jacked a set of duals into the air. "This thing don't need duals when it's empty," he said to his wife. "I'll use the outside wheel of each set of duals and move them to the trailer. I'll have enough wheels to get her out of here."

"Hello, is this your truck?" Ronnie didn't answer, instead tugged at a lug nut. "I'm a newspaper reporter, the Boyne Citizen." He jotted on white paper attached to his clipboard.

"My husband Ronnie," Jacqueline said. "I'm Jacqueline Perkins. We know the owners of the truck. They're inside. His wife drove the truck in here. Her husband was injured. We're taking care of the truck for them."

"Jacqueline and Ronnie Perkins, then." He wrote swiftly. "I caught these events on my radio." He nodded toward a Chevy panel truck that carried 'Boyne Citizen' and a telephone number. A long aerial stood up from a fender. "A little girl driving, was it? What is her name?"

"Not a girl, not a little girl, Mrs. Dosia Platt drove that monster to here because Del Platt, her husband, was injured. They're inside."

A lug nut clacked onto the pavement. Jacqueline scurried to retrieve it and placed it into a kettle she'd pulled from behind the truck seat, wanting to be sure her man had enough nuts in the end to mount the wheels on the trailer. I'd bet they got Perfect Circle piston rings in this truck," Ronnie said. "Like I got in the Crown Vic. They'd hold good even on a hot drive like this."

The reporter looked at Ronnie then scribbled at his notes. Piston rings? "Thank you," he said. Piston rings? His eraser rubbed his forehead then his eraser began editing his notes. He pursed his lips, glanced at Ronnie: "Dele here, I'd think." The reporter moved toward the hospital entrance. Ronnie went gleefully on removing nuts.

Inside the hospital, Doctor Helms at last had time for Nathan and the others. "I'll be transporting him by air to the University Hospital at Ann Arbor." The reporter, now with a 'Press' sign and his name and 'Boyne Citizen' pinned to his shirt, jotted furiously.

"I've had left seat time in a twin as a student pilot," Nathan said. "If you'd like company in the cockpit. I'm his brother, Nathan."

"Twin Cessna?"

"Sure, the Bamboo Bomber, with wooden wing spars."

"You're welcome in the cockpit. Ladies, there'll be room in the airplane for you. Officer Baker will transport you ladies to the airport. An emergency room tech will be in there with Del. Nathan, you'll ride with me." They drove away, leaving the reporter still writing on his clipboard.

At her store, Auburn telephoned Helio and Anna Mae Outhe, assuring them that Del was alive and being flown to Ann Arbor; that Dosia,

Nathan, and Luisa would be there with him. She asked Anna Mae and Helio to contact Del's parents. She carefully gave them her telephone number and the directions to her Walloon Lake store.

The reporter pulled in at the store and took pictures of the truck before interviewing Auburn.

In the air, Nathan and Doctor Helms could converse freely back and forth by means of their head sets. "Going to college interrupted my flight training," Nathan said.

"The army taught me to fly," the doctor said. "Martin Marauders, the B-26. Over Normandy was my first combat. After I finished med school and my practice began to pay, I bought this Cessna and outfitted it as an aerial ambulance. We've been getting a couple of medical flights a year."

"As to his wound sir, I was an army medic."

"Oh, triage?"

"No, typically, our patients came one or only a few at a time. Head injuries were most often associated with automobile wrecks. His wound doesn't look fatal to me. I'm not nosy, sir. I'm worried that he's still unconscious."

"Rightly so. His condition worries me, as well. There's a good trauma team at Ann Arbor. I believe they are the best in the world on head injuries. Does it look to you that the chunk of metal may have entered the cranium?"

"Frankly, sir, no. It looks like it smashed out the side of the eye socket then went to the outside of the skull. There it scraped along the outside of the skull to lodge under the temporalis muscle in the area of the temple. That bulge could merely be the temporalis muscle being pushed outward."

"I agree. Temple wounds can look ugly and not be dangerous. However, being hit there or being hit hard any place on the skull can result in a tremendous jarring to the brain. It's called brain trauma, or brain bruising. There could be intracranial swelling and bleeding. His being still unconscious, admittedly, has me worried."

With the airplane still in flight to the University Hospital, three ladies were barreling for Ann Arbor. Aunt Edith, that fireball Edith, had a Roadmaster hitting only the high spots. Naddy James, Del's mom, sat in the passenger seat wringing. "Can it go faster?" Her face was red from tears. Her hanky was wet as a sponge.

"Edith, please slow down." Anna Mae was about to insist that her sister relinquish the wheel. We might get there before him. Gosh sakes. Or they won't know anything if we get there too soon."

Edith passed a string of car, kept her foot in.

"Enough! Edith, we must live for him! For them!"

She eased off on the throttle. Tears streamed down her face. She wiped across her eyes with her hand.

"There, ahead there. Pull in there." Naddy and Edith piled into the rear seat. Up in front, Anna Mae kicked gas to that big Buick. She'd be slower than had been her sister, but she sure wasn't inclined to dally.

Meantime, at Perch Lake near Bruin City, Helio pulled into Louie's yard. Louie and Sid were ready. In seconds they were jacking up the red Reo and its Fruehauf semi trailer. They removed the wheels. Leaving the tires mounted, they chained the wheels to the rear deck and hoist of their powerful bright Yellow Beast, a Dodge four-wheel-drive Army surplus truck. All three crammed into the seat. Sid barreled out, heading for a store located at Walloon Lake. Helio held the directions. Louie held a map open in his lap. Each man was armed as well with a flashlight. Evening drifted to night. Dawn's early light would herald their arrival at the store near Walloon Lake.

Meanwhile at the hospital in Ann Arbor, nobody dared tell them they were too many, that waiting room capacity was limited. Anna Mae, Edith, and Naddy had, indeed, beaten the aircraft and its precious passengers to the hospital. They were there to meet Del, Dosia, Luisa, and Nathan in the area of the emergency entrance. Before going up in the elevator, Aunt Edith grabbed Nathan and they fetched folding chairs from the trunk of the Roadmaster. That family crowded around as closely as they could to every place anyone took their Del. As dawn lightened the eastern sky, they took turns to go for breakfast and they all ate breakfast but still there was no word of Del.

At Walloon Lake store Helio, Sid, and Louie walked around the valiant big green Mack, noting the wear on the now singlet rear tires. Helio spoke quietly, in a near whisper. "Better pair these with my newest Coopers. I'll show you which." Helio walked on as in a daze. His friends were patient, knowing of his concerns, his pain. They peered with him at now warped exhaust stacks turned gray and blue gray and with tinges of purple where once had been beautiful gleaming highly chromed twin exhaust stacks. Helio walked aft and began an inspection of the Lufkin. "One heck of a semi trailer," he said. "She held the load safe for that little pig iron trucker."

If any paint was left around where the tandem duals had burned, exploded, disintegrated, and where the wheel rims had ground away into red hot steel and unimaginable pyrotechnics, if any paint remained there it was shrouded in soot and molten rubber and not visible to the men.

While they were inspecting the rig, Auburn had answered the store's telephone. A lady named Luisa had telephoned to say that Del lived, that they thought he'd mend up and be okay. Auburn and Phil, her husband, walked quietly from the home portion of their Walloon Lake store. There was no hello, no introduction as they came to stand quietly with those men, with grieving Helio, with his friends who were obviously also Del's friends, and Dosia's.

They stood quietly watching as Helio walked a little away. He spread his arms to the sky and a low warble flowed from deep within his soul. It flowed to the sky and a bird flew in upon the notes of his refrain to alight upon the roof of the truck. His eyes followed that tiny bird. He turned to his friends. "We Indians ask of the Manitou a sign that He has heard us pray," Helio said. "Her man will be alright."

All murmured prayerful thanks, yet all stood quiet, feeling that Helio had more to do.

That faithful Athabascan walked again around the Lufkin, around the Mack, seeing the damage yet with each step he seemed to stand taller, prouder. Then Helio stopped and looking at Auburn, and he said, "She drove him through, huh? She did all of this bringing him through?"

"She's a real tiger," Auburn said.

"Yes," Helio said. "My little girl.

"My little girl,

She's sure some little girl."

The end.